THE FAIRY HANDBOOK TO SPELLS AND SALVATION

(Book 2 in the Stolen Spells series)

by

Tish Thawer

www.amberleafpublishing.com
www.tishthawer.com

The Fairy Handbook to Spells and Salvation Copyright© 2023 by Tish Thawer. All rights reserved.

No part of this book may be used or reproduced in any manner whatsoever, including Internet usage, without written permission from Amber Leaf Publishing, except in the case of brief quotations embodied in articles and reviews.

First Edition
First Paperback Printing, 2023
ISBN: 979-8864485156

Cover design by Molly Phipps of We Got You Covered Book Design
Edited by The Girl with the Red Pen
Character Illustration by Cameo.Draws

This book is a work of fiction. All characters, names, places, organizations, events and incidents portrayed in this novel are either products of the author's imagination or are used fictitiously. Any resemblance to actual persons, living or dead, events or establishments is solely coincidental or used herein under the Fair Use Act.

Amber Leaf Publishing, Missouri
www.amberleafpublishing.com
www.tishthawer.com

Praise for *The Witch Handbook to Magic and Mayhem*

"No one writes magic like Tish Thawer! What a wonderful, heart-wrenching adventure she penned in *The Witch Handbook to Magic and Mayhem*!"
~ **Casey L. Bond, author of *Where Oceans Burn***

"Tish Thawer has me under her spell once more! With stunning imagery, engaging characters, and an intriguing plot that will have you on the edge of your seat, *The Witch Handbook to Magic and Mayhem* should be on your must-read list for 2023!"
~ **Stacey Rourke, Award-winning Author**

"Whimsy and worry make this an exhilarating ride. Thawer has created another mesmerizing world where the good guys and bad guys may not be exactly what they seem, and the twists and turns keep you wanting more."
~ **Brynn Myers, Paranormal Romance Author**

"There aren't enough words to describe how much I love this story. The sisters are fantastic. The story is simply just magical. With plenty of twists and turns, this story is one that you will not want to put down."
~ **Goodreads Reviewer**

Praise for *Weaver*

"Visually stunning, Thawer's *Weaver* is a fresh YA Fantasy that will capture your heart and convince your mind dreams really do come true."
~ **Stacey Rourke, Award-winning Author**

"Atmospheric. Magical. And swoon worthy. Thawer's YA Fantasy is full of *Practical Magic* vibes and will have you rushing to bed in search of a Weaver of your own."
~ **Belinda Boring, International Bestselling Author**

"Lush and atmospheric, *Weaver* is a beautiful, carefully-crafted YA fantasy."
~ **Casey L. Bond, Author of *House of Eclipses***

"An illustrious YA Fantasy that blurs the line between dreams and reality, obscuring together two worlds into one visionary romance."
~ **Cambria Hebert, Award-winning Author**

"A beautifully written YA fantasy, wrapped in darkness and love. *Weaver* is full of stunning imagery and unforgettable characters that will keep you turning the pages until morning."
~ **Rebecca L. Garcia, Author of *Shadow Kissed***

"Spellbinding and packed with mystery and breathtaking landscapes, the world of the Weaver will assuredly enchant you."
~ **Cameo Renae, USA Today Bestselling Author**

Praise for *The Witches of BlackBrook*

"Tish Thawer's intriguing story line is weaved and crafted into a magical and spellbinding web that kept me up until the wee hours of the morning biting my finger nails and cheering for the sisters. Strong story line and well-developed characters that will sweep you away. I was completely floored by this amazing book and I recommend it to everyone!"
~ Voluptuous Book Diva

"Tish Thawer is an amazing wordsmith. I have devoured several books by her and she never disappoints. The blend of history with contemporary is just genius and I can't wait to see what this author will come up with next. Add this to your list as a must-read recommendation from me! An EASY 5 out of 5 stars!"
~ NerdGirl Melanie

"Overall, The Witches of BlackBrook was a grand slam for me. I was so enchanted by this spellbinding tale of hope, love, and a bond that can't be broken. There was something special about it and I honestly think it had something for all different types of readers. Whether you're into romance, historical, paranormal, new adult, etc. the author effortlessly weaves so many elements together to create a flawless experience for whoever picks it up. If you're looking to be enchanted and escape your mind for a couple hours, I highly suggest picking up The Witches of BlackBrook and diving on in!!"
~ Candy of Prisoners of Print

"Come Fairies, take me out of this dull world, for I would ride with you upon the wind and dance upon the mountains like a flame!"

~ William Butler Yeats

I
Spells

One

Ferindale

Lily

"All hail, Lily of Ferindale! Your true and rightful Queen!" Alder shouted to the crowd below, his hand resting at the small of my back.

I forced a smile onto my face, going through the motions like we both agreed to do.

"It's almost over; just wave." The pressure and warmth of Alder's touch was the only thing holding me in place.

Standing tall on the balcony with him by my side, I waved to the boisterous crowd of fairies, grateful for their cheers. Three months ago, our fathers killed one another in the castle of the Dark realm. Afterward, Bennett—who I thought was my friend—stole the crone's magical book and escaped without a trace.

My smile faltered.

Things could have taken a very different turn, but thankfully, both our kingdoms were happy to accept me and Alder as their new

King and Queen. Now, officially crowned, we could begin merging our two realms into one… a harmonious *Fae* Kingdom, just as Gideon envisioned.

"Let's get you inside." Alder guided me off the balcony and back into the glittering stateroom.

It took countless days to magically rebuild and learn the layout of the Light castle once we verified the crone was gone. Just like Bennett, she had disappeared and we hadn't been able to track either of them down.

I flopped onto the white leather couch, pushing the ridiculous amount of tulle that comprised my skirt out of the way. "Have you received word from any of the search parties?" I asked hopefully.

Alder dropped onto one knee and eased the blister-inducing shoes from my feet. "Not yet, but I expect them to return in the next few days."

My brows furrowed. "And what are we supposed to do until then?" I quickly learned I wasn't cut out for all the meetings and events that came with being Queen.

Alder's hand slid up my leg, caressing my calf with gentle strokes. "I could think of a few things to pass the time."

I laughed, true joy bursting from my lips.

I couldn't thank the Goddess enough for bringing Alder into my life. He had captured me, took me to prison, then saved me from my demented father and explained who he really was. We'd been together ever since—him the leader of the Dark fae, and me the rightful Queen of the Light. But those labels didn't matter anymore, or they wouldn't soon enough.

Gideon wanted us to unite the realms, and to honor his sacrifice, that was exactly what we planned to do.

Closing my eyes, I leaned back into the plush cushions and let myself enjoy Alder's ministrations. Wearing heels was never my thing, and the ligaments stretched tight along my ankles proved they still weren't. "Thank you; that helps." I rolled my left ankle, stretching it even more as Alder moved on to massage the right.

"Have you thought about what you'll do when we *do* find Bennett?" Alder's gaze dropped to the floor. He needed an answer but obviously hated to ask.

I took a deep breath and let the scenarios plaguing me replay in my mind.

I considered imprisoning him, of course. Perhaps in the same cell we'd spent our first few days in below the Light castle. I'd also thought about sitting down over dinner and letting him explain. Hopefully he'd have a good reason for betraying me. And finally, even though I hated to admit it, I thought about executing him for his crime against the crown—a warning to everyone in the realm. But as memories of our time together replayed in my head, I knew I could never do it. Bennett was my friend, and at one time, I thought even more.

"I'm not sure," I replied lamely.

Alder's thumb stroked gentle circles around my ankle bone. "I know it's difficult to think about, Lil, but everyone in the realm will expect some form of punishment."

My eyes snapped open, meeting his with a fierce gaze. "I don't give a damn about what others might *expect*. I am not my father, and I won't be pushed to do something I don't want to do." Pulling my foot from his hand, I slid off the couch and marched barefoot back to the balcony.

The crowd had dispersed, but the celebrations continued and could be heard across the city. Happy voices full of mirth and glee filtered out of the pubs and inns, while music and songs sung on gilded breaths floated from private homes.

"I want things to be different now. Simple. Peaceful." I spun to face Alder, his sorrow-filled eyes rising to meet mine. "I want things to be the way Gideon wished them to be."

Rising from the floor, he strode across the marble tile and pulled me into his arms. "So do I, Lil, but if Bennett was planning this all along, he can't be allowed to roam free. He must pay for what he's done to you, not to mention what his clan might do now that they have the book."

Damn it. I'd spent the last week trying not to think about that, but he had a point. So far, nothing out of the ordinary had happened. No dark spells or evil witches had appeared. Nothing to reveal Bennett's plans were nefarious in any way. Only the memory of his words that his outcast clan had wanted the book to gain favor with the crone and perhaps the King. But now, with my father gone and the crone in the wind, perhaps *favor* was no longer needed. Perhaps I could speak to his clan and find out why they'd been cast out in the first place and set things right.

I stepped out of his embrace and raised my chin. "I'll make my decision once he's caught. Like we told the Guard, he's to be brought back alive and unharmed."

Alder dipped his head, yielding to yet another of my desires.

"Are there any other festivities we need to attend, or can I go change out of this ridiculous dress?" I smacked the tulle at my sides, making it puff out even more.

Alder laughed, the sound lifting my spirits. "You can do whatever you want, Lil. You're the Queen now."

The Queen. I took a deep breath. It was going to take a lot more than fancy dresses, coronation ceremonies, and long-ass meetings to wrap my head around all that came with the title. But for now…

"Then I think I'd like to return to our room." My cheeks reddened as I met his heated eyes.

"Whatever you wish, *Princess.*" Alder's voice deepened on the familiar moniker he'd given me, warming me from head to toe. The nickname may no longer be correct in reference to my title, but it still had an effect on me. As did his kiss…

His feather-light lips touched mine as he ran a hand down my arm, entwining our fingers and leading me toward our room.

Two

Támar - Three Months Ago

Bennett

The moment I fled into the woods with the crone's stolen spell book in hand, I dropped my glamor, letting my true face come to the surface for the first time in years. My heart ached as Lily's cries echoed on the wind behind me. I thought about turning around, giving her back the book and apologizing for everything I'd done—all the lies, deceit, and misdirection—but this was something I had to do. Something I'd been *tasked* to do a long time ago. Still, the desire to return to her nagged me all the way home.

Reaching the border of Támar, I tiptoed through the shadows into our village and slipped inside our hut with no one the wiser. "Hello, Mother."

"Ah! My beautiful boy, you did it. I'm so proud of you!" With a gleam in her eye, Gretchen—my true mother—took the book from my hands and laid it atop the wooden table in the center of our hut.

I looked around the open space and inspected the home I hadn't seen in over three years.

Nothing had changed.

The thatched ceiling and walls needed to be repaired, but the wooden posts and stone base of our modest hovel appeared to be holding firm. Two cots lined the far wall—one for me and the other for Mom. The empty space was where my father's used to be.

I looked at my mother and fought the lump rising in my throat as she ran her finger over the cover of the witch's handbook to magic and mayhem. Her hair was the same washed-out brown rat's nest as the last time I saw her, and it broke my heart. This task had taken a toll on her, too.

"My son, I have no doubt you will succeed. Being chosen by the clan is a huge honor and will serve you well once you return with the book." She gripped my shoulders and forced me to meet her gaze. *"Your success will guarantee favor with the crone… and save my life."*

I shook my head and pushed the memory away. The frantic look in her eyes haunted me every day, but now, another pair of eyes drew the sorrow from my soul.

Lily.

Just thinking her name caused my chest to tighten. She was the only person who knew the real me, and even that was a lie. Striding to the round weathered mirror that hung on the far wall, I took in my true face.

Running my hands along the shaved sides of my head, I flipped the longer, platinum blond strands on top over one ear how I liked, then turned left and right, pleased to find my face and body had maintained their thicker bone structure as well. Lifting the loose cotton shirt over my head, I smiled, noting the tattoos that marked each of my achievements within our clan still covering my arms and chest. The raven, its feathers, and various ferns that wound around my right shoulder and down across my pec would always be my favorite. I received it when I was ten—when my shadow magic first flared to life and settled deep in my bones.

Spy-magic my mother had called it, but it was just the witch's version of fae shifter magic, of the glamors they cast to alter their appearances. I was destined for this mission the moment the magic flowed into my veins. Part fae, part witch, and the perfect spy. I hung my head and wondered what tattoo I'd get for betraying my best friend.

Lily was the only person outside of my clan who had ever seemed to care for me, but now, she would probably never speak to me again.

I lifted my eyes back to the mirror and sighed. With golden skin and muscles to spare, I was the complete opposite of the nerdy plant-boy she knew me to be. I wondered if she'd seen the real me, whether she would have chosen this warrior instead of the other—*Alder*.

I pulled the shirt back over my head and strode to the door. With Mother still stroking the book and muttering to herself, I needed some space. "I'll be back later." Her mumbled response faded against my back as I left our hovel—my home once more.

Támar was a village in the northern reaches of the Light Kingdom, and for as long as I could remember, it was the seat of my witch's clan. We didn't have a high priestess, only elders, which didn't mean much, since they were basically the oldest witches among us and nothing more. We were a simple village with no need for trinkets or offerings and rarely had a dispute among us. I often wondered if that was why we were shunned. We had nothing to offer the Light crown or their crone—until now.

At this point, though, what did it matter? According to Lily and Alder, soon there wouldn't be a *Light* or *Dark* Kingdom to grant favor any longer. Once in power, they'd unite the kingdoms like Gideon asked them to do.

Taking a breath, I looked through the trees, remembering how much I loved the sunrises here. Soft light filtered through the forest, speckling the path before me in the pastel colors of early dawn. It was something I wished I could share with Lily. Hanging my head, I kicked a pinecone from the trail, shooting it directly into the fire of our closest neighbor. "Sorry!" I called out, raising a hand in apology as the wood snapped and popped beneath their black cooking pot.

"Bennett… is that you?" The old man tending his soup waved me over.

"Hello, Callum. Yes, it's me."

"My goodness, boy. It's good to see you returned! Your mother has missed you greatly."

I glanced over my shoulder at our hut and huffed. *I doubt that very much.* "It's good to be back," I offered, even though the falseness of the words coated my tongue as soon as they left my mouth. "How have you been?"

With both hands, Callum stirred the pot with a large wooden stick. "Still cooking."

"How have things been since I've been gone?" I didn't want to appear rude or uncaring, but I could tell by the rest of the rundown huts that nothing much had changed during my absence.

Callum's mouth twisted into a grin as he looked around the village in the early morning light. "All is as it's always been, as you can see."

I scanned the other huts along the tree line and offered a sad smile in reply.

The old man's shrewd gaze swiveled back to me. "But now that you're back, I have no doubt exciting times await. I can only assume you've succeeded in your task to find the book?"

Any warm, fuzzy feelings I had fizzled out the moment he mentioned the book. I wasn't sure if I should tell him it was merely a few feet away, though I couldn't imagine what harm it would do. The entire village was aware of my mission from the day it began. "I did."

Callum's smile widened a fraction, but thankfully, he went back to stirring the soup and let the subject drop. I took the silence between us as my opportunity to leave. "It was nice seeing you again, Callum. I'm sure we'll catch up more soon."

He nodded slowly. "Yes, you too. And I'm sure we will."

He held my eye as I turned away, his words nagging at the back of my neck as I neared the forest's edge. I had no doubt that as soon as Mom got her shit together, the rest of the elders would be notified I'd obtained the book, and the decision of what to do with it would be made. Initially, I assumed I would have accompanied Mom and the elders to the Light castle to present the crone with her missing book, securing favor for our clan and sparing my mother's life. But now… I had no idea what would happen or what they planned to do.

Lily's face instantly formed in my mind, and I imagined handing her the book and receiving *her* favor instead.

Perhaps my mission wasn't over yet.

Three

Essex, CT - Present Day

Aster

"Practice safe hex!" I handed my customer their stack of books and followed them to our purple front door. Lifting a hand in goodbye, I clicked the lock behind them as soon as they were out of sight. "Okay, that's it." I flipped the sign in the window to *closed*. "Everyone gather around. It's time to collect our supplies for the trip."

My twin sisters, Fern and Iris, met on the rug in the center of the room, their straight, raven hair cut to two different lengths the only distinguishing characteristic between them. Out of the blue, Iris had asked Mom to cut hers shorter earlier this month, and as I looked at her now, I thought it suited her perfectly.

"Where's Daisy?" Iris asked.

I glanced around the bookstore, looking for my youngest sister's pointy black hat. Now that everyone knew Lily wasn't *truly* the baby of the family, our dynamic had definitely changed. With

Mom hyper-focused on the store, I became the stern know-it-all who watched over all my siblings, while Daisy, now the youngest, continued to be her bubbly, somewhat flighty self.

"I'm here!" Daisy called out as she descended the stairs, her frizzy brown hair flying wildly behind her. "I can't wait to see Lily and Alder again. This is going to be the best summer vacation ever!"

I took a deep breath and wasn't sure if *vacation* described our upcoming trip to Ferindale the best. After what happened in the Fae realm, Lily and Alder altered our portal so we could visit them whenever we wanted, but this was our first time making the trip. The fact that we were doing so without Mom still didn't seem right, but after watching her grieve the loss of Gideon over the past three months, I understood her reason for staying behind. It was still too soon for her to return to the place where he had died.

It was quite a surprise to find out that Gideon—the Dark King—was the father of my remaining sisters based on a deal to protect our magical wards. Fifteen years spanned our births, and similar to a magic square, the protection was pivotal in keeping Lily hidden from her true father—the Light King. My resolve strengthened when I thought about his demise. After going mad at the loss of his wife, he cast his only daughter—Lily—into our world. And now, with both Thadius and Gideon gone, Lily and Alder had accepted their destinies and planned to rule their respective kingdoms together, uniting them as one.

"Yes, well, I hope we get some fun *vacation* time in too, but remember, we're going to assist Lily and Alder in the search for

Bennett, the book, and the missing crone. Hopefully we can destroy the damn thing before she—or any other rogue witches—cause more damage to ruin the peace Lily and Alder are trying to build." I returned to my desk and shoved the few books I'd gathered into my bag, piling them on top of the clothes I'd packed earlier this morning. This time I focused on everything related to fae magic instead of witches specifically, and hoped combining the two would yield better results. "Iris, your turn."

Joining my sisters back on the rug, we waited for our magical shop, *Hexx*, to shift and morph into Iris's crystal store. Books flew from the shelves, disappearing into thin air as bins of crystals appeared along the same walls. Pillars of selenite now lined the counter, while crystal balls of fluorite, onyx, and smoky quartz wobbled on their stands as the shop settled into place.

"Okay... is it weird for anyone else that our sister is *literally* the Fae Queen?" Iris's question came with a smile as she gathered the crystals she wanted to take.

"Shocking? *Absolutely!* Weird? *Maybe a little.*" Growing up with Lily as our sister witch, her fae powers remained suppressed on this side of the portal. But now that she'd taken her rightful place as Queen, it was an adjustment we'd all have to get used to. "Come on. Let's finish up so we can get going."

Returning to the rug with her patchwork bag filled to the brim, Iris's blue eyes sparkled as Fern's flower shop blossomed around us.

Bouquets of white roses and lavender filled the air with their familiar scents as Fern made her way to the cupboard near the back of her shop. "I'm going to bring a few restricted plants with me, so please be careful if you need to go into my bag. I don't need any of you accidentally poisoning yourselves."

"Same," Daisy piped up. "I'm taking some vials of henbane, belladonna, and mandrake, in case we need to subdue Bennett now that we know he's part witch." An awkward silence settled over the shop as Fern finished packing her selected plants and Daisy's apothecary morphed into place. Rows of home-brewed tinctures shimmered in the afternoon light as the setting sun limned the bottles' surface. "I still can't believe what he did," Daisy scoffed.

"None of us can." I adjusted the glasses on my nose. "And I can't imagine what Lily's been going through, knowing he's still out there." I put my arm around Daisy, giving her shoulders a slight squeeze. "But that's why we're going, right? To help her find him and keep the kingdom safe."

"Right." She shrugged, attempting a smile that didn't quite reach her eyes as she heaved her canvas bag onto the crook of her arm.

Guiding everyone to the hidden entrance at the back of the shop, I led us down three flights of stone stairs to the basement, winding underground until we reached the wooden door far beneath the earth. I pulled the heavy skeleton key from around my neck and jammed it into the old metal lock, twisting until the secret door opened to reveal the fairy portal inside.

Blue light pulsed from behind a metal gate with filigree scrollwork to fill the room with an otherworldly glow.

Before, we had no idea where it led, but now, we knew it connected our world to the Light Kingdom in Ferindale. Since Lily and Alder had used their magic to alter it, stepping through for this trip would take us directly to the Light castle and our sister had planned.

"Leaving so soon?" Mom's sweet voice sounded behind me, pulling at my heartstrings.

I'd heard her footsteps on the stairs as soon as I opened the door. It was like she could sense the fae magic, which I supposed was no surprise. For generations, our family had been sworn to protect the portal's existence, and it remained our duty today.

"Yes. I told Lily we would be there before sundown." I moved through my sisters and fell into my mother's embrace. "Are you sure you don't want to come with us? We'll miss you so much."

Mom's chest rose and fell beneath me as she took a deep breath. "I'll miss you too, but someone has to watch the shop. And…" she lowered her head, "I'm just not ready." Tears shone in her eyes and I pulled back, nodding that I understood. "Now come here, girls. Give me a hug and let's get you on your way."

Mom took turns hugging us tight and kissing our heads, whispering something private into each of our ears. Returning to me, she pressed her lips to my cheek and leaned in close. "Protect your sisters, and help Lily the best you can." She paused. "And especially watch out for Fern. She hasn't been herself since we returned." I drew back, ready to snap my head in Fern's direction, but Mother held my chin, her gaze serious and penetrating.

"I will," I whispered.

I had no idea what she meant and hadn't noticed anything off about my sister. But if Mom sensed something was wrong, I would definitely heed her warning.

"All right, ladies. It's time to go." Mom reached for the metal door and unlocked the magical clasps that held it in place.

The blue fairy portal pulsed brightly from within—coming alive, as if it too, knew something I didn't.

Four

Ferindale

Lily

"Lily!"

Daisy's frizzy brown hair and pointy hat was in my face before I even had a chance to say hello.

"Hi!" I returned her hug and greeted everyone as the rest of my sisters stepped through the portal. "It's so good to see you all." Hugging each of them in turn, their familiar warmth brought tears to my eyes. "I've missed you all so much."

"We've missed you, too!" Daisy gushed. "So, what's it like being Queen?"

I hissed a sharp breath in through my teeth. "Not sure I can answer that yet."

"Why? What's wrong?" Aster's question was far more serious than Daisy's.

"Nothing's wrong... per se. I just don't think anything I've done can be considered very *queenly* yet." I waved a dismissive hand in the air. "At least not in my mind. Now come on. You must be hungry. We can talk more over dinner."

Guiding everyone through the halls and toward the dining room, I grinned as their faces beamed in wonder. We hadn't made many changes to the castle except to remove all traces of my father and his crone. But since they'd only seen one small portion of one specific hall, I was happy to show them the true beauty of the place. Alder and I had designed a new joint crest that would grace every banner and building across the land... as soon as we were officially married—a topic for another time.

"Everything is so beautiful." Daisy ran her hand along the white marble wall as we continued down the glittering corridor.

"Thank you. But I do miss the dark, natural vibe of Gideon's castle, too," I admitted.

"Have you and Alder talked about changing things here to add more details from his home?" Aster raised a brow as she took in the silver banner hanging above the dining room door, just as it had before.

"Of course we have," Alder answered for me as we entered the room. "Lily and I will merge our kingdoms in every way possible, including the decor of our two realms. No need for Light and Dark anymore when they both complement each other so well." Reaching for my hand, Alder pulled me into his arms, addressing my sisters again only after placing a kiss upon my cheek. "I take it there were no issues with the portal?"

"No issues at all," Fern supplied, dropping her bag by the door.

The rest of my sisters followed suit, smiling wide as a swarm of servants rushed to gather their things and move them to the family quarters we had prepared in advance.

"Take a seat and let's eat! I'm starving." I moved to the head of the table where Alder pulled out my chair, his gentlemanly ways warming my heart. "Thank you all so much for coming!" I addressed my sisters. "I can't tell you how happy it makes me to have you here."

Glancing around the table, I struggled to keep my smile in place as I noticed the empty chairs. It would have been so wonderful to have Mom, and even Sybil, the Acrucian Coven's High Priestess here. My eyes lingered on the final empty chair at the far end of the table. *And most of all, Gideon, of course.*

From his seat beside me, Alder squeezed my hand beneath the table, acknowledging my thoughts through our shared blood bond. *"It's hard for us all. I'm sure they wish your mom could be here too,"* his words whispered through my mind, but no one spoke as the elaborate meal was served.

Freshly baked breads in handwoven baskets, roasted meats on silver platters, jams and jellies in crystal bowls... As the elaborate meal was served, I suddenly wondered if my sisters would think less of me now that I had more.

"So, has there been any news about Bennett yet?" Aster tore into the subject with the same vigor with which she tore into her bread.

Taking a sip of wine, I swallowed and answered with the embarrassing truth. "Not yet."

"We have multiple search parties scouring the region," Alder added firmly.

Meeting Aster's gaze, I recalled a memory I had in the Acrucian forest... how *I* was disappointed in *Sybil's* efforts to find the book. My cheeks heated at my embarrassing behavior, because *now* I understood.

"But that's why you're here! We can make a plan and use our magic to locate him." I slid a bite of meat from my fork between my lips, offering her a closed-mouth grin.

"I brought everything we need!" Daisy beamed. "Maybe after dinner you can show us where to set up?"

Aster interrupted before I could respond. "It's been a long day. We should all get some sleep and plan to set up after breakfast tomorrow." Meeting my eyes again, she winked. "Don't you agree?"

"I do." I smiled back, realizing this was her usual way of saying she wanted to speak with me alone. "Let's enjoy our dinner, and then I'll show everyone to your rooms."

Alder's knee brushed mine beneath the table as we dug into our meal and did our best to make pleasant conversation with my family from another world.

"That was exhausting." Alder collapsed onto our bed, then brushed a sweep of fire-red bangs out of my eyes with a gentle swipe of his fingers. "I wasn't around them much the last time they were here. Are they always that... animated?"

I think he was trying to avoid the word *annoying*.

"Yes and no." I rolled onto my side, meeting his gaze. "I think they're just happy to be here." I paused. "Aster is, of course, more serious than the others, but that's because she carries so much responsibility when it comes to us all."

Alder's hand glided over my shoulder and down my arm. "What did she want to talk to you about?"

I closed my eyes, reveling in his touch, then answered honestly but withheld the details. "A warning she received from our mother." I wasn't ready to cast *any* of my sisters in a negative light until I learned more.

He tensed. "A warning?"

"Yes, but it's nothing to worry about. I just need to spend some extra time with all of them tomorrow." I reached for his hand, entwining our fingers. "I hope you don't mind."

"Of course not." He placed a kiss on the inside of my wrist, setting butterflies alight in my stomach. "Take all the time you need.

I'll be meeting with the Guard in the practice arena to go over the next territories I want them to search."

"Where will you be sending them?"

"Up north to Cromwell, Vizount, and Támar."

Five

Lily

After a flurry of activity, breakfast, and a trip back to their rooms to gather their things, I guided my sisters to the basement space that had been established as my workroom. The stone floors cooled my feet through the flat slippers I preferred, and the wood cabinets and time-worn tables gave it the perfect feel to remind me of home.

This was where the true search for Bennett and the crone would begin.

"This is lovely." Fern lifted a hand to the rafters but refrained from touching the dried flowers hanging above her head. Her eyes traveled to the cabinet in front of her, going wide at the multitude of colorful vases sitting on the shelves.

Aster meandered to the old oak table in the middle of the room, spreading out her books and claiming the spot with sharp precision. Daisy unpacked and sorted her bag of bottles and herbs on the granite countertop near the deep sink, cheerfully humming to herself beneath her breath.

"Thank you," I responded to Fern. "I haven't had a chance to study the flowers in the region yet, but I imagine they are pretty spectacular." I waved a hand at the empty glass containers. "I was hoping we could gather some fresh bouquets together later this afternoon."

"Oh, Lil, I would love that!" Fern spun and met my eyes, a true smile lighting her face.

"What about the search for Bennett?" Aster's pointed question quickly brought our heads out of the clouds—or in this case, out of the garden.

"I say we start with the usual… a locater spell." Iris pulled her favorite pendulum from a velvet bag, while Daisy scattered a mixture of salt and herbs on the large worktable that would serve as our altar, creating a mini circle to focus our magic.

I flicked my hand at a nearby shelf and smiled as my candles floated through the air and landed in place. Green for earth, blue for water, yellow for air, and red for fire. All the elements represented and working together as nature intended.

"Neat trick. I see that your magic has gotten stronger." Aster smiled, nodding in approval.

"Um, yes… you could say that." As a matter of fact, my magic had gotten *so* much stronger since becoming Queen, it was another reason my workspace was located in the stone basement. Safety.

Being Queen didn't come with a handbook and it certainly didn't mean I had control of my magic all of the sudden. It still required discipline and strength of will, and to be honest, I was glad my sisters were here to help me gain a little more of both.

"Well, then we should be able to make short work of this and locate the traitor within the hour." Aster slid into position next to me as the rest of my sisters surrounded the table.

With each of us focusing on our specific magic, I cast the familiar spell into the ether, hoping the combined energy would hasten the result. Sparks flew from the candle's flames and landed in the salt and herb circle, causing it to burst to life. We all gasped as the fire sputtered and sizzled around the table, then burned through the circle like one of the sparklers we used to play with as kids. In a span of seconds, our workspace glowed brightly before falling completely dark as the final ember fizzled out.

"Well, that didn't work." Daisy's sweet voice didn't lessen the annoying truth.

"No. It didn't, and I wonder why." Aster raised a brow in my direction, glancing around the table until her gaze rested on Fern's downcast face. "Fern, what's wrong?" she asked.

Fern shook her head, her long dark hair swaying side to side. "I'm not sure. I felt a pull in my chest when the circle caught fire and… I don't know. There was this weird buzzing in my head." She closed her eyes and pressed her fingers to her temples.

Aster and I left the circle, moving closer to Fern. Resting a hand on her back and chest, we sandwiched her between us. Closing my eyes, I focused my revelation magic, hoping to see what the strange pull could be.

Sparks of light fizzled behind my eyes and recalled the memory from Fern's point of view. The pull in my chest and buzzing in my head mimicked how she described it, but I was ready.

Holding onto the magic, I followed the thread, looking for where it originated. Finally, a low voice broke through the buzzing to whisper on the wind like shadows blowing in through an open window and creeping up the walls. "*I'm sorry...*"

"Ouch!" I yanked my hands back as a strong snap of energy severed the connection.

"What are you doing?" Aster asked, her hands still resting upon Fern's back and chest.

"I..." I stammered, wondering if Fern had heard the words, too.

"Why did you stop?" Aster continued, her brow raised in confusion.

"Because of that crack of energy that almost fried my hands." I rubbed my palms together and tried to massage away the pain.

Aster dropped her hands to her sides. "Interesting. I didn't feel a thing."

Six

Lily

"I've never seen this color of flower before." Fern knelt, snipped the glowing magenta trumpets from beneath the tree, and added them to her overflowing basket.

"Me either," I agreed. "They are beautiful, I just wish I knew their name. I think I'm going to have to do some major studying in my spare time." Like I had any of that.

"Do you have a library here? Perhaps there's some botanical books we could look at later this afternoon." Fern smiled and stood then continued further down the back garden path.

The walls of the castle surrounded the large space with manicured walkways winding throughout the mini forest of white-barked trees. Bright pink blooms graced their limbs year-round and wandering beneath their canopy felt like walking through a dream. With almost florescent green grass and luminous flowers covering the forest floor, you'd never know you were still inside the castle grounds. But even with its meticulous design, it remained a wild place and had quickly become one of my favorite getaways.

"So, regarding this morning…" I wanted to talk to Fern alone about what happened, but so far, all we'd managed to discuss was the foliage.

"What about it?"

"You said you heard a buzzing in your head. Is that all?"

"Yes, I told you already." Fern stopped to snip a cluster of shimmering purple tulips growing near the path.

"So, you didn't hear anyone speaking to you?" I handed her my basket, swapping it out for her already full one.

"Nope. Just a strange pull in my chest and buzzing in my head." Her eyes darted back to the ground.

"Fern, come on. You can trust me. I won't tell anyone… not even Aster." I stood still, waiting for her to reply, and gasped when she looked up at me with tears pooling in her eyes.

"I'm sorry," she whispered.

"For what? *Did* you hear something?"

"No. Nothing except the buzzing." She paused. "But I *do* think someone, or something was trying to communicate with me." She stood, leaving her basket on the ground and reaching for my hands. "And whoever it is, desperately needs our help."

"Why do you think that?"

She shook her head, distraught, then released my hands and bent to gather her flowers again. "The pull in my chest… I know there's more to it that I can't explain, but someone out there needs our help. That's all I know."

I took a deep breath, needing to treat light here. "Fern, you know what I'm going to say, right? That this could be Bennett or the crone trying to manipulate you to get to me."

"I know, but that's what I'm trying to explain. The connection allowed me to *feel* what they were feeling, and I'm telling you, there was no malcontent or harm behind the thoughts. Whoever this is needs our help and is sincere in their intent."

Shit. Aster was never going to buy this, and honestly, I'm not sure I could either. Especially after Mom's warning.

"Come on. Let's finish our walk." I pulled Fern back onto the path and meandered deeper through the swaying trees. "I'll make you a deal. I won't say anything for now, if you promise to tell me if it happens again."

Fern wound her arm through mine and shifted her basket to her other hand, smiling as if all was right in the world. "I promise."

Bennett

Today was the day. I'd finally worked up the courage to reach out to Lily, and with the fire stoked and my ingredients ready... it was time.

Concentrating on the connection we shared, I sent two simple words through my spell, targeting Lily with all the truth and feeling I carried in my soul. *"I'm sorry."* When my fire sparked, I knew it worked and hoped eventually it would make a difference. I wasn't dumb enough to approach the castle in Ferindale yet, but after discovering the crone was missing and the threat to my mom's life was no longer in play, I absconded with the book again and left my clan and mother behind. Returning to Lily was the only thing I wanted. With a few more spells, hopefully she'd understand why I did what I did, and more importantly… forgive me.

It was the rainy season in Devonshire, and while the moonbiens and morphineas loved the constant drizzle on the lake, it only added to my depression of being on the run.

Returning to the Dark Kingdom was my best bet to avoid discovery, especially from my own clan. They would never cross into the Dark territory, even if it was to find me or the book. But being so close to Dartmoor was a risk, one I'd have to move on from soon. I thought about returning to the Dark castle itself, seeing as it had basically been abandoned after Alder and Lily moved to Ferindale to unite the kingdoms, but I couldn't bring myself to do it. There were too many painful memories there. It was where I lost Lily. And while the fault was ultimately my own, I couldn't help but wonder if the blood bond between her and Alder had never been enacted, if things might have ended up differently.

I shook my head, tossing the thoughts aside. Scooting back against the tree and under its protective bright-blue boughs, I closed my eyes and reinforced my glamor so I wouldn't be discovered as I continued to daydream. Nothing could break their connection now, but the least I could do was try to win her forgiveness as the man I truly was.

No more glamor, no more lies, no more assigned missions—just me, the half-breed fae witch warrior with all my regrets laid bare before the Queen.

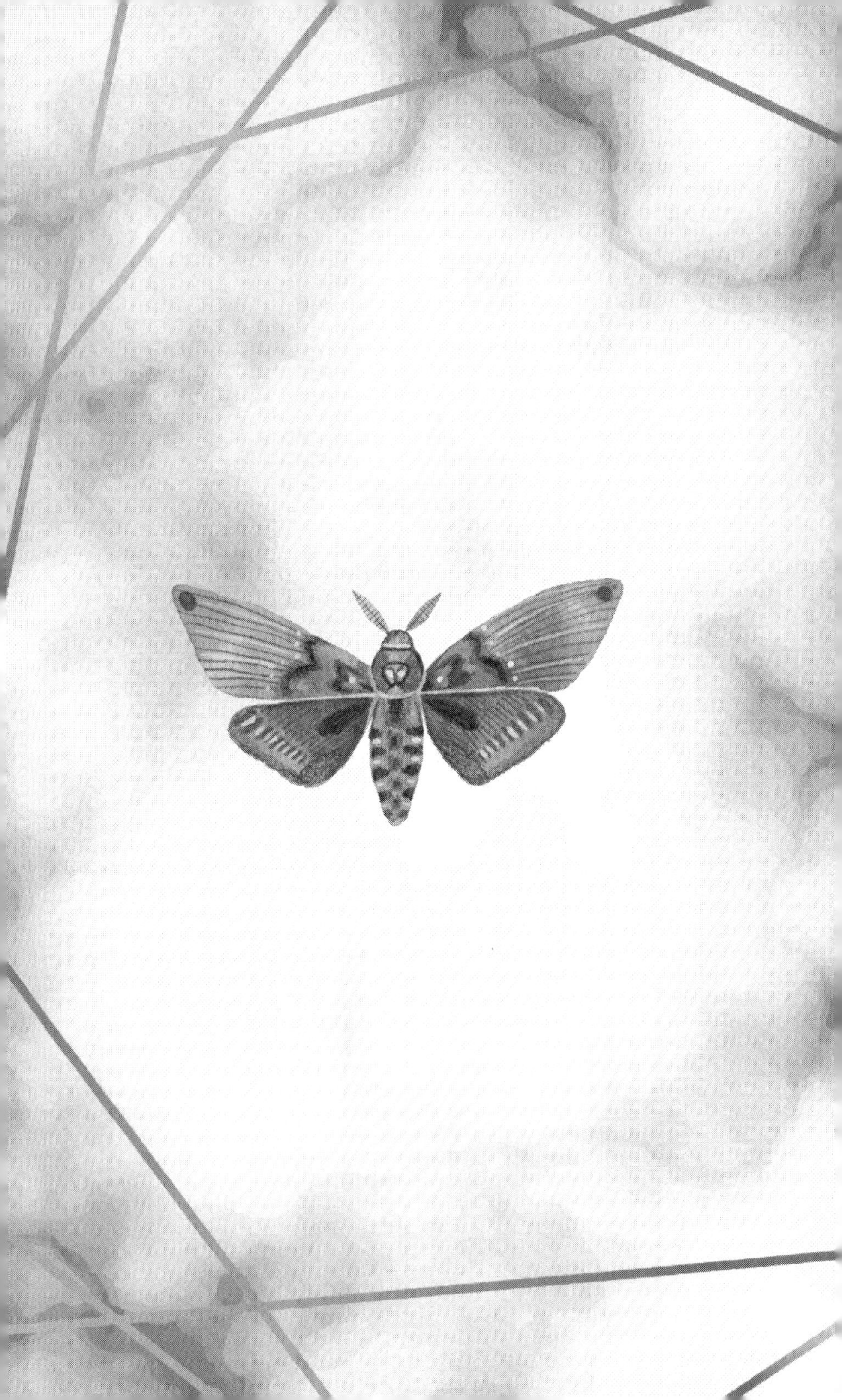

Seven

Lily

"How was your day, *dear*?" Alder teased, his voice falling in soft waves against my skin as I stared into the bathroom mirror. He was shirtless and sweaty, his bronze skin glistening in the reflection under the fairy lights.

"It was… okay. How was yours?" I turned to face him and propped myself against the marble vanity behind me.

Striding across the room, he came to stand before me with a sexy smirk plastered on his lips. "Better now that I can do this." He leaned down and brought his mouth to mine. The kiss was soft at first, then deepened as a low chuckle rumbled from his throat. Lifting me off the floor, he pulled me against his slick chest. "Time for a shower."

"What?" I burst out laughing, faking a struggle. There was no arguing, and who would want to? We both needed and wanted this, and as Queen, I was slowly learning not to deny myself the things I craved.

Running a finger down one of his antlers, I threaded my hands into his thick black hair. "Seriously, how was training?"

He set me on my feet in the all-glass shower and reached past me to turn on the water. "It was fine, but unfortunately, I didn't receive any further news regarding the search." He gazed down at me with hooded eyes. "How about you? Learn anything new?"

I studied the planes of his beautiful face, the angle of his jaw, his oh-so-kissable lips, and decided now was not the time to be discussing Bennett. "No. Nothing of relevance."

"Good. Because I'm not in the mood to talk." His lips met mine again as he guided us beneath the warm spray and began peeling the clothes from our wet bodies.

"Me neither." I lifted my arms over my head, and once my shirt was gone, all else was forgotten.

Lily

"I don't care what you think, Aster. I'm telling you the truth!" Fern's stern words matched her gaze as she looked up from the table, pinning me with a *help me* stare.

"Good evening, everyone," I greeted my sisters. "I hope the rest of your afternoon was enjoyable." I walked the length of the carved wood table and took my regular seat at its head.

"Oh yes, it was enjoyable. Relaxing, even. But a complete waste of time!" Aster snapped. "We should be doing more to find Bennett and the crone, instead of picking flowers and taking showers."

I reached up and smoothed a strand of my still-damp hair behind my ear. "Yes, well. There are other things in the kingdom that require our attention." I motioned to Alder.

"Yes, like preparing my men for battle in case a threat was to arise." He angled his head in Aster's direction while reaching for my hand beneath the table, giving it the light squeeze of comfort I'd grown accustomed to.

"Yes, but don't you agree if we spent more time trying to find Bennett and the crone, the need for military preparations would no longer be required?" Aster stabbed a piece of meat on her plate with a silver fork.

"I believe a strong protective force is necessary for any kingdom, regardless of its current *issues*." Alder's nostrils flared as he raised a glass in the air. "To our continued efforts, both physical and magical."

The rest of my sisters raised their glasses and shouted, "Here, here!" All but Aster, of course.

Since arriving here, my oldest sister seemed sterner than I remembered. Harder around the edges somehow. I wondered what was going on back home and vowed to discuss it with her tomorrow once we'd all had time to rest.

"Here, here." I added my confirmation to Alder's toast and raised my glass, then addressed Aster directly. "Tomorrow, we'll set up another spell. And we'll do the same the day after that, and the day after that, for however long it takes. But I will not neglect, or minimize, the rest of what needs to be done around the kingdom to help keep us on the path to peace. Nor will I spend the entire time you're all visiting holed up in the basement out of fear." I grinned at all my sisters seated around the table. "Yes, Bennett is still out there, but nothing has happened in the months since he's been gone. The crone has disappeared and is hopefully dead, and I never get to see you guys. I want to enjoy our time together, so that means taking walks, and having dinner, and…"

"Hosting a ball!" Alder interrupted boisterously.

"What?" I gasped.

"I'm sorry I didn't get a chance to tell you earlier." He squeezed my hand beneath the table again. "The other reason I went to the training arena today was to select the guards who will attend our Samhain Ball." He shrugged. "Not only is it a traditional celebration across the realm, but I wanted to celebrate your family's visit and acknowledge publicly that Fern, Iris, and Daisy are my half-sisters through Gideon."

Giddy smiles and squeals erupted around the table. The girls were obviously excited about the prospect—all but Aster, of course. And for the first time since their arrival, I tended to agree with her.

The memory of the last ball I attended here and how everything had gone so wrong rose to the surface. However, it was also what brought Alder into my life, and for that, I was grateful.

Returning to their meals, the girls' conversation turned to party dresses, sparkling decor, menu items, and more, while I leaned forward and placed a kiss on Alder's cheek. "Thank you. I think a ball will do everyone some good."

I caught Aster's eye and hoped more than anything I was right.

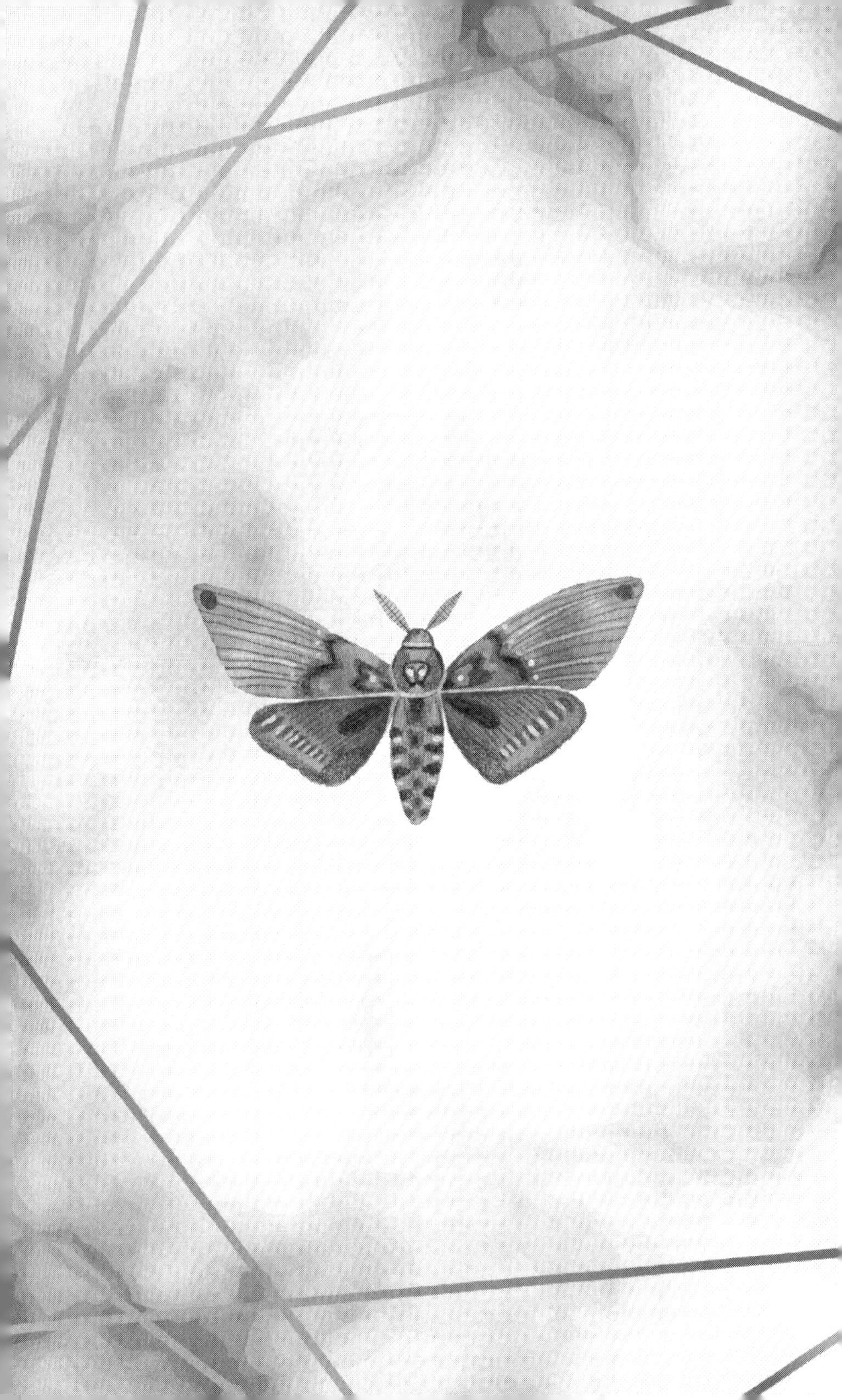

Eight

Lily

"We need to try a different spell. This *locater* one isn't working." Aster stomped from the altar and tossed the remnants of her tea down the sink.

Our morning session in the basement was proving to be just as unfruitful as yesterday's. I surveyed the space and all the gathered ingredients lining the shelves and tables and took a deep breath. They reminded me of home, but also gave me an idea that stemmed from the adventure which brought me here. "Maybe we should try the spell Sybil used to boost Bennett's connection to the book but alter it instead to boost his connection to me."

Aster raised a brow. "Do you think your connection was that strong? Something that would linger even after what he did?"

I shrugged. "I don't know. Maybe?"

Fern shifted away from the altar and moved to take a seat in the chair across the room.

"What do you think, Fern?" I asked.

"What? Oh, yeah, maybe it could work."

I ignored Fern's flippant response and started gathering the items I'd need.

My old wooden pestle felt at home in my hand, as did the anise, angelica, and the pinch of mushroom I'd watched Sybil add to the mix. Grinding the herbs, I tried to remember if the leader of the Acrucian Coven spoke any words to activate the spell, but I didn't recall seeing her do so. It was only her instructions that lingered in my mind… *"Drink this and concentrate on finding the book."*

Daisy handed me a cup of tea and I stirred in the herbs.

"Should we talk about this?" Aster spoke up again.

"What's there to talk about? If this works, it should induce an astral vision that will show me where Bennett is, just like it did when we found the book's hiding place." I shook my head, trying to keep the sting of that memory at bay.

Aster nodded, silently agreeing and letting the subject drop.

I slid into the wooden chair in front of the old oak table and downed the potion like a shot of whiskey before turning my focus fully on Bennett.

Memories of our time together rushed into my mind. Him falling across the threshold of our magical store, his stormy colored eyes landing directly on me. His tall, athletic build, and his affinity for Adidas over Chuck Taylors. His short chestnut hair, and his nerdy plant-filled dorm. The way his hand felt in mine as we roamed the Essex countryside. The way my body felt against his lying in the bed at the Sessile Oak Inn. But mostly, the sorrow in his eyes as he disappeared into the Dark forest with the book, marking himself as a traitor.

Outside of the vision, I felt my heart clench as the memory of his deception took center stage, playing on repeat across my mind.

"Lily, come back. Lily, wake up!"

Shaken awake, I snapped out of the memory spiral to four pairs of panicked eyes.

"Oh, thank the Goddess. Are you alright?" Daisy smoothed the hair from my face and removed the cup still resting in my hand.

"It's okay. I'm fine." I leaned forward, then dropped my head and braced my arms on my knees.

"There you go, just breathe." Iris rubbed gentle circles on my back, the feel of the warm stone in her hand quickly aiding in my recovery.

"What happened?" Aster's question felt soft. Hesitant.

"I'm not sure. After I took the potion, I focused on Bennett and was hit with a wave of memories. For some reason, I got stuck there." I straightened in the chair, disappointed with the whole encounter. "I didn't learn anything new about where he is now, though."

"That's okay. Maybe we can use a different combination of herbs and try again," Daisy offered kindly.

I pushed to my feet and crossed the stone floor to the large selection of bottles and herbs lining the shelves of my fully stocked storage cabinet. "Daisy, you're right. Help yourself and mix up whatever potion you think might work."

Daisy bounced on her feet with a grin that stretched from ear to ear, then quickly got to work. She pulled some of her own ingredients out of the stash in her bag, then mixed them with a few of the new options she'd selected from mine.

"Aster, if you don't mind, would you go to the kitchen and ask Gretta to prepare us some lunch? I'd like to spend the rest of our afternoon working on this until we get it right."

The corner of Aster's mouth tipped up, as if she couldn't contain her smile at my reaffirmed work ethic. "Of course. I'll be back shortly."

I lifted my chin, grateful she didn't balk at my request, because in reality, I simply needed some time to talk to Fern alone.

I think I was the only one who noticed how pale she was after I took the potion and came out of my vision. She remained in the chair across the room, not moving but clearly affected by something. A light sheen of sweat shimmered on her brow, but she remained still, holding her tongue.

With Daisy and Iris occupied at the worktable, I crossed the room and propped my back against the wall beside my sister. "Fern, are you okay? Did something else happen when I cast that spell?"

She was silent for a moment, then looked up and met my gaze with an ice-blue stare. "Yes. Something else happened. And this time, I *did* hear a voice."

I slid down the wall and crouched beside her. "What did it say?"

"*'I'm sorry'* and *'Please let me explain'.*" Fern's eyes brimmed with tears. "The sorrow behind the words, Lil." She placed a hand over her chest. "It was heartbreaking."

I held her gaze and looked deeply into her watery eyes. I had no doubt the emotions she felt were genuine, but I couldn't deny I thought she was being used. "Fern, you have to realize this is probably a trap."

She shoved out of the chair. "I *do* realize that, Lily! And I have no idea why this is happening to me, but I'm telling you... the emotions I feel when the connection is made are so strong, it's almost overwhelming."

I took a deep breath and rose to my feet. Could this be Bennett? Could he have changed his mind about turning the book over and now needed our help?

"What are you two going on about over there?" Daisy interrupted our conversation from across the room, then waved us over before I could respond. "Lil, whenever you're ready to try again, I think this combination will work."

Fern grabbed my hand and gave it a squeeze. "Whatever is happening concerns us both, and we need to get to the bottom of it."

My head bobbed in agreement as I smiled at my sister. She was a badass, and despite the warning from Mom and Aster, I knew I could trust her. "You're right. Let's do this... together."

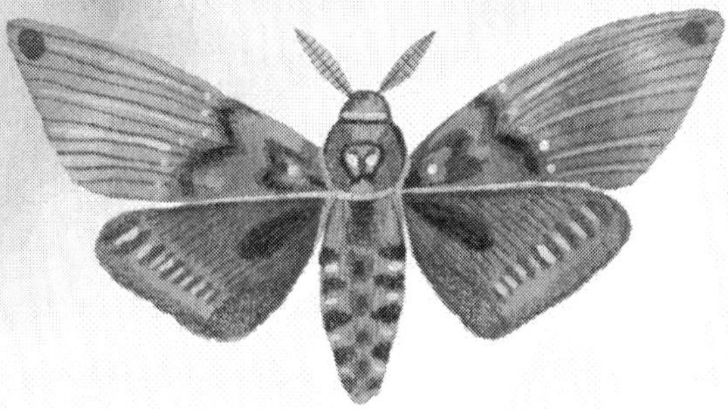

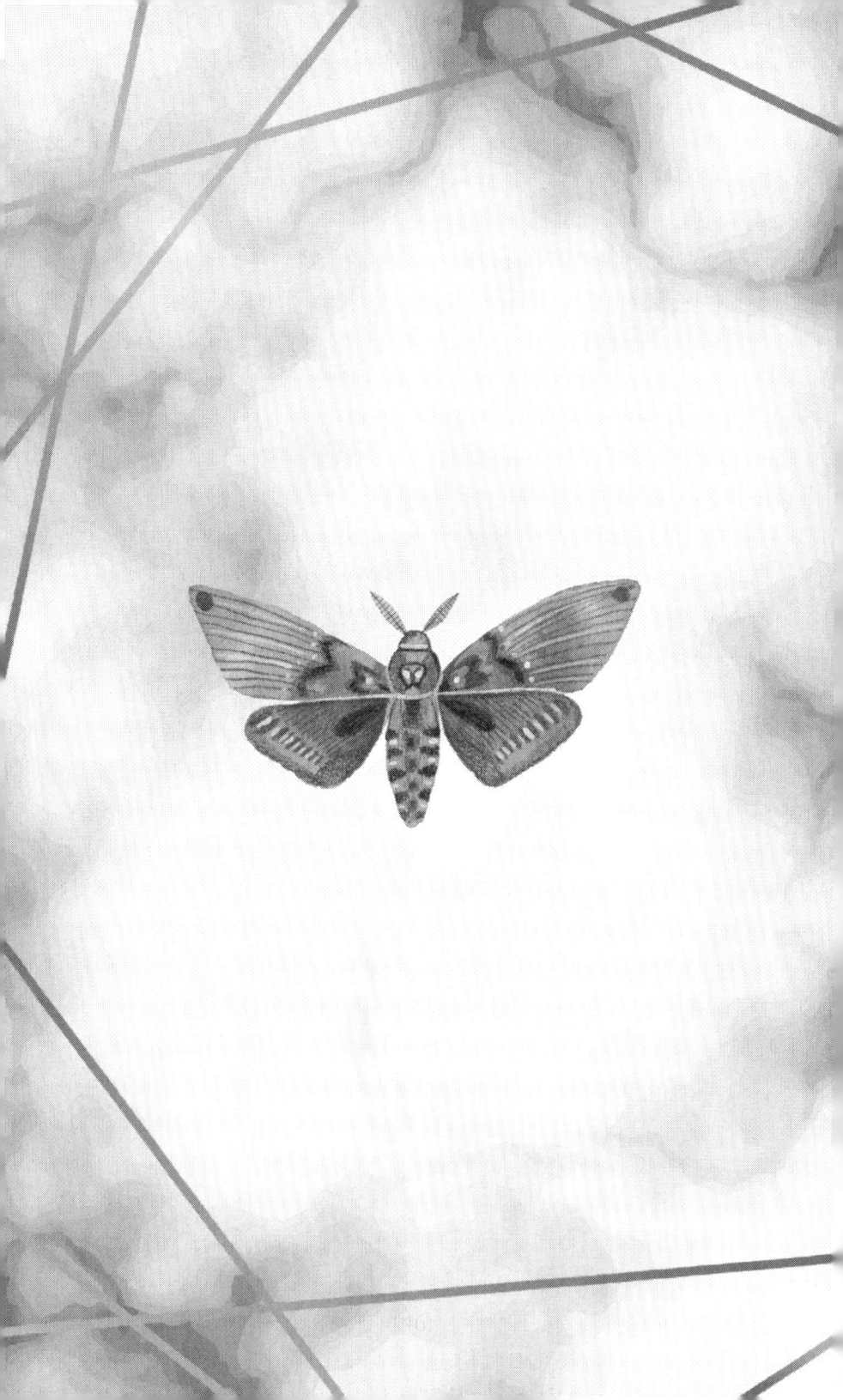

Nine

Lily

"I've used some Dittany of Crete to aid in the astral projection, which should help protect you during the link. I've also crushed in some pomegranate seeds to boost the overall divination and to grant your wish for the spell to work." Daisy handed me the cup again, beaming.

"Thanks, Daisy. I should have known better than to attempt this on my own." For goodness sake, we all had our specialties, and this was hers. What was I thinking?

As if she read my mind, Daisy ran a hand down my arm. "Come on, Lil. We may have our unique affinities, but we're all witches at our core. Magic runs through our veins, and with the lessons learned from Mom and the guidance from the Goddess, we each can do what's required when need."

She was right. After accepting my place here and unlocking my full fae magic, my original witch powers blossomed as well. Now, seeing as I was usually alone, I'd learned to depend on myself and trust my instincts even more. I looked around the safety of my basement and offered everyone a lopsided grin. "You're right, but

I'm still glad you're all here." I retook my seat as Daisy, Iris, and Fern surrounded me, creating a circle of their own.

"Bottom's up." I grinned and downed the tea. This potion went down a little smoother, but the jolt I received was anything but.

I shrieked, tossing back my head as an electrical current raced down my chest, arms, and legs. My insides burned like fire, and I couldn't open my eyes. Shouts filled my head, but I was unable to tell if they were coming from my sisters or from the vision into which I was being forced.

Inhale. Exhale.

I forced myself to take a deep breath, and the burning began to subside. *Just a few more.*

Inhale. Exhale.

Inhale. Exhale.

There, that's better.

A light sting continued to travel through my veins, but it was something I could work past with a little more concentration.

Focusing deeper on the vision, I once again followed the thread attached to whatever kind of magic this was. Sparks flew behind my eyes, but thankfully, I didn't feel their sting. Only the warmth of friendly thoughts and a kind embrace.

"Forgive me," a distant voice whispered.

The echo sounded vaguely familiar, but I couldn't be sure if it was Bennett or not. "Bennett?" I called out into the ether.

"Lily. Forgive me," the voice repeated.

Whether it was him or not, I had no forgiveness to offer a disembodied voice. "Come to the castle so we can talk. I invite you to our Samhain Ball. Turn yourself into the Guard, and I guarantee no harm will come to you."

"Forgive me." The words repeated, then faded away as the connection broke apart.

Gasping, I lurched forward, almost falling out of the chair.

"Lily! Thank the Goddess you're back." Daisy's voice hitched, and I looked up to find her eyes shining with tears.

"I'm okay. I swear."

She shook her head. "It's not you—"

I followed her gaze, then dropped to my knees as soon as I saw Fern passed out on the floor beside me. "What happened?" I reached for my sister, brushing her raven hair away from her face.

"We don't know," Iris supplied. "After you drank the tea and screamed, Fern started to convulse and then passed out." Iris sniffled and grabbed Daisy's hand. "We couldn't wake either of you."

Daisy pulled her into a hug, offering what comfort she could. "She'll be okay. Just stay strong. Your twin bond will help guide her back."

"That's just it." Iris shook her head. "I haven't felt our bond since we originally returned home from here."

"What?" Daisy took a step back. "And you're just now telling us?"

"I talked with Mom about it, and she said not to worry. That perhaps she was just taking some time to find her own way… magically."

My eyes returned to Fern's prone form lying on the cold stone floor. Could that be why Mom told Aster to keep an eye on her? To give her space so she could find herself *magically*? What did that even mean? "Okay, well, if Mom said not to worry, then I guess we won't." *For now.* "Daisy, can you bring me a wet cloth, please."

"On it."

Daisy laid the cool towel in my hand seconds later. I leaned forward and placed it across Fern's forehead, whispering, "Come on, Fern. Come back to us."

"Lunch is served!" Aster returned to the room with a flourish, balancing a large silver platter filled with sandwiches and drinks on both her hands. The moment she saw us, her smile fell and concern transformed her features. Sliding the tray onto the counter, she stomped across the room. "What the hell happened?" She bent down and placed a hand on Fern's chest. "Lily, explain."

"I don't know what happened. Daisy prepared another potion for the spell, and after I took it, I was caught up in my own vision. I had no idea what was happening to Fern."

Her hawk-like eyes snapped to Daisy. "Fine. Then *you* tell me what happened."

Daisy sniffled, then relayed her account. "Just like Lily said, she took the potion and was caught up in a vision, but at the same time,

Fern started to convulse and fell to the floor. We tried to wake them both and couldn't, but Lily eventually came to on her own."

Aster's gaze returned to our ailing sister, but her words were directed at me. "Did you learn anything new, or at least make a connection with Bennett?"

"I… I'm not sure," I stuttered lamely. "Fern and I have both been hearing voices during our spells, but I can't make out whether it's Bennett or not."

Aster jerked upright, springing back to her feet. "Then that's enough of that! No more *connection* spells, or whatever you're calling them. If you don't even know who it is you're connecting to, the risk is too great. Wouldn't you agree, *Your Highness?*"

My head ticked back as if I'd been slapped. "You know what, Aster? Don't be a jerk! The spell we were trying came straight from the Acrucian Coven, and it's not like we're a bunch of amateurs here." I crossed my arms, feeling defiant and annoyed—but she was right.

We took too big a risk, and now Fern was paying for it.

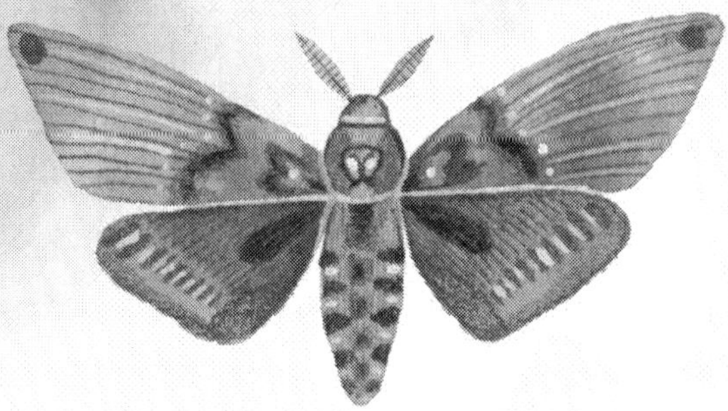

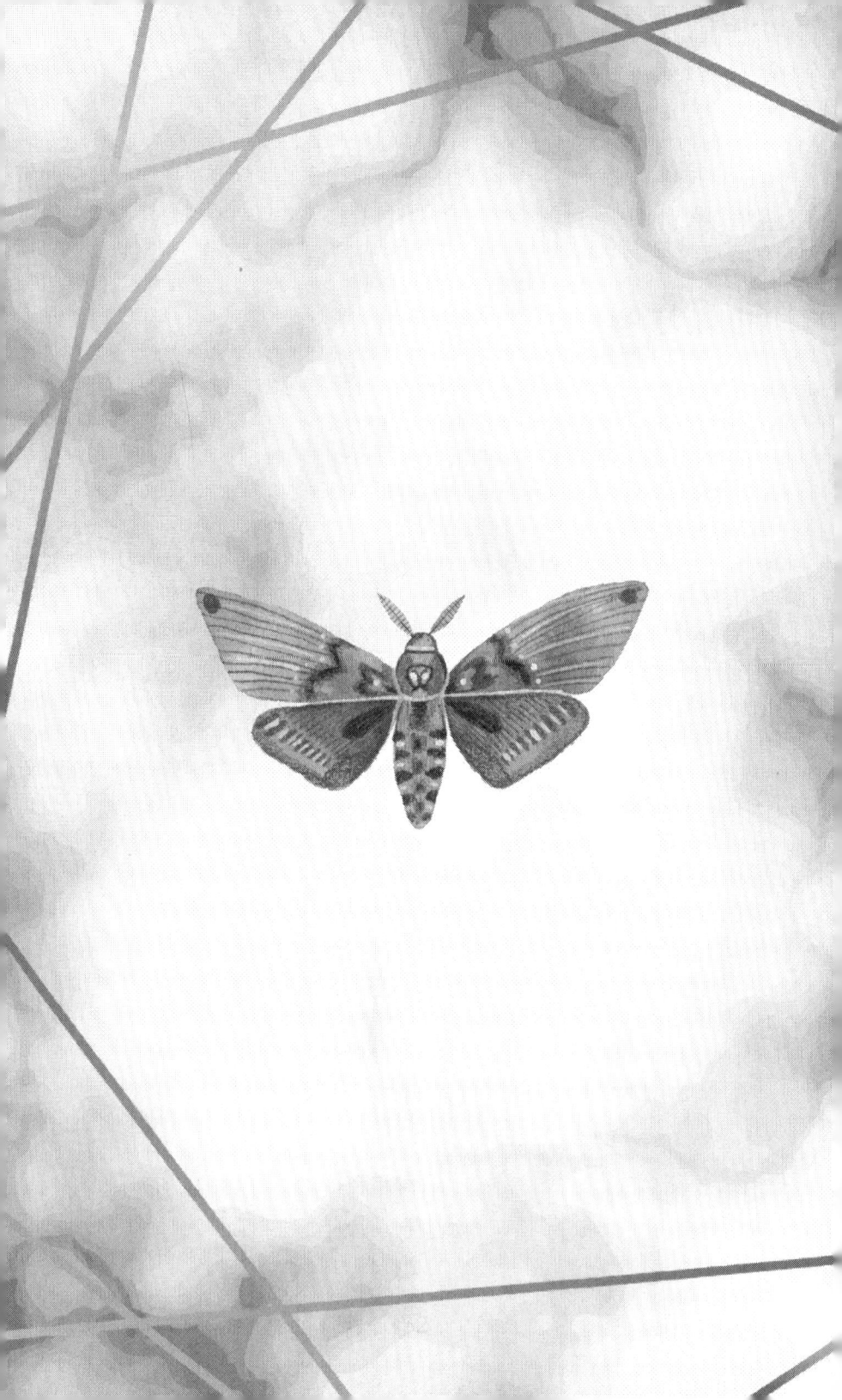

Ten

Lily

"Gretta, please bring me another bowl of fresh water and ask Daisy to come join me." I dabbed a cool cloth across Fern's forehead.

After being further reprimanded by my big sister, we all agreed to move Fern into my bed chambers so the staff and I could keep an eye on her day and night.

"Yes, ma'am. I'll be just a moment," Gretta replied before quickly shuffling from the room.

I allowed the silence to wrap around us like a weighted blanket as I stared at my sister. I imagined her waking and smiling up at me with her bright blue eyes, but instead, she remained unconscious, her long dark hair feathered out across the crisp white pillows of mine and Alder's bed.

I was close to all my sisters, but Fern and I shared a special bond. I could hear our laughter in my head as we giggled like fools, weaving together flower crowns for her shop while sitting in the candlelight of mine. Our bond was light-hearted, filled with joy and mutual interest for what the other did. She provided the flowers and helped dip my spell candles in their petals, while I provided the scented candles that magically led her customers to pick their perfect blooms. My heart ached at the memories of all our time spent together inside the safety of *Hexx*.

The laughter, the fights, the discovery of something new each time our magical shop would shift into a new season. In autumn, pots of mums would replace the hydrangeas in Fern's shop, while black candles and pumpkin spice wax melts would pop into existence in mine. It was our favorite time of year, and whenever we could, we'd spend hours kicking through the leaves in the forest behind our home. The shop was our safe place, and as I stared at my sister now, I missed it and my life back in Essex, Connecticut more than I ever thought I could.

When the door creaked open, I quickly wiped my eyes.

"Gretta said you wanted to see me." Daisy's voice was soft and comforting as she set a bowl of fresh water on the table beside the bed.

"Yes. Thank you. I thought we could try something else with your herbs. Perhaps a dream bag under the pillow to help guide her back to us. Or maybe a piece of moonwort placed beneath her tongue to help her speak the words to break through whatever is holding her under." I shook my head, hot tears stinging my eyes again. "Honestly, anything you could think of that might help."

Daisy placed her hand on my shoulder. "If that's what you'd like me to do, I'll do it. But you heard what Aster said... She doesn't want any of us using magic or doing any more spells until she finishes the research she's doing with her books."

I pushed out of the chair and walked into the elaborate bathroom. White marble countertops and glittering silver fixtures greeted me, but today, their shine did nothing to brighten my mood. Stopping short, I realized how much I longed for the dark, moody feel of Gideon's castle and the comfort it lent. "Never mind. You're right. We should wait like Aster said." I spun around so fast, I almost lost my balance. "Can you please go find Gretta again for me?"

"*Sure...* but are you alright?" Daisy took a half-step toward me but stopped when I spun back around to face the sink.

I splashed my face with cold water which helped my rising temper, but it did nothing to cover up my lie. "Yes. I'm fine. I just need to speak to Gretta and make some arrangements for the Ball." I played it off as if it was part of my queenly duties and hoped Daisy bought it.

"Okay, I'll send her right back. See you at dinner?" Daisy's lingering question made it obvious she was still unsure where my emotions lay.

I took a deep breath and gathered myself. "Of course. And let me know if Aster discovers anything from her books before then."

Daisy smiled and slowly left the room, while I returned my gaze in the mirror and fell further into the dark.

Bennett

Wet leaves squelched beneath my boots as I trekked through the forest that would lead me back to Dartmoor. I told myself I could hide out near Devonshire Lake for as long as I needed, but when the entire Dark Kingdom was saturated with torrential rains, my plans were forced to change. Now, despite the warnings I'd given myself, hiding in the Dark castle seemed like the smartest thing to do. After Alder's surprise arrival the last time we were there, I'd followed the hidden corridor from the main bedroom back through the tunnels and found that the secret entrance emerged into a dilapidated barn just outside of town.

Trudging over rain-soaked logs and saturated foliage provided a workout I happily welcomed, and I felt the burn as my legs strengthened back into peak shape. Slipping and sliding my way through the grass, I crested the final hill to reveal the barn below. Its worn exterior suggested an air of neglect, but I wasn't stupid enough to think the crown didn't have someone watching it, seeing as it led straight into the heart of the castle.

I posted up in the tallest tree near the forest's edge and began my new mission. I watched a few random farmers move their herds of cowkrieps back and forth across the field, but oddly, no one ever approached the barn. As the sun began its descent, I looked out over the Dark Kingdom with true appreciation. The vibrant colors painting the sky reminded me of my time here with Lily, and how she often commented that the clouds reminded her of cotton candy.

The dying rays of pink and purple light faded with the sunset, and all I wanted was to hear her sweet voice again.

I tried to reach her every day with a new spell to tell her how sorry I was, but I had no idea if my messages were getting through. And worse yet, I had no idea if she would forgive me even if they were. I heard nothing back through the connection, but at one point thought I sensed a feeling of understanding or perhaps sympathy radiating from the other side. It was that feeling that kept me going—kept me trying to contact her and reveal my truth.

A snap of wood pulled my attention back to my current predicament, and I braced for impact as the limb I was perched on finally gave way. Landing on my feet, I took off at a full run and dipped into the barn through the gaping hole in the wooden front door.

Age-eaten planks and tattered feed bags lined the floor at the back of the barn. I raised a hand to shield my eyes from the falling straw stirred up by a gentle breeze blowing through the cracks in all four walls. Moving my way to the rickety staircase in the back, I carefully climbed into the hay loft, thankful it smelled dry and clean instead of wet and musty like I expected.

What I *didn't* see was the door that led to the secret passageway into the castle, but as a yawn overtook me, I stretched my arms and back and admitted to myself how exhausted I was. I needed to rest, then I could look for it tomorrow.

Kicking the hay into a pile, I patted it into the shape of a makeshift bed and laid down. I closed my eyes and thought the same thought I had every night for months... *I'm sorry, Lily. Please forgive me.*

Fatigue quickly overtook me and I fell into a dreamless sleep, waking the next morning to pink clouds and a bright blue sky. Surprised by how comfortable my hay bed was, I stretched out, propped my arms behind my head, and imagined Lily lying beside me. Through the cracks in the ceiling, I watched the clouds softly glide across the sky, imagining them carrying my hopes and dreams of forgiveness to the woman currently occupying my heart and mind.

"Don't lose hope. It'll be okay."

I jerked upright, sending a spray of hay into the air. "Lily, is that you?" I concentrated on the words—visualized them piercing the veil and reaching Lily's mind, but there was no response. I waited, focusing harder and pulling on all the magic I could. "Lily, please. Say something."

"Come to the castle."

I gasped. The words fell heavily against my chest like four beating heartbeats, bringing me back to life.

Eleven

Lily

"Gretta, please prepare my riding clothes." I didn't meet her eyes and practically whispered my request.

"Yes, ma'am." By now she knew me well enough she didn't inquire about my intent. "Will anyone be joining you?"

"No."

Gretta sighed—the only physical expression of her concern—but continued to do as I asked.

I needed this. To return to the one place I'd felt safe and at peace in this entire realm—the Dark castle. My thoughts drifted to Gideon and my heart clenched, but it was time. Alder and I had agreed to move to the Light Kingdom since I was its true heir. But after wandering these glittering halls and trying to work my magic in the same basement where the crone had once been, I wondered if it was a mistake. I wondered if we should have moved to Alder's kingdom instead.

"Here you go, my lady." Gretta handed me a thick pair of riding pants and gestured to the rest of the clothes she'd laid out on the bed.

My heart tightened again when I bent to grab them and my hand brushed against Fern's foot. "Please help my other sisters watch over her while I'm gone," I asked Gretta.

In that moment, the heavy wood door to my room burst open. "I think I found something!" Aster came striding in with a thick tome lying open in her hands. "There's a potion the fairies use to break mental blocks."

I looked at Gretta, curious as to why she hadn't mentioned it before. "Go on," I urged my sister.

"It says here it requires root of grimloc, a strand of moonbien hair, and the petals of the vilenflu flower."

Gretta covered her mouth with a gasp.

"What is it?" I asked.

"That must be a very old book, because I haven't heard that list of ingredients since I was a child… and that was a *very* long time ago."

"Do we have the ingredients?" I asked Gretta.

She shook her head. "No, my lady. No one has seen a vilenflu flower for centuries." She visibly swallowed. "The crone and your father had them all burned ages ago."

"What?! Where did they grow originally?"

Gretta hesitated, wringing her hands together in front of her skirt. "In the mountains of Glenmiere… deep in the Dark Kingdom.

After Gideon fled the realm, your father burned all sorts of medicinal crops at the behest of the crone."

The world spun and a heaviness settled in my chest as I thought about the citizens of the Dark Kingdom and all they'd been through. I recalled Alder's words when he was still pretending to be a guard in my miserable father's army… *"After the Dark King vanished many years ago, his people spent most of their time warring between themselves. We just stop the thieves who cross into our borders, looking for an easy score."* I wondered now if they were truly thieves or simply looking for the plants or medicine my father had destroyed.

I turned back to the bed and glanced at Fern's unconscious form. Now, more than ever, I needed her with me. Her flower magic centered around healing the body and mind, so after seeing her lying there unable to help herself—the situation had turned from a hard pill to swallow to an almost unbearable burden to bear. "Please go get Daisy. And Gretta… prepare some riding clothes for her as well." With a firm nod, Gretta left the room in a bustle of skirts.

"What are you doing?" Aster looked around, finally realizing I was preparing to leave.

"I was going to take the day and return to the Dark castle." I sighed heavily. "I need a break, and I thought with the rest of you here, I could go and search Gideon's library for any clues that might help with this entire mess." I flung my arms out wide, mentally including everything that had happened since Bennett fell through our shop's front door. "And before you try to stop me… please remember, I *am* Queen here." I took a deep breath and lifted my chin. "But with this new information, it looks like I'll need to take more than an afternoon away. Daisy and I will venture to Glenmiere and see if we can find anything that remains of the vilenflu crop."

Just then, Daisy entered the room with Gretta hot on her heels. "The *what* crop?" my sister asked.

"Vilenflu. It's a rare flower that may hold our only chance to wake up Fern." I picked up my riding crop. "You up for a ride?"

Daisy beamed. "Heck, yes!"

Aster slammed the hefty book down on the dresser across the room. "Now wait a minute! You can't just pick up and leave," she fumed.

I straightened my spine. "Actually, I can. Alder and Gretta will make sure you and Iris have everything you need while we're gone."

"And where exactly are you going, my dear?" Alder's deep voice echoed from the open door. A smile graced his beautiful face but immediately dropped away when he spotted my riding gear. Striding across the room, his steps ate up the marble floor until he towered over me. Reaching for my hands, he leaned down and whispered, "Seriously, Lil. Where are you going? And were you even going to tell me about it?"

I gazed up into his caring, caramel eyes. "Can everyone give us a minute, please?" I paused. "Daisy, I'll be by your room to get you shortly."

No one said a word as they left me and my king alone.

My breath felt shallow and a knot formed in my chest as I rushed to offer an explanation. "Look, I need a break away from here, and yes, I was going to tell you, but it all happened so fast. Aster discovered an ingredient we need that may help wake Fern up, so Daisy and I are going to travel to Glenmiere to see if we can locate it."

"What?!" He jerked his hands from mine and began pacing the floor of our room. "You think you can just ride into Glenmiere alone and ask for help?" His broad shoulders and wide chest heaved with every breath.

"Well, yes. Why couldn't I? We've announced we're uniting the kingdoms, and everyone has been so accepting of the prospect. Excited, even. Why wouldn't they want to help their new Queen?"

He paced for a few minutes, deep in thought, then stopped right in front of me and ran a hand through his thick dark hair. "Because, Lil. Not every territory in the realm acknowledges the kingdoms in the first place. Glenmiere is home to the Dark Elves, and they are not a tribe to be trifled with." He moved closer and reached for my hands again. "I'm sorry, Lily, but I cannot let you go alone."

I pressed my lips together and took a deep breath, suppressing the urge to rip my hands from his. "While I acknowledge there's a lot about this realm I still don't understand… you have *no right* to tell me what I can and cannot do."

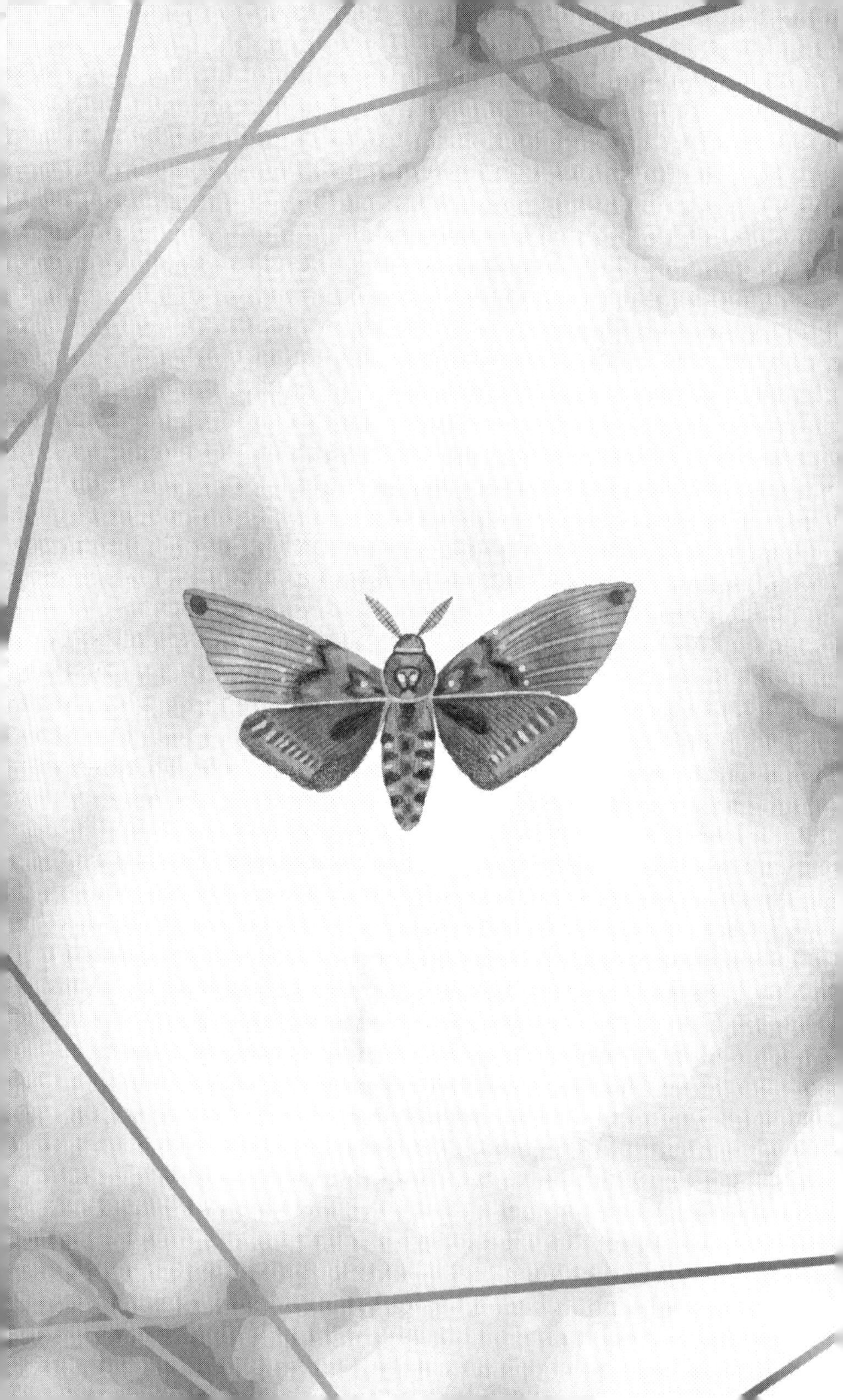

Twelve

Lily

I gently pulled on the reins and eased my beautiful white mare, Luna, out of the stables. "You good?" I called out to Daisy.

"Yep, just getting used to this big boy's action. I haven't ridden in a while." Daisy sat atop one of Alder's favorite black stallions, giving him the reins so Samson could get used to her just as much as she was getting used to him. "I can't believe Alder agreed to let us go."

"Yes, well, it wasn't without concessions." I tipped my chin toward the edge of the barn where one of the guards who would be accompanying us waited. Alder wanted to come with us, of course, but General Niasin—the leader of his Guard who rode before us now—convinced him to stay behind and continue the search for Bennett while overseeing the arrangements of the Ball. After hours of raised voices and argued points, Alder finally agreed with a begrudging acknowledgement that we'd be in good hands.

"Ah." Daisy smiled, then led Samson into step beside me and Luna as we set out on our adventure. "Well, you know what they say… marriage is nothing without compromise."

I laughed. "Very true, wise one. But Alder and I aren't married yet." We both fell silent as the words hung in the air.

"Is that something you've talked about? Is there a specific timeline for something like that here, seeing as you're the ruling couple now?"

"Yes and no. The realm can't do anything about us ruling since it's in our blood. We've both been validated as the rightful heirs, but I guess you could say it's *expected*." I shrugged. "And I do love him, there's no question about that," I rushed to add.

"So, what's the hold up?"

Luna held her head high, maintaining her smooth gait as I pondered Daisy's question. "There is no *hold up*. We've just been busy. Between the coronation, the search for Bennett, all the meetings about joining our kingdoms, and now planning the Samhain Ball, there hasn't been a lot of time to discuss a wedding, that's all." My answer probably sounded defensive, but it was the truth. But so was this… "Honestly, while I do love Alder, I'm not sure I'm ready to be married yet." I slumped in my saddle, feeling guilty for even thinking the words, let alone saying them out loud.

"Why's that?" Daisy looked over at me with genuine concern as she bounced atop Samson.

Hot tears stung my eyes as I let my emotions rise to the surface. "It's barely been six months since I left our home for the first time. I've never had a boyfriend, never left the country before all this, and now… here I am, the Fae Queen of a foreign land expected to marry and unite two kingdoms into one." I shook my head. "Sometimes, it all feels like too much, ya know?"

"I get that," Daisy acknowledged kindly.

"Everything has been such a whirlwind since Bennett fell through our door, and until we find him and this damned book, I'm not ready to move forward with anything, if that makes sense." I wiped my eyes with the back of my hand.

"Of course it makes sense, and I'm sure it would to Alder, too." Daisy paused, then pinned me with a knowing stare beyond her years. "Have you told him any of this?"

I shook my head, refusing to say the word.

"Maybe you should."

I sniffled and looked away. She was right, of course. However, I already knew where Alder stood. He would marry me at the drop of a hat. But admitting to him that I wanted to wait was an unnecessary wound I refused to inflict. I'd convinced myself of this very thing over and over again. We would make the arrangements once Bennett was caught, and I was sticking to my plan.

"Whoa!" a guard called out from up ahead, raising his fist into the air.

I pushed against the stirrups and lifted out of the saddle to see what was going on. A large tree had fallen over the road, which the guards were already working to move.

"Can't we just go around?" Daisy asked as she glanced into the forest on either side of the well-used path.

"Not here, ma'am," another guard replied from behind us. "Too many wolven roam these woods. It's best if we stay on the road. King's instructions."

I bristled at that last part, then reprimanded myself for doing so. Alder knew this world better than I ever would, and he was only trying to keep us safe. *Goddess, what is my problem?*

Daisy and I sat patiently atop our horses while the guards made quick work of the tree. With a squad of ten ahead of us and another ten behind us, our merry band of twenty-two resumed our ride west toward the Dark castle as soon as the road was clear. It was agreed we'd spend the night there before venturing higher into the mountains to reach Glenmiere. Aster had shown Daisy and me what the vilenflu looked like, and as the Queen, Alder and Gretta thought my magic may be the only thing that could bring them back to life. That fact alone was probably the only reason Alder agreed to let me go.

I hung my head as the usual doubts crept in.

My revelation magic hadn't failed me yet, but combined with my growing fae powers that weren't exactly under control… I hoped it would be enough to make this work. I hoped *I* would be enough to make this work.

"Are you excited about returning to the Dark castle?" Daisy's question pulled me from my thoughts.

"Yes. It was where I planned to go before the rest of this trip took shape."

"Really? I didn't know that."

"Yeah, well, like I told Aster… I needed a break and thought I could look through Gideon's library for anything else that might help us with Fern."

"That's a great idea. After we get settled and get something to *eat*, I'd love to help you see what we can find." She winked, making sure I caught onto the fact that she was hungry and food was her number one priority.

"You got it. Gretta sent word to the staff before we left, so everything should be set up by the time we arrive."

"Yay! This really is turning out to be a great vacation." As soon as the words were out of her mouth, she dropped her head and cringed. "I'm sorry. That was a stupid thing to say with everything that's going on."

I realized in that moment, Daisy was just like me—sheltered and confined by our familial duty to protect the portal and our jobs at the shop. "It's okay, Dais. We can still celebrate the little things, ya know."

Alder's beautiful face popped into my mind, and I realized exactly why he'd been so adamant about throwing this Ball. He was trying to give us all something to celebrate amidst the sorrow we'd experienced over the last several months. I squeezed my eyes shut, holding back a tide of emotions and a well of tears. Daisy was right. I needed to tell Alder how I was feeling and would do just that once we were together again. He deserved to hear it face-to-face. Goddess, after all he'd endured, at times, I thought he deserved better than me.

His unending kindness melted my heart, and possibly my resolve. Perhaps the celebration of a Samhain wedding was just what the kingdom needed.

Thirteen

Bennett

Peering through the cracks in the barn's front door, I watched another farmer guide his herd of cowkrieps through the field. My mouth watered as I thought about what delicious meat they produced, but I had no way to get any here. In fact, I had no sustenance here at all, which was proving to be a problem.

I ran out of water yesterday, and with the constant traffic of local farmers through the surrounding fields, I couldn't exactly meander down to the creek to refill my waterskin.

Holding the archaic canteen in my lap, I laughed to myself and thought about Lily. The memory of us hiking through the countryside outside of Essex, England, sharing water from my sleek, double-insulated water bottle seemed like a lifetime ago.

I peered around the barn again and sighed. I still hadn't found the hidden door that would lead into the castle. If I didn't gain access soon, I would have to move on. My hope was to get in, gather some food, and be gone before anyone knew I was there. But that wasn't working out so far.

Movement outside the barn snagged my attention and I rushed up into the hay loft and burrowed into a heap of straw. The barn door creaked open and from my hidden position I saw the uniform of a Light guard, then another and another. Holding my breath, I watched as they ushered someone in under a thick cloak to the back of the barn.

"Stand back, my lady," the lead guard said.

A bright gold light flared in the corner of the barn, and I cursed at my stupidity. Instead of a physical door, there was a magically hidden portal. *Of course.*

Biding my time, I watched four guards escort the woman through the portal before sliding from my hiding spot, sporting a fresh new look. Thanks to my shadow magic, the leathers of a Light Guard uniform now wrapped around my body, and the helmets they wore hid my facial features enough I fit in perfectly.

Shaking off any residual straw, I adjusted the book in the now-glamored pack and raced down the ladder, heading straight for the corner.

"All good?" a deep voice asked from behind me.

I spun to see another four guards hiding someone else between them.

"Yes. All good." I offered a clipped nod, making sure to keep my head down as I stepped aside.

The group of seasoned warriors moved forward, shielding their ward until she stood on the precipice of the portal.

"Go ahead, Your Majesty. The others are waiting there, and we'll be right behind you."

Your Majesty? My eyes locked on the hooded figure and I held my breath, waiting and praying to see if my dreams would come true.

Tossing back the hood of her cloak, Lily smiled up at the guard and thanked him for his service.

My heart clenched in my chest.

She was even more beautiful than I remembered. With her long, fire-red braid resting over one shoulder and her gorgeous green eyes gleaming in the morning light, she practically glowed with power. Or maybe that was just the portal. Still… she looked perfect to me.

"You," the main guard called out, demanding my attention. "Follow us through, and make sure the portal closes completely."

I nodded again. "Yes, sir."

Lily briefly glanced in my direction, and it took everything I had not to lift my head and meet her gaze. Not that she would recognize me, of course. But something deep in my soul hoped that she might.

Following instructions like I was part of the Guard, I stepped in line behind the final warrior and walked through the portal, confirming it snapped closed behind me like it should.

I held in a gasp as I looked around the familiar bedroom. It was just as palatial as I remembered, dressed in dark tones and moody accents—the same as my room had been right across the hall. I watched from the shadows as Lily moved around the space, touching the dresser and the freestanding desk with tears in her eyes.

I longed to reach out to her. To comfort her and tell her how sorry I was for her loss. We'd all experienced heartbreak here in one way or another, but seeing her reaction to the space again sent all my grievances right out the window. Sure, this was where she'd chosen Alder over me... and pushed me away to claim her birthright. At the time, it was something I couldn't forgive. But now, being here and seeing her again... none of that mattered. At least not to me.

"Your Majesty." The lead guard bowed at the waist. "We'll leave you and your sister to get settled. Two guards will be posted outside the door and will accompany you to the dining room once dinner is ready." He ushered the rest of the guards from the room, leaving me to stand frozen in the shadows and looking like a fool. "You too, soldier. Come man the door."

I swallowed hard and hurried from the room, eyes downcast. Sooner or later, someone would realize they'd gained an extra guard in their ranks, but for now... all I wanted to do was follow his directions so I could remain as close to Lily as possible.

Stopping outside the door, I mimicked the other warrior's stance, crossing my arms and leaning back against the wall. Hearing Lily's muffled voice through the door for the next hour was a torture all its own, but when she stepped out and asked if dinner was ready, I almost swallowed my tongue.

She had unbraided her hair, letting it fall in waves down her back, and had changed into dark green leggings and a loose cream sweater that hung off one shoulder. She was beauty incarnate.

"Almost ready, Your Majesty," the other guard answered.

Lily returned to her room, shutting the door and leaving me and the other guard alone. "Have you ever been to Glenmiere?" he asked out of the blue.

I snapped my head in his direction, then looked away before he could focus on my face. "No. Have you?"

I wasn't sure why he was asking, but the pit in my stomach told me it was important.

"No, but I can't wait to check it out on this mission." Excitement bubbled beneath his words. "Can you believe she and that sister of hers will be walking straight into the Dark Elves' tribe, unannounced?" He shook his head. "Gotta say… that's pretty ballsy for our newly appointed Queen."

I flinched as the pull in my gut tightened. If Lily truly was headed there, I didn't know if twenty guards would be enough.

Looked like I'd be playing soldier a little longer after all.

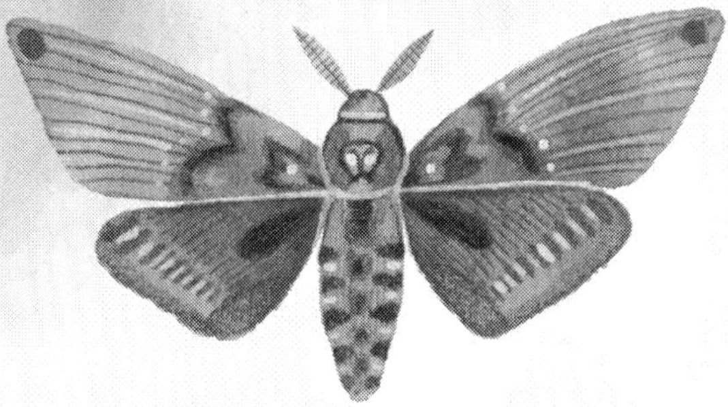

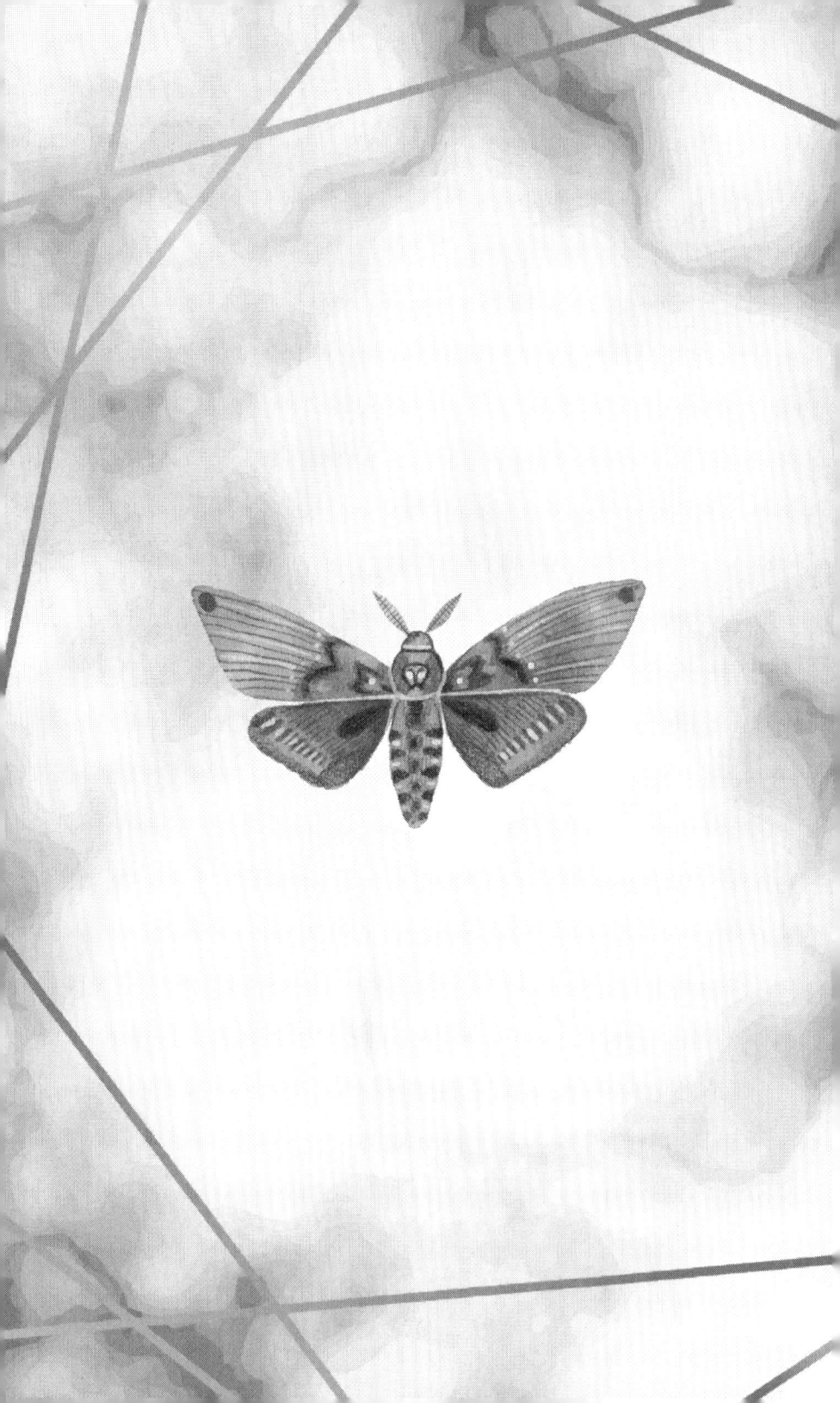

Fourteen

Lily

By the time we were escorted from our room and dinner was served, I was absolutely famished. The rest of the journey to Dartmoor was smooth enough, just longer than expected—which I suppose was no surprise since we were traveling by horseback instead of using a portal.

I'd thought about it, of course. Even argued with Alder about it.

He wanted to use one of the metal balls like Gideon had when he rescued us from the Light castle and took us back to Dartmoor. Alder's plan was to secure the Dark castle and make sure everything was okay, then send the horses and more men to meet us the following day. I talked him out of it, though, mainly because there were only a few portal balls left. Plus, without knowing the state of the castle or warning anyone in advance, I didn't feel right just *popping* in, unannounced. At least this way, Gretta had a chance to communicate with the staff before we arrived. And to be honest, I was looking forward to a ride through the woods.

"Mmm... this is delicious." Daisy moaned beside me, savoring the fresh meat, vegetables, and bread the staff had prepared.

"You've got that right. Nothing like a nice hot meal after a long trip." I smiled and took a sip of my wine. "Speaking of long trips…" I turned to General Niasin who stood stiffly by the large, carved wooden doors. "Do you know how long it will take to reach Glenmiere from here?"

"About a two day's ride northwest, Your Majesty."

I swallowed another gulp of wine. "Then I assume we'll be camping along the way."

"Correct. But don't worry. We'll have all the luxuries you need."

"Luxuries? While camping?" Clearly, I was missing something.

"Yes, ma'am. The King sent another detail ahead to set up camp. He provided the royal tent, cooks, and another twenty guards. You and your sister will be well taken care of."

My cheeks grew hot, and I started to balk at the secret plans Alder had made on my behalf.

"Lily, what is it?" Daisy's kind voice penetrated my rising anger, and I shook my head. "Nothing." I turned back to the guard. "Thank you, General. Sounds like the King has everything well in hand." I took another bite of meat, then laid my napkin across my plate. "If you'll excuse me, I want to freshen up before we start in the library."

Daisy's eyes met mine with a brief flicker of concern, but returned to her plate as she remained seated, happy to stay and finish her meal.

The moment I left the dining hall, I knew a guard would be assigned to follow, but at this point, I didn't care. I'd ignore them here, just like I'd been doing at home in the Light castle.

Home.

I ran my hand down the deep forest-colored walls, drinking in the warmth of the gold, black, and wood accents, and allowed myself to become immersed in the organic, moody feel of the Dark realm again.

How was it that *this* felt more like home than the sparkling world of my birth mother? Maybe it was because I missed Gideon so much. I sighed; my heart so heavy it felt bruised against my ribs.

I kept walking until I reached the glass doors that led into the gardens. The late afternoon light cast deep shadows onto the ferns and foreign plants that grew beneath the trees, while lush, almost tropical flowers bloomed in the raised beds that flowed throughout the rest of the space. Winding my way through the vibrant colors, I came to stand at the end of one path. Stepping up onto a concrete bench, I peered over the wall and could see the spread of gray buildings in the town below. Mesmerized by how they blended with the shadows while still twinkling like stars, I allowed myself this moment of peace and watched the embedded mica sparkle and dance.

"Beautiful, isn't it?" my assigned guard asked from behind me.

"Yes, it most definitely is."

"Forgive the observation, but it seems like you might enjoy the Dark Kingdom better than the Light."

I didn't turn around but wondered what observations he was talking about. Was I really that obvious?

"You might be right. Do you think it wrong of me?" It was freeing to talk about this so openly. And honestly, this was the most any guard had ever spoken to me since I became Queen.

A deep sigh sounded from over my shoulder, then I felt the guard moving closer. "Your Majesty, I think whatever you feel is the right path for you, you should follow it. You have a realm full of people who love you and a family who would do anything for you, so how could you go wrong?"

"I don't know about that," I scoffed. "Look where I have us heading—into a territory that probably doesn't even know I exist and will refuse to acknowledge me as their Queen. Pretty sure the Dark Elves of Glenmiere aren't going to love me." I stepped down off the bench and turned around, hoping to thank the guard for this honest exchange, but there was no one there.

"Hello?" I called out.

Another soldier stepped onto the path from much further away. "Yes, Your Majesty? Do you require assistance?"

I looked back and forth, peering into the shadows but saw nothing out of the ordinary. "No. I'm fine." *Just apparently losing my damn mind.*

Bennett

I was so close to revealing my true self to Lily, but had to disappear when I heard the other guard moving down the path.

Blending into the shadows, I crept back inside the castle and returned to the hall of bedrooms. With everyone currently downstairs, I could easily slip back into the hidden passage and use the portal to return to the barn... *or*, I could stay here, pretend to be a soldier in Alder's army, and follow Lily into an adventure that might get us both killed.

A fresh vision of her swam behind my eyes, and my choice was made. I'd willingly risk discovery and death just to stay by her side and prove myself again.

Removing my helmet, I dipped into my old room across the hall and locked the door. I needed a shower and to rest for the night if I was going to pull this off.

Daisy

I wandered around the dining hall after finishing my meal, gazing up at the hanging plants and beautiful glass ceiling far above my head as I waited for Lily's return.

I knew she needed some time alone, and knowing we were safe here, I certainly wanted to give her that. But walking beneath the starlit sky in the exact place where Gideon lost his life wasn't exactly relaxing to me.

"Excuse me?" I called out to the nearest guard. "If you could please let my sister know I'll be in the library, I'd appreciate it."

The soldier nodded, then proceeded to follow me down the hall as I made my way to Gideon's study. The dual space was the same deep green that flowed throughout the rest of the castle, but with sheets tossed over the large oak desk and the oversize hearth fireless and cold, the room felt dark and ominous and not somewhere I wanted to be. Unfortunately, I couldn't waste the opportunity to further the research Lily and I came here to do.

"Excuse me?" I addressed the guard again. "Would you mind gathering some firewood so we could warm this place up before my sister arrives?"

"Of course, ma'am. I'll be right back."

Ma'am. I laughed and moved to the door and watched him disappear down the hall, wondering if I had time to reach my room before he returned. I needed to grab my notebook to document anything we found here, and I hadn't thought to bring it with me to dinner.

Tiptoeing toward the stairs, I raced up to the next floor and down the hall that led back to our bedroom. Rounding the corner, I stopped short when I saw another guard standing outside the room opposite my own.

I didn't think I'd get in trouble for being unaccompanied, but with Alder giving the orders for his guards to keep us safe, I also didn't want to get anyone in trouble for not doing their job.

Hanging back, I watched as the lone guard neared the room directly across from ours, then slammed a hand over my mouth when he removed his helmet before opening the door.

I'd never really been into beefy guys before, but the tall, broad-shouldered guard with the edgy platinum hair certainly caught my eye.

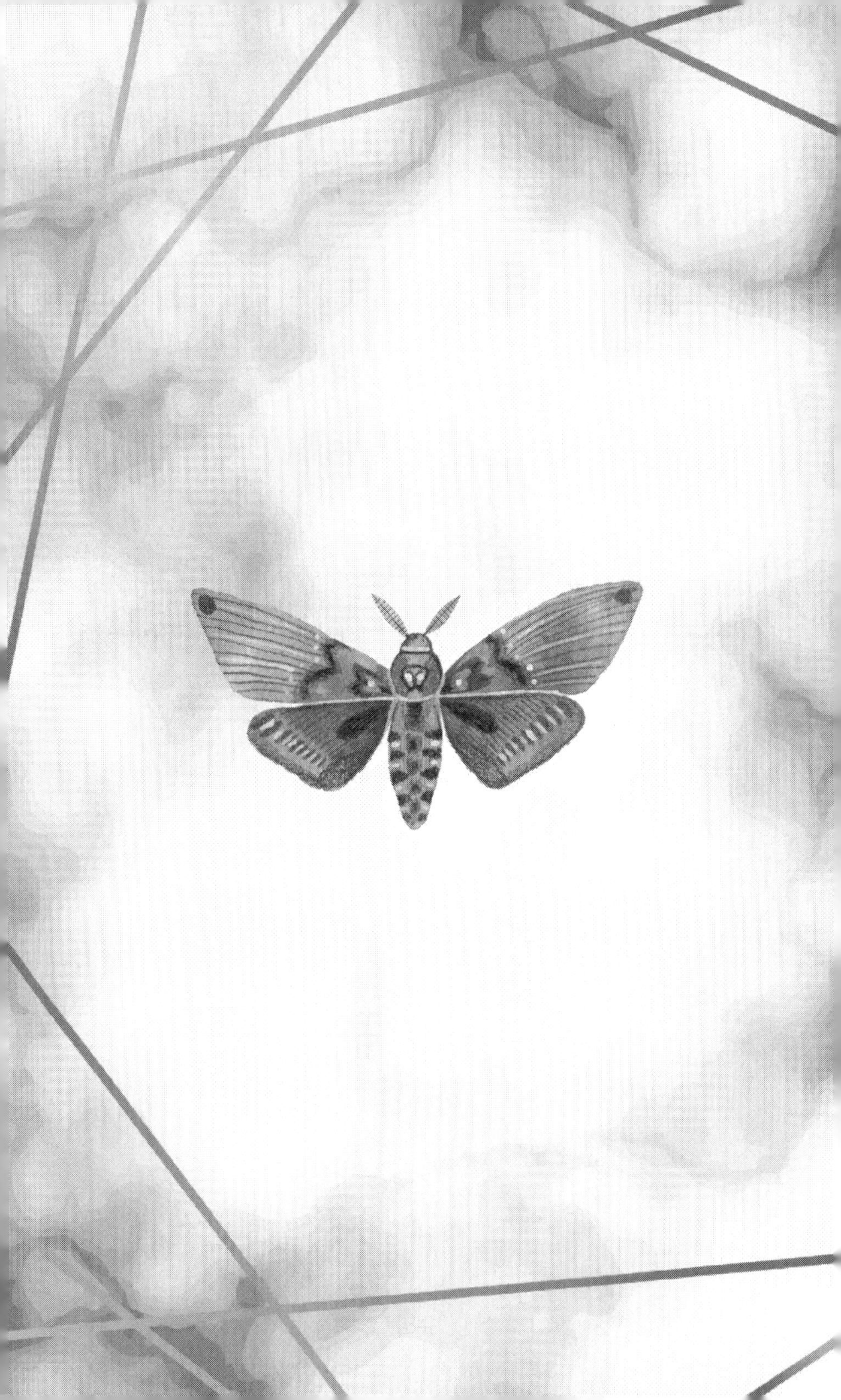

Fifteen

Lily

"Lil, seriously... he was gorgeous." Daisy giggled as she described her latest crush to me. "He had platinum blond hair that hung over one eye and was shaved on the other side, and the way he filled out that uniform..." She fanned herself, swooning.

"Well, sounds like you'll have plenty of eye candy to keep you occupied during our trip tomorrow then." I thumbed through yet another book from Gideon's library before placing it on the desk with the rest I'd discarded so far. "Have you found anything yet?"

Daisy slumped into the oversized chair near the fireplace and shook her head. "Not really. There's a mention here and there about fairy spells and certain herbs, but nothing we haven't come across before."

"Dang it! For whatever reason, I thought we'd find something that could help us here." Crossing the room, I laid down on the leather couch and folded my arms over my eyes. This was turning out to be a huge waste of time.

"Don't lose hope, Lil. There's plenty more books for us to check out." I peeked at Daisy as she stared up at the floor-to-ceiling bookshelves and took a deep breath. "I'm just not sure we can get through all of them before we leave tomorrow."

"My point exactly." I sat up, then firmly planted my feet back on the onyx floor. "I wanted to come here and relax. Take my time, and see if I could find something of real use." I waved my hand in the air, gesturing wildly at the impossible task. "But now, we barely have time to scratch the surface before heading on to Glenmiere."

Daisy kept her eyes plastered on me, but she didn't say a word.

"Sorry. I'm just worried I'm making all the wrong decisions." I took a deep, weighted breath.

Rising from the chair, Daisy set her book on the desk and joined me on the couch, wrapping her arm around my neck. "Lily, if anyone has insight to what the right thing to do is, it's you. Being Queen may have unlocked your fae magic even further, but in your heart, you're still the white witch Mama raised."

I closed my eyes and allowed her words to sink in.

A warm pull from deep inside me flared, anchoring me back to the root of my magic. Light and revelation was what we needed here, and Daisy just reminded me I was full of both. "Thanks, Dais. Now let's see if I can shine a little light on things."

I jumped up from the couch and marched toward the wall of books, where I pulled on my magic to guide my hand and words. With an open palm, I moved in front of the shelf, then muttered the words that floated into my mind. "*Hidden past, at long last, reveal to me the book to read. Honored fae, show me the way, bring salvation to those in need.*"

I repeated the spell as the magic guided my hand back and forth in front of the bookshelf, stopping when a burning sensation flared in the center of my palm. "Here! This one." I pulled a thick, worn tome from high on the shelf and coughed as a light layer of dust floated down with it, shimmering in the firelight.

Moving back to Gideon's desk, I laid the book on the large oak top. The cover was dark, worn leather, but there were no identifying words on the cover or spine.

"What does it say?" Daisy asked from across the room.

"Hold on. I haven't found the title yet." Cracking it open, I gently peered inside. The pages had yellowed with time but were still in good shape. I flipped through the first few, noticing they were blank, but then saw something scribbled in the lower corner a couple more pages in. It looked like a name—*Gwenlyth Trelayne*.

"Come here and have a look at this." I waved Daisy over.

She eagerly joined me and read over my shoulder. "Gwenlyth Trelayne? Who is that?"

I shrugged. "I have no idea."

"Well, what else is inside?" Daisy urged me on.

Flip by flip, I leafed through the book, becoming more and more frustrated with each blank page. I closed the cover after reaching the end. "What the hell?"

"Relax," Daisy huffed. "It is a *fae* book, ya know. One you just found by using your revelation magic." She lifted a brow. "Why don't you try that again?"

She was right, *again*, and obviously, I was just frustrated and tired. "Okay, you're right. Here we go." I held both hands over the open book, hoping the same spell would work again with a slight adjustment to the words. *"Hidden past, now found at last, reveal to me your words to read. Honored fae, show me the way, bring salvation to those in need."*

My palms warmed as I held them over the book. Squinting, I watched in awe as writing began to take shape on the page, then screamed when tiny sparks flew from my hands, lighting them on fire instead. "No! Shit, shit, shit!" I used the long sleeves of my sweater to pat the pages until the flames were completely smothered.

"Holy shit, Lil! Are you okay?" Daisy raced forward and slammed the book shut.

My chin dipped to my chest and I pulled away, embarrassed. "I'm fine. Can we please just go to bed now? I'm tired and not quite feeling myself."

Daisy gently laid her hand on my shoulder. "You're right. It's been a long day, and we both need to rest."

"I couldn't agree more," a deep voice sounded from the doorway. General Niasin stood with his arms crossed, disappointment marring his face. "My men tell me you've already managed to slip past them."

A lopsided grin pulled at my lips. "Sorry, General. Just needed a little girl time with my sister and some light reading." I picked up the heavy tome from the desk, ignoring the smell of singed paper.

"*Light* reading?" The General chuckled. "Whatever suits you. Now let's get you both secured in your rooms. We leave tomorrow right after breakfast."

I clutched the book to my chest and looked around Gideon's study one more time. My memories of him were alive here, and walking away from all the things he'd collected over the years had me longing to spend more time in his castle than I originally planned.

Lost in thought, I stumbled on the stairs.

"You okay?" Daisy asked.

"Yes, I'm fine."

With heated cheeks, I recalled my first encounter here with Alder which just so happened to take place in the same room we were headed to now.

As I pulled the paper-thin dress up over my head, Alder's sultry voice stopped me cold.

"I don't know... I can't decide if I'm going to like you better in black, or if I prefer you in the white instead," he teased me from the shadows just behind the bed.

Pushing open a hidden door, he strode breezily into the room with a flame alight in his hand, like it was no big deal.

I gasped and tugged the dress back down. "What the hell are you doing here? They'll kill you if you're caught."

He flopped down onto the bed. "I had to make sure you were alright."

I gaped at how casually he lounged in my new room.

"Where were you when the crone ambushed me? I thought you said you'd keep me safe," I accused.

"No, I said…" he drawled, *"that you'd always be safe as long as you were with me… which you weren't."* His tanned skin glistened in the glow of his flame, the bright warmth of his honeyed eyes threatening to melt me where I stood.

I had no idea at the time that he was the heir to the Dark throne, but now that we were together, being back here just felt right.

Caught up in the memory, a light laugh bubbled from my throat.

"Are you *sure* you're okay?" Daisy asked again, eying me suspiciously.

I faked another stumble. "Yes. I'm okay. Just ready for bed."

Thanking the General once we reached our room, I quickly changed and crawled between the sheets, squashing the more vivid thoughts roaming the back of my mind. Being here was exactly what I needed, and it felt good to confirm that decision to myself. This was where Alder grew up. The place where Gideon ruled. And the one place I felt safe and relaxed. *This* was home—not the Light Kingdom to which I was promised.

With talks of our union already underway, I didn't think a move would make a difference, but knew it wasn't something that could happen soon. We had to get the vilenflu back to Fern, find Bennett, and figure out who Gwenlyth Trelayne was now, and how I could use her book to help.

Another image of us living here floated into my mind and settled between the cracks of my heart. I closed my eyes, wrapped in a sense of peace I hadn't felt in a long time, and smiled up into the dark.

Sixteen

Lily

"Holy shit! I had no idea it would get so cold this fast." Daisy pulled a fur-lined hood down over her ears as we climbed the rocky trail that led out of Dartmoor.

The higher we rode into the mountains, the harder the terrain became. Jutting rocks could be seen in the distance, and the evergreens lining both sides of the trail were already tipped in a light layer of snow.

"And it's only going to get worse the higher we climb," the General shouted back from atop his large, gray-dappled horse.

The body heat from our mounts helped keep us warm, compounded by the fact that Gretta had insisted we be properly outfitted and made sure the staff fetched us all we'd need. After serving us a delicious breakfast, they filled our thermoses with warm coffee and tea before sending us on our way. We followed the General and his men to the stables first, then out of the castle and onto the path that would lead us to Glenmiere, officially kicking off the next leg of our journey.

I watched Daisy breathe warm air into her hands and rub them together to help keep her warm. Settling into my saddle, I wisely kept my mouth shut. I no longer needed to worry about the cold.

Since fully accepting our roles as King and Queen, the blood bond allowed me and Alder to share more than just thoughts. His fire magic was now a part of me. It was also the reason my spell went array last night, and another reason why my magical workspace had been established in the stone basement of the castle. I hadn't exactly mastered the element just yet.

At the moment, it was simply one more thing I was failing at, and I didn't have the heart to tell my sisters. Especially when imagining Aster's condescending stare.

"You're awfully quiet this morning." Daisy led Samson into step beside Luna and me.

"Just taking it all in." I glanced around the forest, sincerely happy to experience another aspect of this beautiful realm.

The plants here were hardier than those in Ferindale and Dartmoor, but still beautiful in their own way. Clumps of flowers that reminded me of a hydrangea bush were scattered across the forest floor, their delicate, creamy white petals covered in a light layer of frost. "Fern would love this." I sighed.

Daisy was quiet for a moment then said, "She really missed you, ya know? We all did, of course, but I think it hit Fern hard. She would sit on your favorite rock in the basement and just stare into the portal for hours on end."

Daisy's words landed like a punch to my gut. The guilt I felt since the day my family disappeared was overwhelming. But this... this would crush me. "I'm sorry, Dais. I wish I could have been with you all at home, or that you could have returned right away, but..."

My sister shook her head. "No. Don't apologize. That's not why I'm saying it. We all understood the levity of what you were facing and what had to be done. I'm just mentioning it because of what Iris said... that she hadn't felt their twin bond since we returned home. I think Fern longed to be here with you, and that may have had something to do with it."

I sniffled and pretended the cold was affecting me. Perhaps Fern *did* long to stay in the Fae realm, but that decision shouldn't have changed her or interrupted the twin connection she shared with Iris. It was all so confusing.

After discovering Fern, Iris, and Daisy were Gideon's daughters, he explained that their powers would remain as they were—based in our mother's witch magic since they were born in *her* world. For them to share any of *his* magic, they would have had to be born here, in the Fae realm, like me.

We tried to discuss it more, and even searched for something that could activate their fae side, but once Gideon died and Bennett stole the book, they were cast back home and our time to investigate had abruptly ran out.

I looked over at my sister, so grateful she was here. Perhaps once this was over, we could do more research and hopefully discover something new that would work.

"Ouch!" I reached around and shifted my pack to stop it from poking me in the hip.

"Okay back there?" the General called out.

"Yes, I just over packed, which turns out is a bad idea for this mode of travel." I forced a smile, then shrugged to adjust the heavy straps.

"Give it to one of my men. They'll be happy to carry your burden, my lady."

I glanced behind me to find the closest guard, but all of them had packs of their own, except one. "Would you mind?" I shimmied the bag off my shoulders and held it out to the side.

Riding up next to me, the warrior didn't say a word but happily accepted my pack.

"Thank you, that's much better." I dipped my head in sincere gratitude.

Catching movement in my periphery, I looked over at Daisy, who was nodding at the soldier and grinning like a fool.

"What's your name?" I turned back and asked, but my words drifted into the frigid air as he'd already returned to his position within the ranks. I winked at Daisy. "I'll try again once we make camp tonight."

My sister beamed, shifting in her saddle like an excited kitten.

Bennett

I'd never experienced this level of torture before.

After getting a good night's sleep, I emerged from my old room, donning the guard's uniform again. Pulling on my magic, I glamored the pack containing the crone's book in the shadows upon my back and crept my way to the stables with a few apples in hand.

As planned, the stable master had all the horses ready, and he offered me one as soon as I stepped inside.

"She's a fine mare. Surefooted, too."

"What's her name?" I wasn't sure if the question was something a true guard would ask, but I didn't care. If I had to trust this animal to keep me safe and bear my weight during this journey, I at least wanted to know her name.

"Soven."

"Soven," I repeated, feeding her one of the apples as I brushed my other hand down her black and white speckled back. "Let's take good care of each other, shall we?"

The mare snorted, which I took as her acceptance of a bargain well struck. Now, two hours into our ride, I sat atop Soven, miserable and cold and forced to stare directly at Lily's back.

I watched as she shifted in her saddle to speak to someone up ahead, then she removed the bag and turned back, speaking directly to me. "Would you mind?" She held her pack out to the side.

Understanding her request, I rode up next to her and took it from her delicate hands. It wasn't as heavy as the pack already hiding within my glamor, but it certainly seemed weighty enough to be carrying something significant inside.

"Thank you, that's much better," I heard her say as I pulled Soven back to our place in line.

I pretended not to hear her next question when she asked for my name; instead, I concentrated on securing her pack to the side of my saddle. But oh, how I wanted to share it with her now.

I imagined rushing up beside her, removing my helmet, and declaring who I truly was, but I knew this wasn't the time or place. Revealing myself now was a guaranteed death sentence. But perhaps once we settled for the night at camp, I could find her and reveal my secret then. I just hoped she'd give me enough time to explain before calling for my head.

Seventeen

Lily

The guards made quick work setting up our royal tent, and I made a mental note to thank Alder in a very special way when I returned home. The elaborate material of the tent reminded me of the Dark castle with its deep green, black, and gold embellishments embroidered along the edges. Two beds lined with furs had been provided for Daisy and me, along with a small desk, a round table, and two surprisingly comfortable canvas chairs.

"This is amazing!" Daisy gawked up at the ceiling and the lanterns full of fairy lights dangling above our heads. The look on her face reminded me of when Mom took us all to the circus back home. Daisy was eight at the time, but she'd never lost that sense of wonder.

A fire had been started in the corner of the tent with its dug-out chimney drawing the smoke outside. The General informed us we'd be expected to remain inside until they signaled for us in the morning, and that our dinner would be brought to us here as soon as it was ready. I appreciated all their efforts to keep us safe, but I had something else in mind.

"I'm going to take a look around. Wanna come?" I pulled the heavy gloves back onto my hands to keep up appearances.

Daisy's eyes went wide. "Um, no! And you shouldn't go, either." She crossed the room in a huff. "What else could you possibly need to see out there? Everything here looks the same. Gray rocks, green trees, white snow, the air turning to smoke every time I take a damn breath…"

Clearly, she wasn't enjoying the frigid temperature of the mountains.

"Fine. Stay here, but I'm going to at least go check on my horse." I pulled up the bottom of the tent near the back and snuck beneath its heavy panel.

A light layer of snow glistened in the moonlight, casting the rocks in an entirely different light. The usual pink tint of sunlight was long gone, leaving the forest bathed in shadows. I moved around the camp stealthily, using the lack of light to my advantage. Multiple fires burned in the snow, set up outside each soldier's tent. Low voices drifted on the wind and provided an idea of everyone's location, which mostly seemed to center around the cook.

Sneaking through the grove on the west side of camp, I reached the rocky embankment where the horses were gathered. "Hi, Luna. Shhh… it's okay. It's only me." My stately white mare raised her head at my approach and gave a slight whinny before settling when she recognized my scent. Rubbing down her neck and back, I petted her muscular form, whispering a spell to help relieve any remaining tension from the day's ride. "There you go, sweet girl. Now you should sleep like a baby." With one more stroke down her back, I turned around and headed back toward camp.

Being out here alone was like a breath of fresh air... *literally*. The mountain air was so crisp and clean, bringing with it a lightness I'd never appreciated before. Stopping in the open space between the woods and the camp, I leaned my head back and closed my eyes. A soft dusting of feather-light snowflakes fell against my face. I'd never felt more alive.

"Well, well, well. What do we have here?"

I jerked my head toward the tree line and tried to discern where that deep, gravelly voice came from. Stepping out from behind the nearest tree, the figure of a wild, hulking man stood in the space where the darkest shadows fell. I froze, debating whether I should run toward the camp, or turn back and try to reach my horse.

"Don't bother running. You're already mine," the man growled, pointing at me with a large wooden staff, tipped with what looked like a chunk of white stone.

I opened my mouth to scream, but nothing came out. I lifted my foot to run but that proved just as ineffective, because despite how much I tried, I couldn't move a muscle. Frozen in place and unable to speak, I tried the only thing I could think of and reached out to Alder through our bond, desperate for him to hear my plea despite the distance between us. *"Help! Someone is invading our camp."*

Silence settled like a blanket over the space where our bond usually lived, and I recalled Alder's words again...

"*No. I said...*" he drawled, "*that you'd always be safe as long as you were with me... which you weren't.*"

Goddess, how had I become so lax? It was the most important rule of our blood bond—it only protected me and connected us when we were together. *Dammit!* I never should have left without him. Now, here I was, alone and vulnerable and completely cut off from the one person who could help me.

With panicked eyes, I watched the wild man stomp into the clearing and head straight for me. He snatched me off my feet, tossing me cleanly over his shoulder, then turned around and quickly disappeared into the forest again.

I continued to will a scream from my throat or writhe out of his grip, but nothing worked. It was as if I was frozen in fear, though I knew that wasn't the case. This had to be a member of the Dark Elves, and I believed I was now under his dark spell.

With no ability to fight or flee, I dropped my head and watched a single tear melt into the snow as he hauled me further up the mountain and deeper into the woods.

Daisy

"Come on, Lil, get your ass back here." I paced the tent, knowing any second a guard would arrive to deliver our food.

Not wanting her to get in trouble for sneaking out on her own, I pulled the old trick of piling up pillows under the blankets to make it look like she was already asleep. Minutes later, a guard entered our tent with a large tray of steaming food balanced between his hands.

"For Her Majesty." He stumbled over his words, barely making it to the table to set down the tray. Bending at the waist, he gave the empty bed a quick bow, then disappeared back out the front flap, barely acknowledging I was even there.

The scent of fresh meat and steaming pumpkin soup wafted into the air, making me salivate. I was starving, and there was no way I was going to wait for Lily before I dug in. Pulling one of the canvas chairs up to the table, I scooped a spoonful of soup into my mouth and savored the rich flavors as they burst on my tongue. Each bite was better than the last, and as I took my time to sample each dish, I prayed Lily would return and join me soon.

"Good evening, Miss. I'm checking to make sure dinner was to your liking." I looked up and almost choked. The gorgeous soldier I told Lily about stood alone before me. His helmet still covered his platinum hair, but I could tell by his stormy blue-gray eyes that it was him.

Gulping down the mouthful of soup, I coughed out my reply. "Yes, thank you. It was all delicious."

He looked at the bed where Lily was supposed to be and directed his next question to her. "And does the Queen approve?"

Standing at attention, he waited for a reply that would never come.

Rushing to fill the awkward silence, I quickly answered for her. "She enjoyed it very much."

My heart was thrumming at the base of my throat as I noticed the pinch of his eyes and the slight movement he made toward the bed. He knew something wasn't right.

"Okay, okay… please wait," I blurted out as I rushed to stand in front of the tent's entrance. I needed to explain before he called in another guard, or worse yet, the General. "She just stepped out to check on her horse. She'll be right back."

He stomped across the tent and flung back the blankets to reveal the pile of pillows. After taking a few deep breaths, he stalked across the space again, coming to stand directly over me. "Daisy… how long has she been gone?"

I crooked my neck back and looked up to meet his eyes, ready to answer his question. Still, I had to force myself to ignore how much I liked hearing my name fall from his lips. "Probably an hour," I estimated.

"Dammit!" he cussed. "The horses are secured no more than five minutes away."

I sucked in a sharp breath and flattened myself against the tent wall. "Oh, no." I couldn't believe this was happening. First Fern fell ill and now Lily was gone… Aster would never forgive me. And neither would Alder.

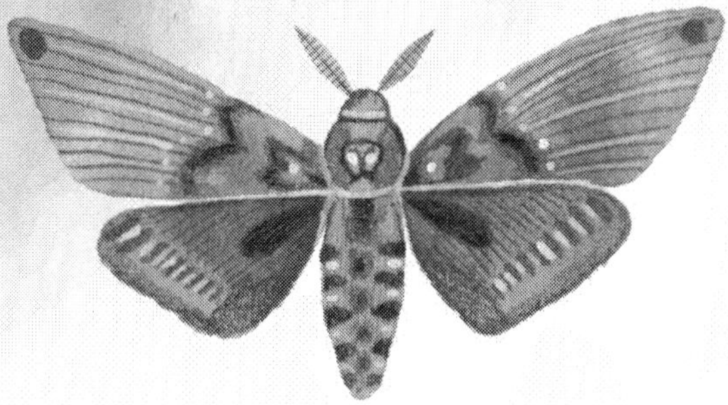

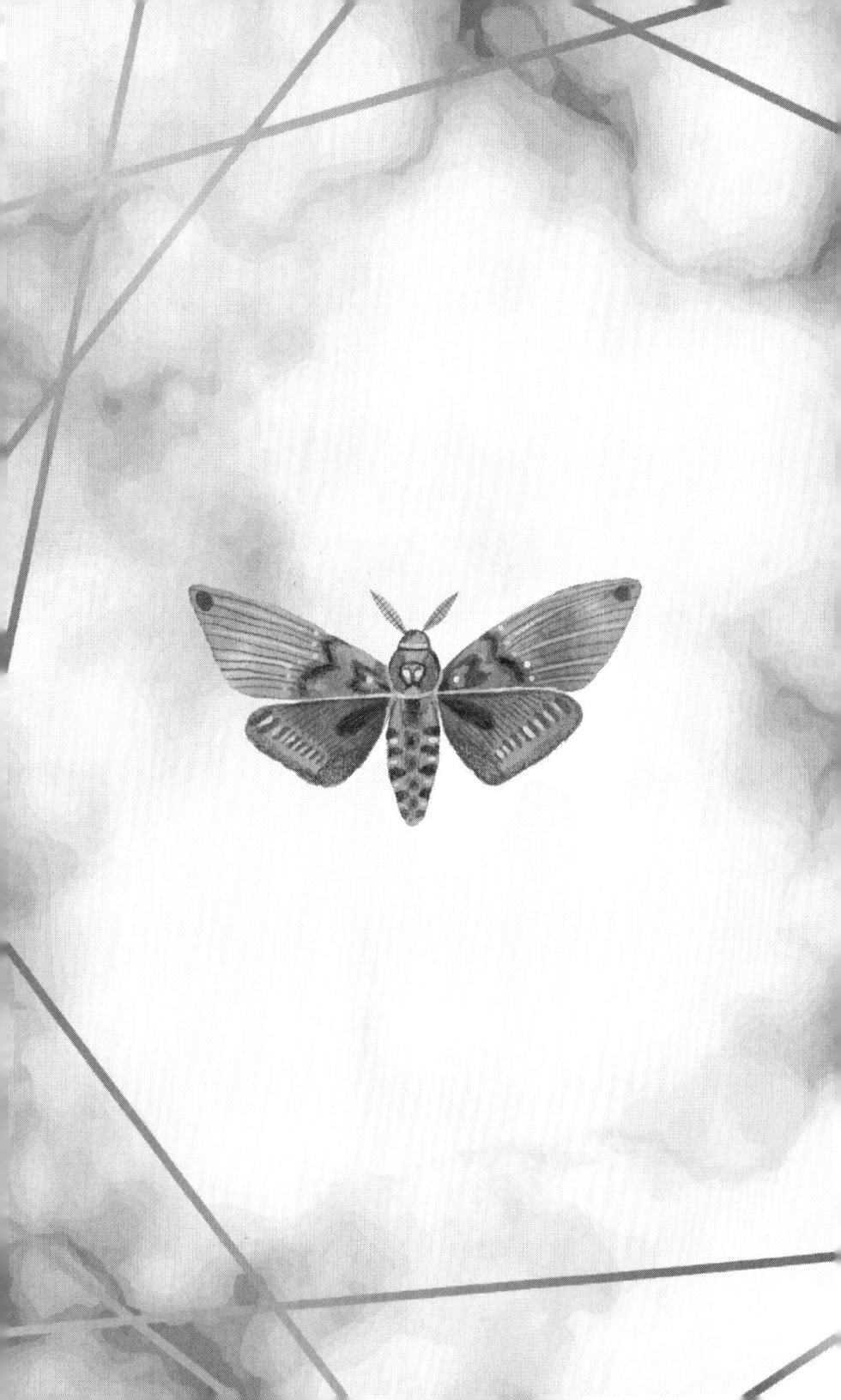

Eighteen

Bennett

I couldn't believe Lily ran off into a foreign territory without telling anyone! "What the hell was she thinking?" Daisy tried to hide her tears as she rocked back and forth from atop her bed inside the royal tent. "I'm sorry," I apologized. "I'm not blaming you, and I certainly don't expect you to know what she was planning to do."

"I understand. I get it! It's upsetting." Daisy wiped her eyes, then crossed her arms over her chest as if the action would help hold her together. "Do you really think something bad has happened to her?"

I swallowed past the lump in my throat. She wasn't going to like my answer. More so, I didn't want her alerting the others that Lily was missing just yet. "Yes, but I think I can help in a way no one else can."

She sat up straighter. "What do you mean?"

This was it… I would have to reveal my true self if I had any chance of saving Lily. I glanced back to the opening of the tent and imagined being dragged out by the arms when they found out who I was.

"Before I tell you, you have to *swear* not to panic."

Daisy hitched a brow. "Probably one of the worst ways you could have started that sentence, soldier."

I chuckled. "That may be, but I still need you to promise you'll stay calm."

She narrowed her eyes on me. "Fine. I promise."

"What I'm about to show you will be a huge shock, but I swear to you, Daisy, I will not hurt you or anyone else. I just need a chance to explain."

"Okkaayy…" She stood from the bed and moved to the chair, placing both hands on either arm like she was prepared to bolt for the door. "Get on with it then."

I took a deep breath and tried to ignore my quivering gut. God, I didn't know if I could go through with this. All the times I'd imagined this moment, it was in front of Lily, not her sister whom I barely knew. Not to mention the huge risk I was taking by exposing myself now. If she panicked and shouted for the guards, there was no way to escape and help Lily. But even if Daisy agreed to keep my secret, once the cat was out of the bag, there was no putting it back in.

I closed my eyes and focused on Lily. She was the only thing that mattered. Using my fae magic, I slid my original glamor back into place and morphed into the Bennett they all knew. I opened my eyes when I heard Daisy's shocked gasp. "Daisy, please. I can explain. And remember, I'm the only one with this magic and your best chance at getting Lily back," I added in a rush.

With one hand over her mouth and the other still tightly clutching the chair, she remained silent as I continued.

"I..." I stammered. "I don't even know where to start." I let my old glamor slip away, changing back into my true self while retaining the guard uniform to keep up my current guise. After all this time preparing for this moment, I could barely find the words. "I guess I'll just start by saying this is the real me and that I'm sorry for what happened. As you just saw, I can shift into different forms. Because of my unique brand of magic, I was tasked by my village to go undercover to find the crone's book. It was intended to buy favor for my outcast witch clan, and more importantly, save my mother's life. But after everything that went down, and with the crone gone, the need is no longer there." I hung my head. "I've spent months trying to reach Lily to explain and tell her how sorry I am for betraying her trust. And to return this..." I reached behind me to the now visible pack on my back and pulled out the witch's handbook to magic and mayhem.

Daisy's eyes went wide as she leapt from the chair, snatching the book out of my hands.

"My clan has no use for it, and if there's any chance it can help with whatever's going on, I'm happy to return it."

Daisy placed the worn book of shadows on the desk and struggled to catch her breath. She stared down at the book, then lifted her chin to glare directly at me. "You mean, you hope it buys *you* favor now. With the new King and Queen, right? That's why you want to return it. So you'll look like the hero in Lily's eyes again, and maybe... just maybe, she'll forgive you for what you did."

I slammed my eyes shut, unable to hide my regret. "Yes. You're right. All I want is Lily's forgiveness, and if returning that book or rescuing her now gets me even a fraction closer to that, then that's what I'll do."

A commotion outside drew both our attention. Daisy ran to the front of the tent and peeked through the slit to see what was going on. "Shit!" she whisper-yelled.

"What's wrong?" I stepped forward.

Daisy turned around and looked me up and down, clutching her chest. "So, is this the *real* you, then? A broad-shouldered, Viking-looking fae witch... Not the tall, nerdy plant guy we all set out to help?"

"Yes, minus the Light Guard uniform." I lifted my chin, vowing to be completely honest with her. "I grew up a witch and warrior, learning all the ways of our small but proud clan. We *are* fae, but our magic is closer to that of witches, simple and earth based—at least everyone's but mine. I was blessed with shadow magic, or *spy*-magic, as my mom liked to call it. It's what allows me to change forms."

Surprisingly, Daisy took my hand and pulled me toward Lily's bed. "Then you better use that spy-magic right now, because Alder just arrived in camp."

Shit!

"What do you want me to do?"

"Use your magic to become Lily and crawl into her bed."

My god, I couldn't believe this was happening. I did as she asked, quickly transforming into Lily and climbing into her bed. "I swear, Daisy, if he grabs my ass or tries to kiss me, I'm going to lose my shit."

"Shut up! Not only is that a stupid thing to say, but if you don't do whatever it takes to go along with this, both our lives are over. Now, just pretend you're asleep and let me do the rest."

I pulled the blankets up to my chin and caught the determination sparkling in her big brown eyes. Rolling over, I turned my back to the front of the tent and prayed we could pull this off.

Daisy

Goddess, why does everything have to turn to shit? I rushed to take a seat at the table as soon as Bennett transformed and crawled into Lily's bed.

"Knock, knock." Alder entered the royal tent, looking very much like the king he was. Standing nearly seven feet tall, his wide chest and broad shoulders barely fit through the small tent flap. Ducking his head, he lifted a hand to make sure his antlers didn't get caught as the material dropped down behind him.

I waved like the ditz everyone thought I was, then raised a finger to my lips. "Shhh… she's had a long day."

Alder glanced at Lily's bed. The muscles in his legs and arms flexed as if his body instinctively wanted to move closer to hers. Thankfully he didn't, thinking better of it when he realized *she* was asleep. "Did something happen I should know about?" he whispered.

"No, nothing specific. I just think the stress of what's happened to Fern, then being back in the Dark castle, and now taking this journey… it's all left her physically and mentally exhausted." I shrugged and nodded with as much sympathy in my eyes as I could.

"I see." Again, his body betrayed him as he looked longingly at Lily's fake form. His fingers flexed, wanting to touch her, and all I could do was pray that Bennett would go along with it if he did.

"Will you be spending the night with us, then?" I asked the question as a distraction, but honestly wondered how he'd gotten here in the first place.

"No. I must return to the castle before daybreak. I just wanted to check on the camp and surprise Lily by wishing her goodnight in person." He smiled, his caramel eyes sparkling in the glow of the fairy lights hanging above our heads. "Guess I was a little too late." Retrieving a small metal ball from his pocket, he started for the door, but then stopped and purposefully stalked to Lily's bed instead. Carefully and gently enough not to wake her, he placed a light kiss in *her* hair, then turned back to me. "Please tell her I love her and to be careful tomorrow."

"Of course. I know she'll be upset she missed you."

With one last look at Lily, Alder turned away, his smile faltering as he exited the tent.

I raced to the entrance and watched as he tossed the metal ball on the ground, creating a new portal right there in the snow. Stepping through, he disappeared and the portal snapped closed behind him. "He's gone," I whispered.

Bennett flew from the bed and dropped his glamor before the blankets even hit the floor.

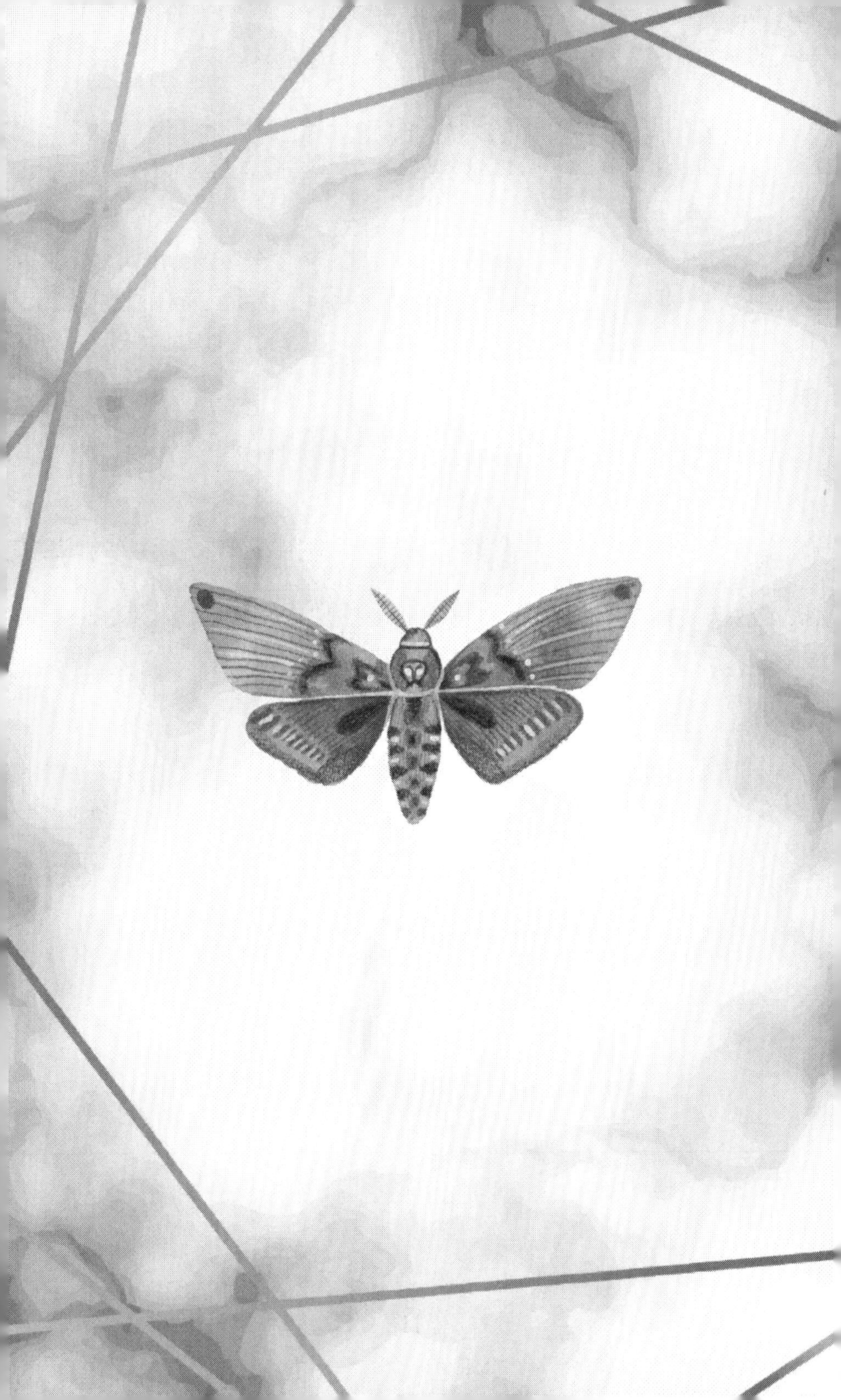

Nineteen

Daisy

"Damn, that was close." I strode back to the desk and took a seat in one of the canvas chairs, then nodded for Bennett to take the other. He'd jumped from the bed the instant the King left, but from the forlorn expression on his face and his sluggish movements, I think Alder's words of love for Lily affected him. "Here's what I think we should do," I started. "It may sound stupid, but I need sleep. I'll need my wits about me tomorrow if all this blows up."

Bennett lifted his chin. "Hopefully, that won't be the case. If I find her by morning, we'll be back before anyone wakes."

I cocked my head. "You may be able to shift forms, but do you have a magical way to see in the dark?" I looked up as if I could see the sky through the ceiling of the tent. "The full moon will help for sure, but you have no idea what's happened or how far she's gone."

His features hardened. "Got it. Understood. I'll do my best." I recognized the emotions bubbling up inside him.

I reached across the desk and took his hand, noticing how he flinched when I did. "I probably shouldn't trust you after what you did, but I know deep down you're a good guy who would do anything to save Lily."

Bennett hung his head. "Thank you. Betraying Lily was the worst mistake of my life, and I'll do everything in my power to bring her back and make this right."

I squeezed his hand and offered a sorrow-filled smile, hoping I wouldn't regret our plan in the morning.

"If anyone asks where you went, I'll play dumb. I figure with as many horses and other soldiers milling around, I doubt anyone will notice you're gone." Bennett nodded absently, and I knew his mind was already on Lily. I stood from the chair and pulled up the edge of the tent where Lily snuck out, nodding it was time for him to go. "Good luck, and stay strong," I whispered as he disappeared.

Crawled into bed, I prayed that trusting him again was the right thing to do. *Goddess, please let him find her, and let my sister be okay.*

Lily

I hung over the shoulder of this fucking brute, jostling for what felt like hours. Still unable to speak or move, I tried over and over to reach Alder through our bond, praying it would somehow work, but with no luck. By this point, I hoped Daisy had told the General

I was missing. I wasn't looking forward to the shit storm it would cause, but I would gladly face it as long as I was back home, safe and sound.

I stared at the footprints left by the Dark Elf in the snow as we trudged upwards—mostly because they were all I could see. Listening closely to every noise and whistle, I tried to pick out something useful to get my bearings, but nothing stood out other than the icy crunch of his boots. He was a big guy, possibly even taller than Alder, and certainly bulkier. The thick furs blanketing his massive shoulders were the only saving grace in my current predicament, softening my impromptu ride and keeping me warm since my access to Alder's elemental magic now seemed to be gone as well. Marching higher and higher up the mountain, the elf didn't even break a sweat. All I could do was hang there like a fucking animal he'd just hunted to eat.

At least he hasn't field dressed me yet.

Goddess, I had to stop these dreadful thoughts, but how could I when I couldn't move?

This was an abysmal situation, and it was all my fault. I should have listened to Daisy and stayed inside the tent, but the whole point of this little trip was to get away from my queenly duties and gain a little freedom while I focused on helping Fern.

So much for that.

On the bright side of things, maybe he was taking me to his village where I could find the vilenflu flower we were looking for in the first place. Not that I could do a damn thing about it in my current state.

Surely, he will lift whatever dark spell he's inflicted me with once we get there, right? I questioned myself, watching more of my tears fall into the snow as my mind supplied a grim answer.

Bennett

I neared the outcropping where the horses were gathered and spotted Soven on the very end. Seamlessly blending into the shadows, I crept between the trees until I reached her, not wanting to startle the rest of the herd.

"Shhh… Hi, girl. It's just me." I gently laid my hand on her neck and led her away.

Mounting her in one smooth motion, I guided the horse deeper into the woods and began searching for any signs of Lily.

My initial assumption was that she'd been taken by the Dark Elves, but in all honesty, I had no idea. She could have become disoriented and lost in the woods, or even worse, fell off one of the mountain's cliffs. The jagged rocks here were beautiful to look at but held plenty of secrets hidden in their deep crevices.

The woods were dark, the moonlight bouncing off the fallen snow the only source of light this late at night. I arrived at the main clearing between here and camp and pulled Soven to a halt.

Two sets of footprints turned into one, confirming my fears. Lily *had* been taken, and judging by the size of the retreating steps, by someone very large.

Dammit!

Leading Soven to the edge of the woods, I dipped my head beneath the evergreen boughs and began my search for the only woman I had ever cared about.

When I'd stolen the book for a second time, my only hope was to return it to Lily and beg for her forgiveness. Now… my only hope was that I'd find her alive.

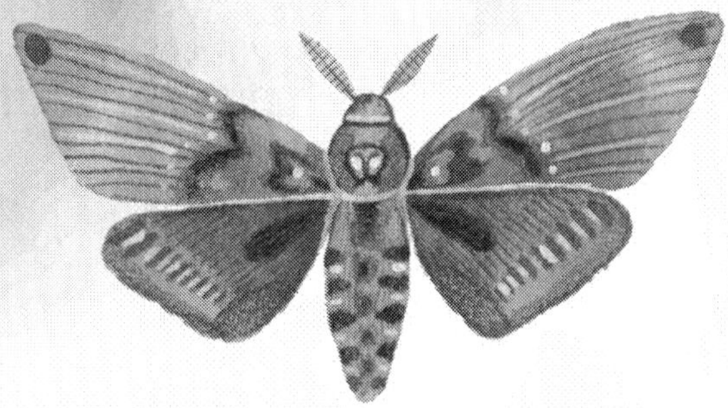

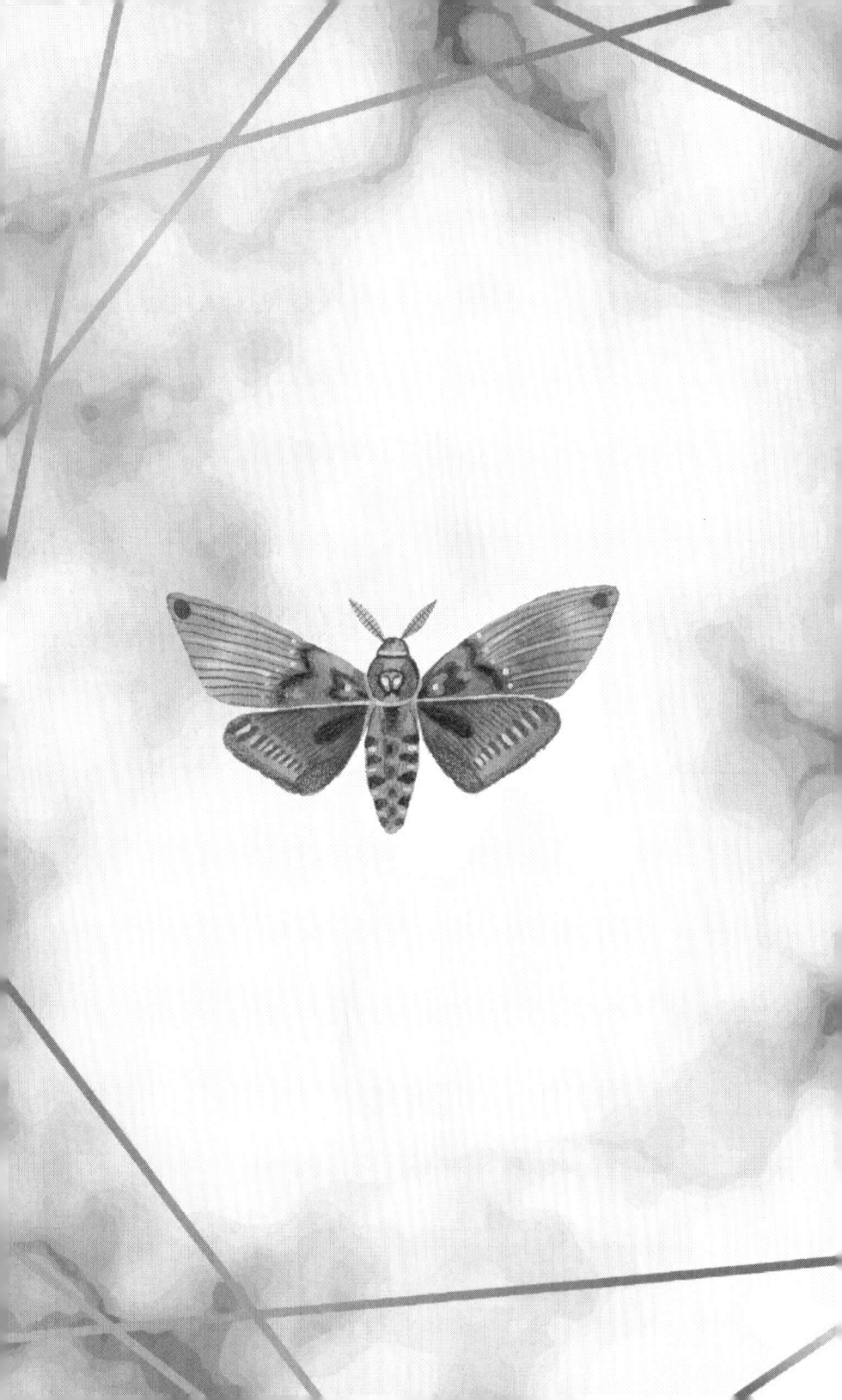

Twenty

Daisy

Morning broke and I was afraid to open my eyes, but as the sun's rays illuminated the tent, I knew it was time to face the day. After Bennett left last night, I fell into a restless sleep. Horrible images filled my dreams, bringing with them a debilitating exhaustion I couldn't escape.

I told Bennett I'd need my wits about me today so I could think fast on my feet, but as I laid there with my eyes closed, all I wanted to do was fall back into the oblivion of sleep and avoid the reality of what I knew was coming next.

I had no idea what type of punishment I'd face for lying to Alder, but I knew it couldn't be good. Would he ever forgive me? Would Aster? Everything I'd done since coming here seemed to have harmed my family in one way or another. I wondered if I should have turned in Bennett and notified the General about Lily last night to avoid further damage.

Too late now.

I'd thought about it the second he revealed who he was, but when I looked into his stormy eyes and listened to his heart-felt plea,

I just couldn't do it. He was obviously telling the truth about his shadow magic—seeing as he morphed from a light-haired warrior into the troubled Yale student we tried to help back home right before my eyes. I was confident those abilities would help him in this task. I just hoped he was telling the truth about everything else.

Pushing out from beneath the layered furs and blankets, I rolled to the side and placed my feet on the chilly floor, fighting back a sting of tears.

Lily's bed was still empty, which meant today was going to be the worst day of my life.

Alder

Being this far away from Lily was hard. Our blood bond only worked in close proximity, which was a side effect of its original purpose—to protect the royal bloodline and *encourage* the King and Queen to remain together during times of strife.

I shook my head. *I never should have let her travel to Glenmiere without me.*

My attempt to surprise her last night may have been ruined, but there was no way I was going to wake her after the stress of the last few days. Not to mention, I still had no new leads on Bennett's whereabouts.

The search parties had cleared the villages of Cromwell and Vizount already, and were now on their way to the northern village of Támar. Hopefully I would have some good news soon.

Showered and dressed for the day in my fighting leathers, I headed to the training facility for a couple hours of light combat before my presence was required in the first meeting of the day. There were a hundred things to plan and complete in preparation for Samhain. In fact, many vendors and artisans already lined the walls outside the castle doors to donate their wares for the upcoming Ball.

Samhain had always been a special time in our realm, but with Gideon and Thadius recently passed, honoring our ancestors was sure to take on a special significance at the celebration this year. With the veil at its thinnest, we'd honor those who came before us and let them know they would never be forgotten.

An image of my mother formed in my mind, and I braced myself for the familiar ache in my chest. I still missed her every day, but now that I knew the truth about why my father left, it somehow made it easier to bear her absence.

"Good morning, Sir." A soldier bowed and greeted me as I stepped into the open courtyard where our trainings took place.

"Good morning," I replied with a clipped nod. "Anyone available for a light workout this early in the day?" The sun had barely risen, and with fall taking hold across the land, the chill in the air made it the perfect time for a workout—not that my men needed it. Once selected for the Guard, we'd all been honed from a young age to fulfill our duties. Still, it would be nice not to sweat through my uniform while I worked off some of the tension I carried with Lily being gone.

Highlighted by the early morning rays, the mountains in the west shone brightly on the horizon, and I imagined her still tucked beneath the furs and blankets in the royal tent. I wished I had another portal ball to make a quick trip there and wake her with a kiss to start her day. Unfortunately, the knowledge of how to make more of the portable devices was lost with my father's passing, and as badly as I wanted to go, I knew using another for such a selfish reason would be a mistake.

"Sir." The soldier lifted a hand from across the courtyard, waving me over to a small group of new recruits.

They couldn't be more than seventeen, though in fairy years, that made them one-hundred and nineteen years old. *Babies.* I chuckled, remembering when I told Lily how old I was and what her response had been.

"Exactly how old are you?"

"By your standards? One-hundred and eighty-two. By fae standards… twenty-six."

"So, it's like dog years? For each one fae year, it's seven human years."

"Are you calling me a dog?"

"What's wrong, puppy? Don't like it when someone calls you a name?"

"No, Princess. *I don't."*

Princess... The nickname I gave her at the time was to poke at who she truly was, but now, it had become a sweet joke between us. I couldn't wait to run my fingers through her blazing hair and whisper it in her ear the next time I saw her.

"Ready when you are, Sir." The soldier grinned and pushed one of the men toward me from within their small crowd.

Stretching my neck from side to side, I watched as the younglings tried not to stare at my antlers shimmering in the early morning light. Lily liked them polished and clean, and so did I. As the first deer-shifter to be King, I was proud of where I came from. After all that had happened, I would never hide who I was again.

"Don't go easy on me," I instructed the poor boy who'd been tossed forward by his superior.

"I... I won't, Sir."

Circling the young guard, I watched his feet and rolled my shoulders, ready to deflect his first move. As anticipated, he lunged forward on his left foot and brought up his right fist in hopes of connecting an early blow.

Sidestepping beyond his reach, I inflicted a light punch to his midsection, smiling as his cheeks turned red. "You're quick on your feet. That's good. Now just work on concealing where your next move is coming from." I didn't want to embarrass the kid, so I offered the instruction as general encouragement. His arm darted out. "Damn," I cursed when his next blow made contact with my chin. "Good. Very good."

We sparred another ten minutes to rousing cheers from the gathering crowd.

"Thank you, Sir. It was an honor to work out with you today." The guard bowed as I brought our session to an end.

"Thank *you*..." I paused. "What's your name, soldier?"

"Dylan."

"Thank you, Dylan... That was exactly what I needed to get the blood flowing this morning."

"You're welcome, Sir. I'm here every day, and at your disposal. It would be my honor to train with you again."

The young man's dark hair and sparkling smile reminded me of Gideon, and the ease with which he moved told me he was on his way to becoming a great fighter.

"It would be *my* honor, Dylan. I'll see you again tomorrow."

I wiped a light sheen of sweat from my brow and walked back into the castle, excited to tell Lily about my new morning routine. She was always encouraging me to do more things for myself, and while I hated being apart, her absence forced me to do just that. Perhaps when she returned, I could convince her to join me as well.

It may seem strange to some, but I was convinced that having a queen who was trained to fight would only strengthen the peace in our realm.

I grinned at the thought, imagining her in fighting leathers as she took on a foe of her own.

Stumbling up the marble steps, I caught myself with a hand against the wall as a vision of her hurt and bleeding blanketed my mind.

Maybe that wasn't such a great idea, after all.

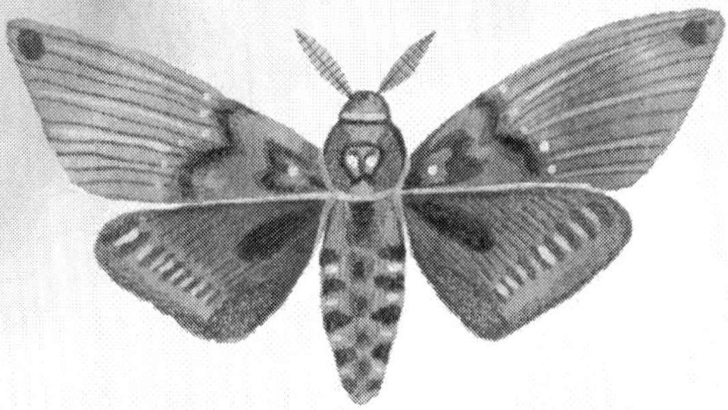

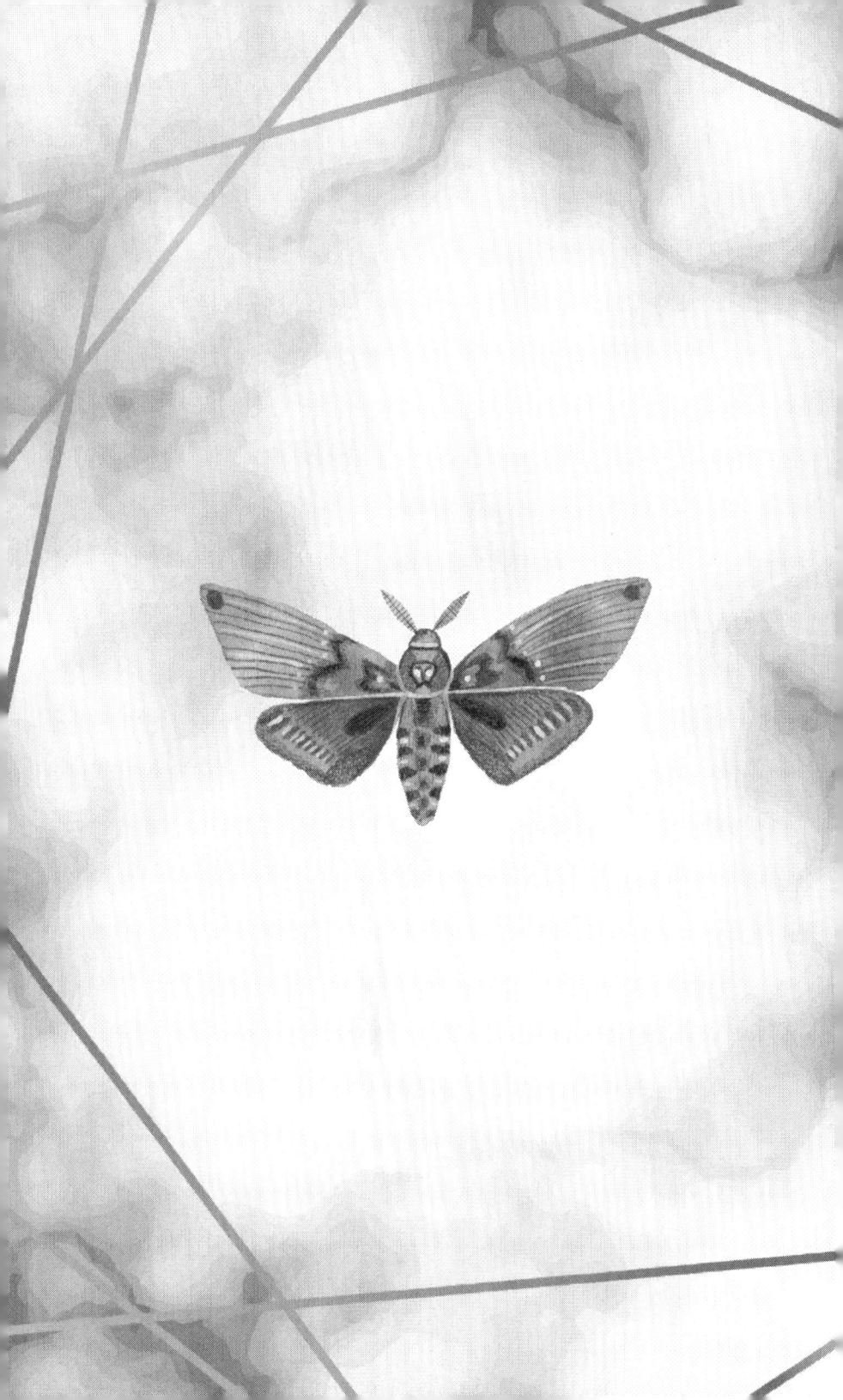

Twenty-One

Bennett

Following the tracks the Dark Elf left in the snow, I crouched behind a large spruce tree high in the mountains and watched helplessly as the huge man hauled Lily into their stronghold.

The outlying village we passed through last night reminded me of Támar, with its simple huts and yurt-like tents, but the carved, stone building they'd just disappeared into sat high on the side of the mountain, reminding me of lairs occupied by the dwarves.

I had no recollection of a war between the two factions, so I assumed they found a way to work together and now lived in peace. I hadn't seen any dwarves yet, so I figured my only option was to glamor myself into one of the Dark Elves and try to find a way inside.

Pulling my shadows around me, I morphed into a beast of a man to resemble the one who had taken Lily. Furs hung from my shoulders and wrapped around my legs, while a head of long, stringy black hair was tied tightly at the back of my head. The points of my ears were longer and sharper, which was the only trait our two races shared, from what I could tell.

The morning sun shone on the mountain's face, lighting it up like the Light castle's wall. Somehow, though, it still seemed dark and foreboding to me. The carved door into the stronghold had to be at least twelve feet tall and just as wide. My hope was that it didn't require some ancient password to enter. My preference would be to wait and observe the movement of others before exposing myself, but if I didn't go now, I'd have no idea where Lily might end up.

I secured Soven safely to a tree and discovered Lily's backpack still hanging at her side. Slinging it over my shoulder, I stomped out from behind the tree and marched toward the mountain with a large, gnarled staff in my hand. The Dark Elf had used one to aid his steps, but I wondered now if it was to aid his magic as well.

Once fully glamored, the pull of their dark energy coursed through my veins, strong, but not malicious. Staring up at the mammoth door, I placed a hand on its flat surface and gave it a push.

Surprisingly, it parted before me.

A long hall lined with pillars of granite opened up before me, and at its end, the elf still carrying Lily over his shoulder lumbered toward another door.

I rushed to catch up, staying to the left side of the hall in case I needed to slip behind one of the massive pillars to hide. Stopping when the elf did, I watched as he tapped a smaller stone door with the tip of his staff, then waited to see where it led.

The booming sound of grinding stone echoed through the space as the small door and the entire wall it sat in collapsed into the floor to reveal an enormous cavern gaping beyond.

Set deep inside the mountain, the glow of fire bounced off the stone, lighting it like the inside of a dragon's belly and thankfully keeping it just as warm. I crept forward the rest of the way and peered down over its edge.

Stone steps cut into the side of the wall led from the drop-off down into the cavern below. Lily's red hair caught my eye about two flights down. I discarded my staff and stepped into the belly of the beast. Descending after them, I noted multiple cages cut into the mountainside, each sealed with a metal grid for a door.

This was not good.

After another flight down, the Dark Elf stopped to open a cage door.

It's now or never.

I sprinted down the remaining stairs and walked towards him as he deposited Lily inside. "Anything to report on this one?" I asked, hoping the question was general enough that it wouldn't give me away. There were no other prisoners in the cages I could see, but I had no way of knowing if that was typical or not.

The enormous elf glanced over his shoulder, barely acknowledging me. "No."

I opened my mouth to address him again, but was caught off guard when he shoved me inside. Before I could react, the cage door clanged shut.

"You don't think I can feel the slick of your magic, boy?" He reached into the cage with his staff and tapped it against my chest, melting my glamor away.

Returned to my true state, I pushed the platinum hair out of my eyes, readjusted the pack on my back, and lifted my chin to meet his condescending scowl. "Just tell me why you took the girl."

"No," he repeated his one-word answer.

I grabbed the flat metal bars with both hands and gave the door a shake. "Tell me what you're going to do to us!"

"No."

I hung my head and sighed, playing as if I was already defeated. "Then at least tell me how you could sense my magic."

He paused, appraising me through hooded eyes. "Where do you think your shadow magic comes from? You've got Dark Elf blood running through your veins, boy." He pointed his staff at Lily, grumbled something under his breath, and walked away.

Holy shit. There was no way I was part Dark Elf. How could I be? My mom was born into our witches' clan, and my father was a witch as well, though from another village. They met when they were young during one of the clans' routine trading days, and I was born a few years later.

No. This elf was simply messing with my head.

Easing the pack off my shoulders, I turned around to check on Lily.

She was lying unconscious on a hard stone bed that jutted out from the wall. Her red hair tumbled over its side, cascading down until almost touching the floor. She was as beautiful as ever.

Kneeling beside her, I took her hand in mine and made a promise I wasn't sure I could keep. "It'll be okay, Lily. I promise I'll get us out of this." Placing my lips to the back of her hand, I let my emotions swell.

This was my first time alone with her in months. I could only hope she wouldn't despise me once she woke up and learned the truth.

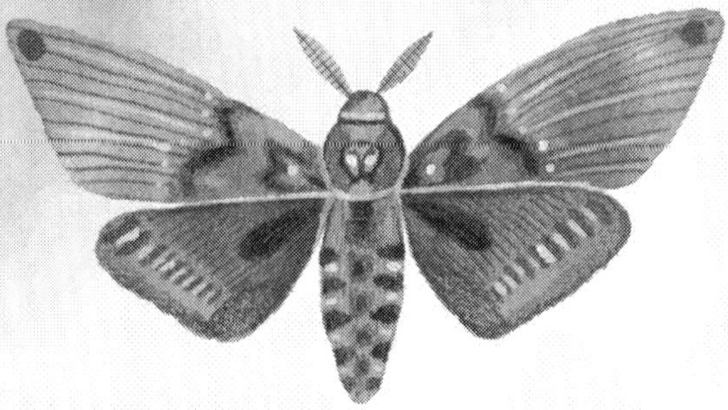

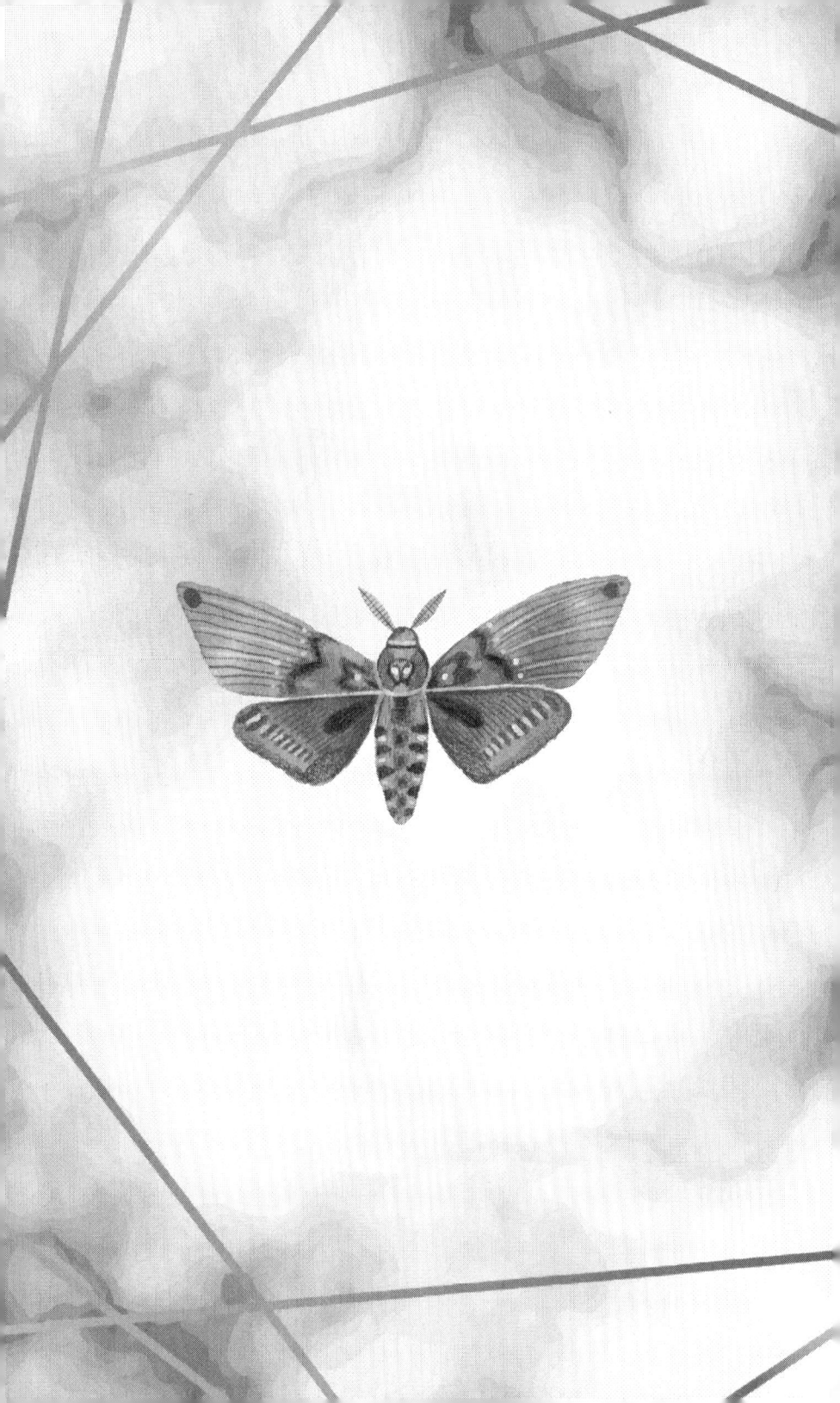

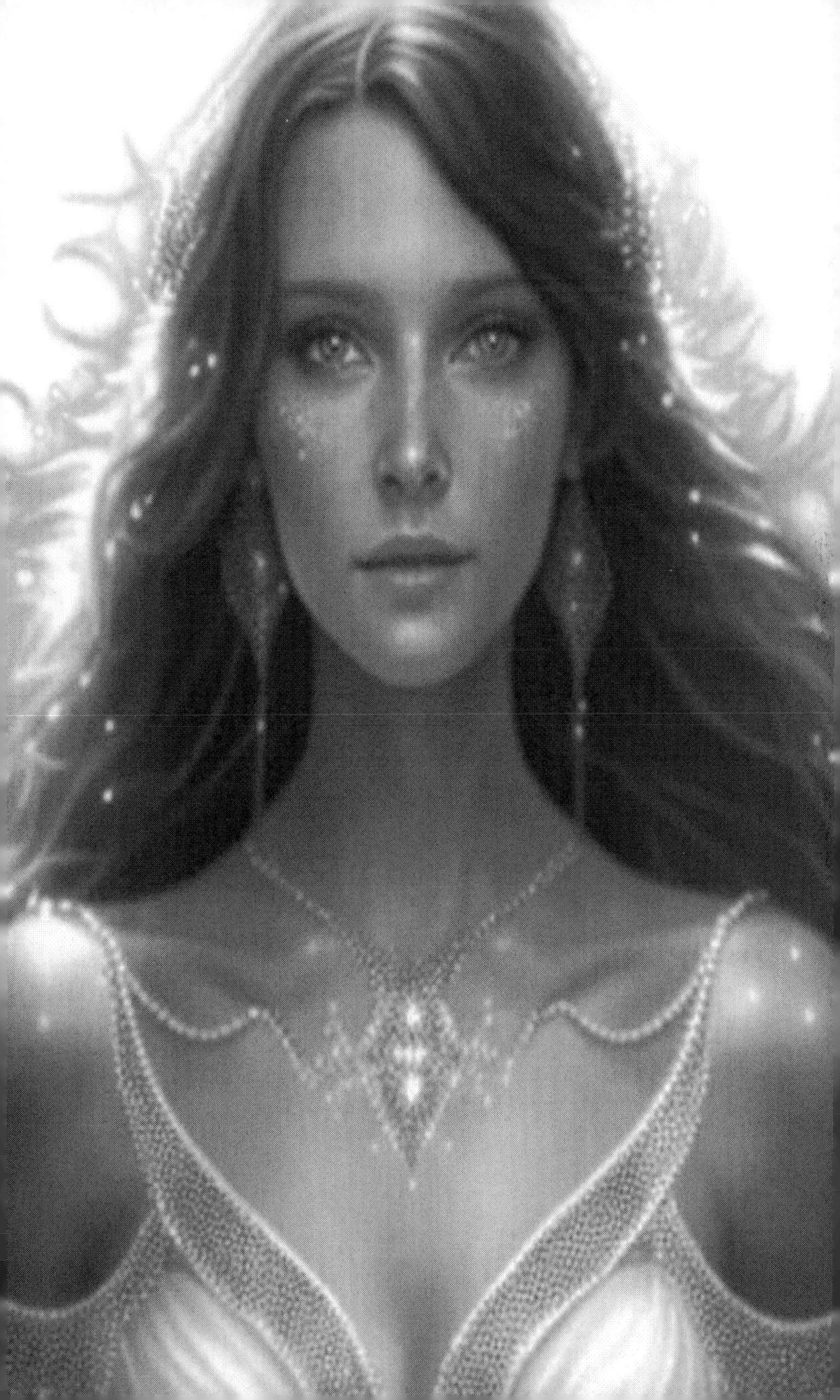

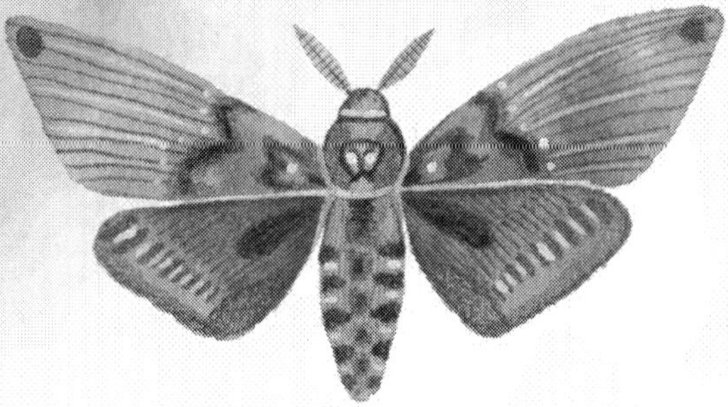

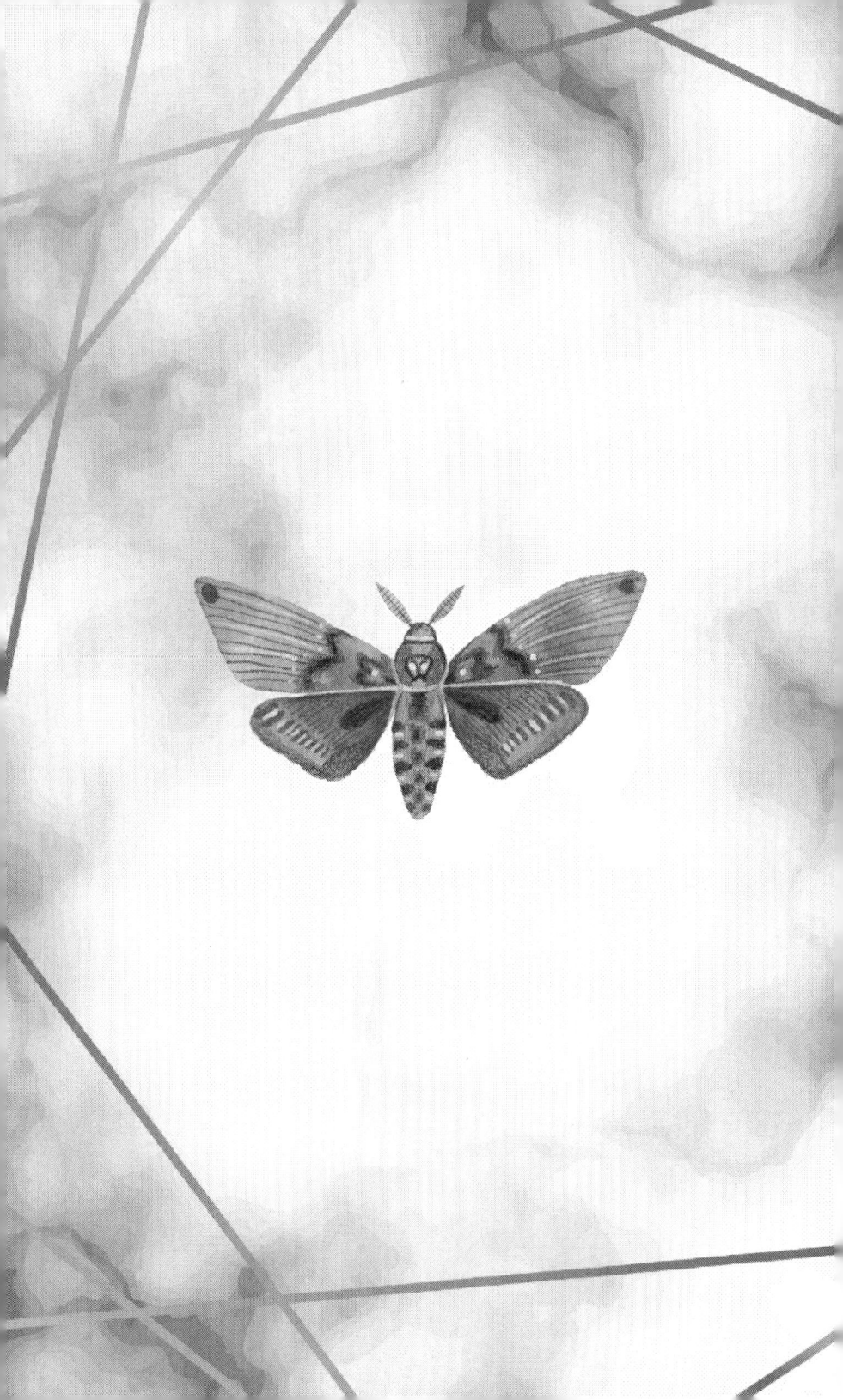

II

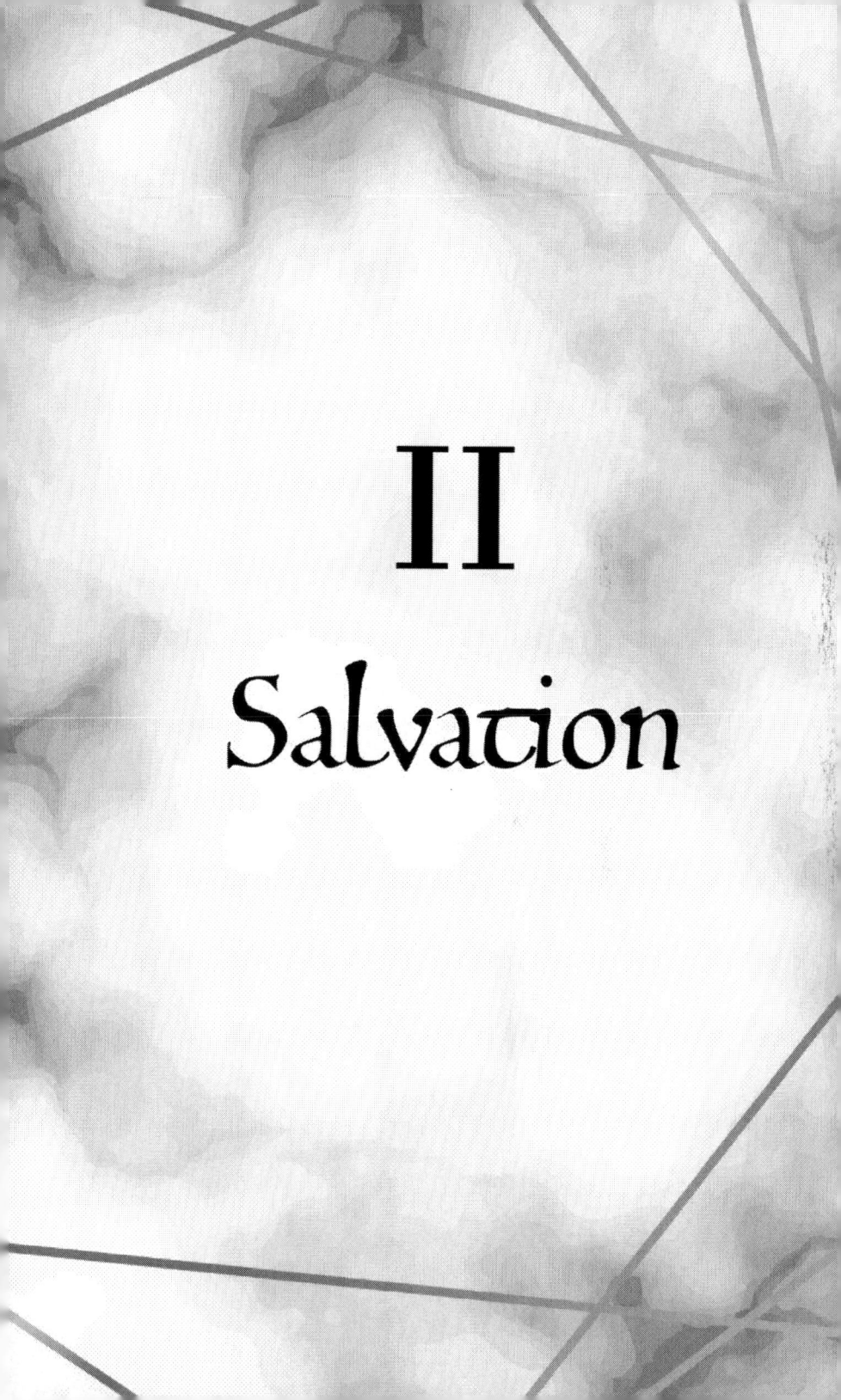

Salvation

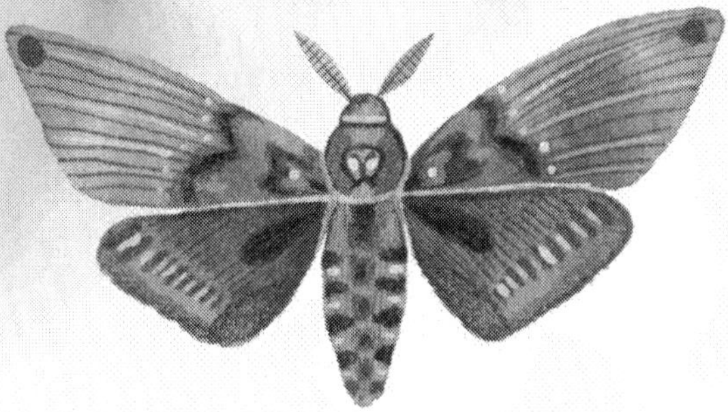

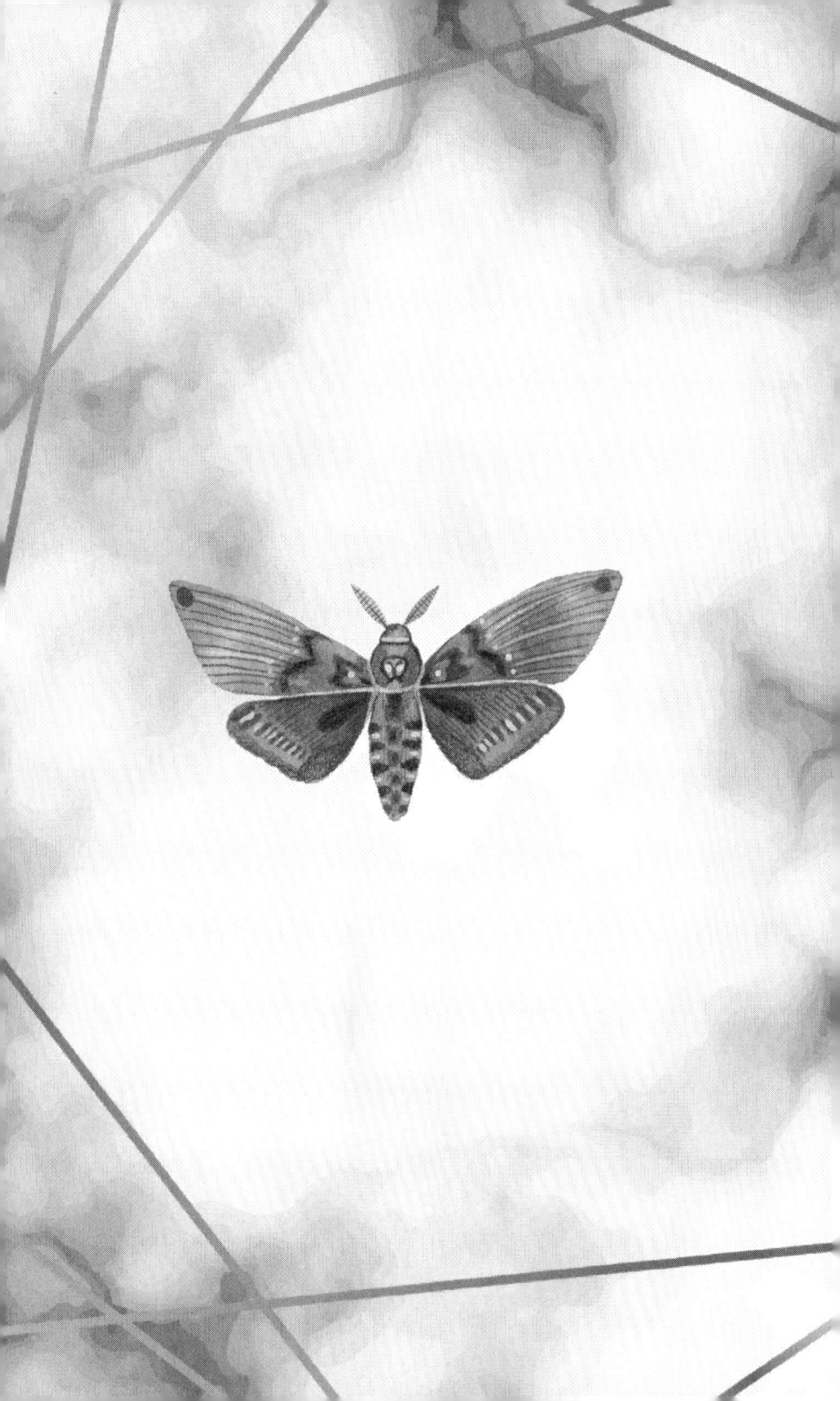

Twenty-Two

Daisy

Creeping out of the royal tent, I squinted into the morning light. A light fog laid over the camp, like a pastel cloud kissing the ground. Movement from the cooks' quarters caught my eye, and I ventured toward them with a knot in my gut.

"Good morning," I whispered.

"Morning, ma'am. Would you like some coffee?"

"Yes, please. And thank you," I rushed to add, feeling oddly emotional, like this would be the last nice thing anyone would ever do for me.

All last night I contemplated how this would unfold, and I thought if I remained calm and notified the General that Lily had gone for a walk early this morning and hadn't returned, it would play out better than if I ran from the tent crying and screaming. In fact, Bennett may be headed back with Lily right now, so causing an uproar seemed like an irresponsible thing to do.

"Could you please tell me where the General's quarters are?" I asked the cook, then took a sip of hot coffee to fortify my nerves, letting it burn all the way down my throat.

"Just over there, ma'am." He pointed to a meager tent mixed in with the others, sitting just a little further back.

"Thank you." I took two steps forward, then paused to savor another sip of coffee. Tilting my head to the sky, I suddenly appreciated the crisp mountain air as it stung my cheeks. It reminded me I was alive. Wild and free. I wondered if that was why Lily loved it so much.

She claimed she needed a break, but I hadn't realized how badly she meant it. The thought of being relegated to a life of servitude had to be overwhelming, especially when that life was all so strange and new.

We'd spent our whole lives protecting the portal back home, but with it being dormant until this year, we mostly lived like normal girls and women—well, as close to normal as growing up a witch could be. Living amongst the fae, in *their* world, and being immediately thrust into the role of their Queen… Yeah, I was surprised Lily hadn't run away before now.

My reminiscing and pondering ended abruptly as soon as the General stepped out of his tent. He met my eye across the camp and immediately headed straight for me.

"Ma'am, is something wrong? Where is your guard?" He lifted his eyes to survey the camp beyond me.

Swallowing hard, I shared the story I'd rehearsed in my head. "Good morning, General. I believe the guard is with Lily. She wasn't in our tent this morning when I woke, so I assume she went for a walk."

The General's eyes widened. "What? No. None of my guards would have allowed that. Not here. Please, let me accompany you back to your quarters."

Setting my coffee cup aside, the General rushed me through the snow and back to my tent. Once inside, he took a quick look around, obviously searching for anything amiss. "You said she was gone when you woke?"

"Yes, sir."

"But she was here when you went to bed?"

"Yes," I lied. "We ate dinner, then turned in early. Tired from the day's ride."

Hmm, he mumbled to himself, still looking over every inch of the space.

My muscles coiled when his gaze drifted over my pack. The witch's handbook to magic and mayhem laid hidden inside. If the General were to discover it and recognize it for what it was, this entire charade would be over in a heartbeat.

"Please remain inside while we do a quick search for the Queen."

His clipped instructions had me shrinking back onto my bed. Pulling my knees up to my chest, I wrapped my arms around them and closed my eyes. I listened to the ensuing commotion outside and knew it would only get worse.

Please come back soon. I prayed Bennett had already found her and they were on their way back, but something deep inside told me that wasn't how this was going to go.

Lily

My back ached when the elf laid me down on a hard stone slab. Forcing my eyes to remain shut, I listened as my Dark Elf captor exchanged words with another. Suddenly, the door slammed shut, and there was movement next to me inside the cell.

"You don't think I can feel the slick of your magic, boy?" the elf said, followed by a thud and a gasp from the other one.

I was desperate to open my eyes, but terrified to do so. I wanted to know who this other prisoner was, but I didn't want to give away the fact that I was awake.

"Just tell me why you took the girl," the man said in a voice I didn't recognize.

I flinched at his mention of me.

"No," the Dark Elf replied.

The door to our cage rattled. "Tell me what you're going to do to us!" the man demanded.

"No," the elf replied again.

The man—who was apparently now my cell mate—sighed, seemingly defeated. "Then at least tell me how you could sense my magic."

I listened closely as the elf replied, "Where do you think your shadow magic comes from? You've got Dark Elf blood running through your veins, boy." Mumbling something else under his breath, the elf fell silent, then I heard him stomp away.

You've got to be kidding me. First, I was kidnapped by a Dark Elf brute, and now I was imprisoned with another one?

Silence filled the space, the stone turning cold and pressing down upon me like a blanket meant to freeze me to death. I squeezed my eyes shut and tried not to move a muscle as the man in the cell moved closer to my side. His warm breath caressed my cheek, and it took everything in me not to jump up and slam my fist into his face. Suddenly, I realized I could. I felt lighter now, like the Dark Elf's oppressive spell had been lifted, allowing me to move. But I stayed rigid, not ready to deal with this asshole yet. I needed more time to learn what I was up against.

I cringed internally as he whispered, "It'll be okay, Lily. I promise I'll get us out of this."

Time froze as he pressed his lips against the back of my hand. *Fuck.* This person knew who I was.

The pressure in the air around me receded and light shuffling against the stone told me he moved away and was probably lying down on the opposite side of the cage. With all the willpower I could muster, I kept as still as a statue and did the only thing I could think of—reach out to Alder again.

A tear escaped the corner of my eye when the connection remained flat.

Goddess, please help me, I prayed, guilty for what I'd gotten myself into.

Twenty-Three

Daisy

Thankfully, the General believed my story, but only after seeing the footprints in the snow leading away from camp. He came to the same conclusion Bennett had... Lily was taken by the Dark Elves.

With a full search thoroughly underway, I returned to the royal tent as the morning sun dipped behind the clouds, turning the landscape as stark and ominous as the situation I was in.

Out of the forty soldiers in our camp, a group of twenty were tasked to follow the trail through the woods, while another five were sent back to Ferindale to report directly to the King. It was a full day's ride through Dartmoor and then onto the Light Kingdom, and once Alder learned the truth, all hell would break loose. I imagined he'd use another portal ball to immediately return to camp, but until then, I was determined to do all I could to help both of my sisters from here.

Sitting at the small desk, I pulled the witch's book of shadows from my pack and laid it open in front of me. There had to be spells in there that I could use to set things right. There just had to be!

Flipping through the pages, I forced myself to ignore the bits of hair and blood stuck here and there, focusing only on the spells for communication. Halfway through, I found what I needed.

A talisman to infiltrate one's mind certainly sounded nefarious—especially while reading it directly from the crone's own book—but if it allowed to me reach Lily, it was exactly what I wanted to do. First, I'd need to find Lily's pack and gather something personal of hers to root the spell. I looked around the tent and a hollow feeling settled in my gut when I realized the last person to have her bag was Bennett.

He was the soldier she'd handed it off to during the ride up, and knowing what I did now, all I could hope for was that he left it in his assigned tent and didn't carry it straight to Glenmiere with the fairy book of Gwenlyth Trelayne strapped to his back.

Peering past the front flap, I had no idea which tent was Bennett's since they all looked the same. Made from light gray canvas material, a sea of temporary quarters littered the camp. I focused instead on the small fires outside, and finally spotted one with low-burning coals, like it hadn't been stoked all night long.

Tiptoeing through the snow, I made my way to Bennett's quarters and quickly ducked inside. Scrambling around on the frigid ground, I looked under the single bed, beneath the thick wool blanket, then stood up and inspected the rest of the space. There was nothing here. Besides the cot, there were no other furnishings, so unless he had glamored it with his shadows, the pack was gone.

Dammit! Without something personal of Lily's, I had no way to make the spell work.

Poking my head outside, I made sure the remaining soldiers were still gathered around the General's tent before slinking back to my own. He'd informed me a guard would be assigned to watch over me at night, which meant I had to figure this out before the sun began its descent.

Digging inside my own bag, I prayed to the Goddess I had something of my sisters inside. I pulled out my small cache of herbs, then fumbled through the rest of the contents until my fingers wrapped around something I thought might do the trick.

A small white candle from Lily's shop, poured by Lily herself which I carried with me for casting circles on the fly. I hoped the connection to my sister would be enough.

Spreading out one of the fur blankets, I sat cross-legged on the ground and created a small circle by sprinkling my salt and herbs. I held the candle tightly in one hand and recalled the last circle I cast in the basement of the Light castle. The image of it sparking and fizzling out threatened my resolve, but I shook my head and pushed past my fears. *This time, it will work*, I told myself, then spoke the crone's spell out loud.

"Blood to blood, the connection's made. With this spell, I invade. Mind to mind, I speak to thee, through Macha's will, so mote it be."

My head snapped back, my eyes and mouth going wide. Dark energy swirled through my veins, brought on by invoking Macha's name, no doubt. I knew enough about fairy lore to know she was associated with the crone aspect of The Morrigan, but was one of the goddesses I never thought I'd be calling on.

The dark energy of my spell peaked, and I called out Lily's name. "Lily! Can you hear me? Please. It's Daisy, and I need to know if you're okay."

The connection snapped and sizzled in my head, confirming it was alive, but I couldn't hear or see a thing. It was like she was there, but not. Like her magic was somehow cut off.

A scream bubbled from my throat as I wondered how the Dark Elves could be powerful enough to subdue the one true fairy queen.

I swiped a finger through the salt and herbs to break the connection. If I couldn't reach her using the crone's own spells, that either meant I wasn't strong enough to do this on my own, or not fae enough to access the magic required.

Tears spilled from my eyes as I returned the candle to my bag and laid down on the bed.

I hoped Bennett had already reached Lily and they were on their way back, but with the connection spell failing, I had no way of knowing. *Unless...*

I jumped up, flung the tent flap open, and raced back to Bennett's quarters. He may have taken Lily's pack but if I could find something of his, I could recast my spell to connect with him instead.

Rummaging through the blankets, I tossed them onto the floor and searched the bedding for something of Bennett's.

Thank the Goddess. There, on the pillow, was a strand of his platinum blond hair. I picked it up between my finger and thumb and held it tightly as I walked back to my tent.

If I couldn't reach Lily, then the least I could do was try to reach Bennett and hope I'd have better luck.

Setting up my circle again, I laid the strand of hair across my palm and repeated the crone's spell.

"Blood to blood, the connection's made. With this spell, I invade. Mind to mind, I speak to thee, through Macha's will, so mote it be."

Nothing happened.

The energy I felt before didn't even start to build.

I repeated the words again.

"Blood to blood, the connection's made. With this spell, I invade. Mind to mind, I speak to thee, through Macha's will, so mote it be."

Again… nothing.

I looked at the hair in my hand, wondering what I was missing. Then, it dawned on me. *"Blood to blood…"*

When I cast the spell to connect to Lily, it reacted because we were related by blood. But that wasn't the case with Bennett. With Bennett, I'd have to spill *my* blood as a sacrifice in order for the spell to work.

Taking a white bone knife from my bag, I sliced my palm and laid the hair back across it.

"Blood to blood, the connection's made. With this spell, I invade. Mind to mind, I speak to thee, through Macha's will, so mote it be."

My head snapped back, and a scream escaped my lips as Macha's dark energy swirled through my veins again.

Twenty-Four

Bennett

I moved away from the stone bed and sunk down against the cold wall across from Lily's sleeping form. I promised her everything would be okay, but honestly, I wasn't sure.

I had no idea how to get us out of here, or why they took Lily in the first place. If this was a political thing, and they knew who she was, we may be in trouble. But if the Dark Elf just happened across a girl alone in the woods, we might have a chance. Though, the idea of why he would take a random fae woman in the first place made me cringe. I didn't want to think about the possibilities, but the thought had already taken root. I shook my head, swallowing hard. If they tried to hurt her in any way, I would be using my *slick* magic to glamor myself into a bear and eat out their fucking hearts.

My gaze returned to Lily, refusing to settle anywhere else. My plan to rescue her, reveal myself, and beg for forgiveness was in arm's reach… literally. But looking at her now, I wasn't sure I could go through with it. She was a captive audience, for sure, but this wasn't how I imagined telling her the truth.

I hung my head.

I wanted to have the book in hand so she could see I was sincere about returning it. And even though I would let her know Daisy had it back at the camp, I still didn't think having a heart-to-heart from the inside of a prison cell was the best idea. Then again, how would she take it if I continued to lie?

"Who are you?" Lily's sweet voice drifted across the cell, but for the first time ever, it carried a sting.

"That's a difficult question to answer," I admitted honestly, my natural voice deeper than what she was used to.

She sat up and folded her feet beneath her on the stone bed, then leaned back against the wall. "Doesn't seem too difficult to me. I heard what that brute said… you're a Dark Elf, too." She looked me up and down. "But if that's the case, then why the hell are you wearing a uniform of the Light Guard? … And why are you so much smaller than the brute?" she tacked on.

I thought, perhaps, she would recognize me as the guard who took her pack during the ride up, but with my helmet in place at the time, it was obvious she didn't. I *was* happy, however, I at least retained my clothes after the elf had stripped me of my disguise, but mortified because if she heard that exchange, then she was awake when I kissed her hand as well.

"That's not *quite* as hard to explain." *This is it.* If I started off by showing her my shadow magic and morphing into the Bennett she knew, maybe she would accept who I was and then I could explain why I did what I had to do.

Taking a deep breath, I reached for my magic, ready to remove my glamor, but was met with a sickening emptiness.

"So... explain," Lily demanded.

I tried again, allowing the thoughts of my normal clothes to flow across my skin. Usually, that was all it took.

Again... nothing happened.

"Something's wrong with my magic." I frowned, realizing our situation had just gone from bad to worse.

Lily took a deep breath and closed her eyes, snapping them open a few seconds later. "Shit. Something's wrong with mine, too."

When I pushed to stand and she did the same, it reminded me how well we used to work together. Moving to the opposite ends of the cell, we searched our enclosure for anything that could be used as a disrupter to our magic. Unfortunately, nothing but smooth stone surrounded us.

"I don't see anything out of the ordinary, do you?" she asked.

"No. Nothing."

She sank back down onto the hard stone slab. "Then I guess I have no choice but to go with... 'the enemy of my enemy is my friend'?" She ended the statement as a lingering question, and when a tiny grin pulled at the corner of her mouth, I just about lost it.

I urge to slam my lips to hers was overwhelming. I either needed to kiss her or scream at the top of my lungs, *"Lily, I'm sorry! It's me, Bennett. I had no choice when I took the book. It was to save my mother's life, etc., etc., etc...."*

But I did neither. Instead, I lied again.

[151]

Reclaiming my seat on the unyielding rock floor, I looked up into her beautiful green eyes. "I know who you are, my lady. And to answer your question from before, I'm in a Light Guard uniform because it's my duty. Unfortunately, I've done a piss poor job at protecting my Queen."

She inhaled, her chest rising and falling with relief as she took a deep breath. "Let's keep my title to ourselves, shall we?"

My head bobbed absentmindedly as I agreed.

"You know my name, but what's yours?" she asked.

I threw out the first thing I could think of, which was the nickname of one of my childhood friends. "Bash. Short for Sebastian." I smiled and lifted my chin, thankful for this time together, yet regretful of the way I knew it would end.

Lying to save my mother was one thing, but lying to Lily's face was another. She was never going to forgive me now.

"What the...?" My head filled with a dark buzzing energy, saturating my mind with an inky blackness I'd never felt before. I grabbed both sides of my head as it crept deeper, slinking its way into every corner.

"What's wrong?" Lily asked, dropping to kneel beside me.

"I... I don't know. It's like someone with dark powers is reaching out to me, but I can't hear what they're trying to say." I pressed against both temples, struggling against the pain until I finally passed out.

The last thing I heard was Lily's sweet voice calling my fake name. *"Bash!"* I swore right then to tell her the truth the next chance I got.

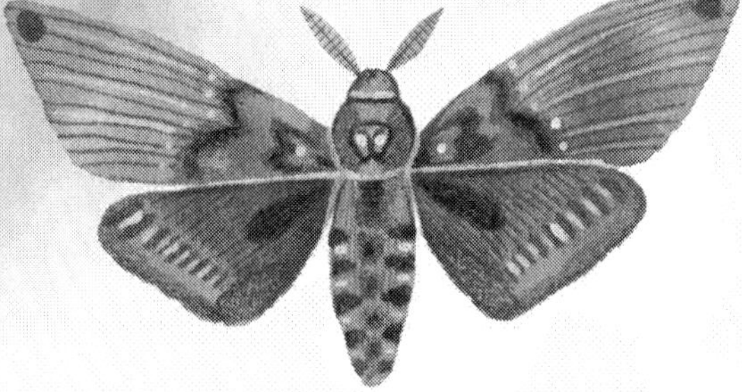

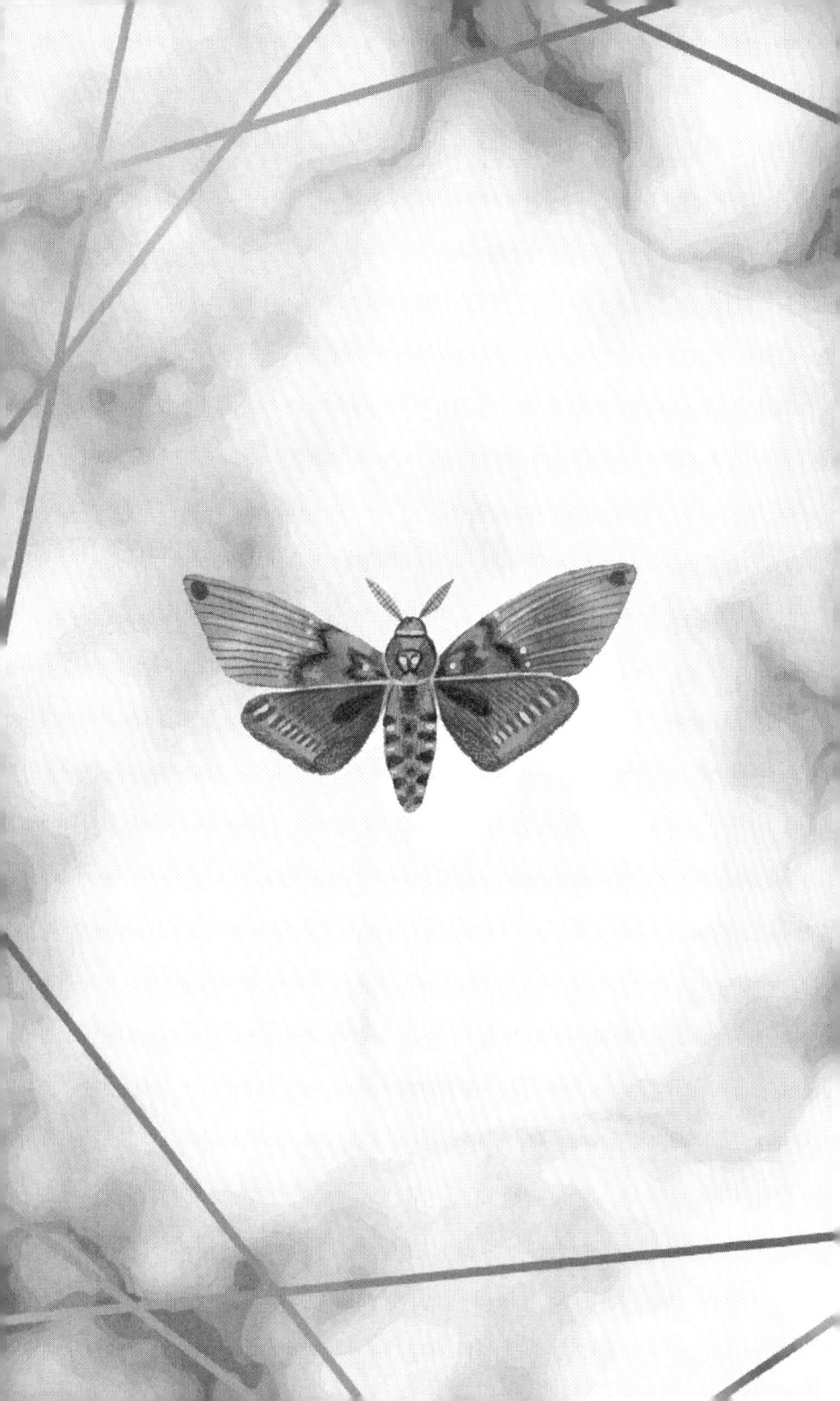

Twenty-Five

Alder

"What?! NO!" I seethed again after hearing the soldier's report. Everything in me yearned to tear the world to shreds, but I refused to show anger toward my men. I'd been on the receiving end of too many of Thadius's rage-induced outbursts, and I would not subject any of my guards to that, despite how their news had broken me.

"Where was she last seen?" I asked.

"In the royal tent with her sister, Sire."

I reached into my pocket, my fingers gripping the portal ball I always kept at the ready, then meted out my instructions. "Rest for the night, then return to the camp tomorrow. I'll inform the General you're on your way."

The five guards bowed, then led their horses toward the stables.

I rushed inside, needing to find Aster and inform her what was going on. When I reached mine and Lily's room, I found Aster and Iris hovered over Fern, while Gretta ran from the bed and headed back toward the bath.

"What happened?" I asked. A frenzied energy filled the room, and I could tell by the flush of Fern's skin something was wrong.

After Lily left, I'd hardly spent any time here except to check on them when I had a free moment.

"We're not sure," Aster answered in a clipped tone. "Yesterday morning, she began muttering words under her breath and developed a fever."

"What was she saying?"

Aster met my gaze with a cold stare. "Something about blood to blood, and Macha's will."

Oh, shit. "That's not good."

Iris's voice hitched and she held back a sob, while Aster snatched the wet cloth out of Gretta's extended hand. "Clearly, Alder, but why don't you enlighten us and tell us who Macha is and how soon Lily should be back with that goddamn flower?" Aster snapped.

My throat tightened, but I forced out the truth. "Macha is a dark witch, and the Fae goddess of death. You *might* recognize her from our lore as one of The Morrigan. She is also the deity the crone called on for her dark spells."

Aster's jaw flexed but she remained silent, tending to Fern as she waited for the next part of my answer, which I dreaded giving.

"And I've got more bad news," I added.

Iris moved closer and reached for Aster's hand.

"Lily is missing from the camp. They think she's been abducted."

The Fairy Handbook to Spell and Salvation

Iris collapsed onto the bed, throwing an arm over Fern as if to protect her from any more hurt. Aster, however, walked straight over to me.

"I assume you're going there now?" she asked matter-of-factly.

"Yes. As soon as I leave you." My fingers flexed on the portal ball still clenched in my grasp.

Aster straightened her spine and raised her chin defiantly. "Then I'm coming with you."

"What? No." I repeated my earlier response, but for very different reasons. I couldn't have another of Lily's sisters out there to worry about. As soon as I reached camp, I would to check on Daisy and then organize my men. Every moment was precious, and wasting time coddling a sibling wasn't in my wheelhouse. "I don't think that's a good idea."

Aster crossed the room and slid a small notebook into her skirt pocket. "I don't really care what you think." She walked back to Iris and Fern, placing a kiss on both their cheeks, then addressed Gretta next. "You have earned my trust, and I ask you now... Please take care of them while we're gone."

Gretta dipped her head, her eyes shining beneath her chestnut lashes. "She'll remain in good hands."

Aster practically floated across the room as she came to stand in front of me with a steeled look in her eyes. "Let's go."

I looked to Gretta—one of my mother's oldest confidants—and with a furrowed brow, accepted the clipped nod of her head that this was the right thing to do. "Fine. Let's go."

Pulling the portal ball from my pocket, I tossed it into the corner of the room. White light burst from within, followed by a scattering of snow spilling onto the marble floor. Taking Aster's hand, we stepped through together, emerging in the mountains and right in the center of the camp.

Daisy

I knew facing Alder would be horrible, but when I spotted my oldest sister emerging from the portal with him, I suddenly wished I was the one who had gone missing instead.

The King pointed to the royal tent and called out for a guard to show Aster the way before disappearing into a crowd of his men.

Scrambling to the desk, I stowed the crone's book back in Bennett's pack and quickly stuffed it under my bed. The last thing I needed right now was the pressure of figuring out a way to explain how I had the book Bennett stole.

Aster pushed into the tent, shivering from the cold.

"Goodness gracious, Aster! Why in the world don't you have a coat? Here." I wrapped one of the fur blankets from Lily's bed around her shoulders.

Gathering the edges in front of her, she glanced around the tent. "Left in a hurry," she supplied through chattering teeth.

"Come here," I instructed as I pulled a chair in front of the small fire, recognizing the oddity of *me* taking care of *her*. I stood close by and waited for the questions to begin.

"Do you know what happened?" Aster rubbed her hands together while keeping her eyes locked on the flames.

"Yes and no. When I woke up yesterday, Lily was gone. I assumed she left early with a guard to go check on her horse. Obviously, I didn't go with her, and obviously she didn't come back. That's all I know." My response was rushed, but it felt good to get through it, even if it wasn't the whole truth.

I needed to stick to the story I'd told the General or I'd be in even more hot water than I already was. Once everyone found out what *really* happened, I'd probably never be allowed in the fairy realm again. I looked up and found Aster watching me like a hawk.

"Daisy..." she drawled, "do you know anything about the goddess Macha?"

My eyes went wide, which instantly gave me away. Practically collapsing to the floor, I sank down beside my sister's chair and begged for forgiveness. "I'm so sorry, Aster. I was only trying to reach Lily after she disappeared."

Remaining quiet for a moment, she studied the fire before turning to meet my pleading gaze. "Your spell worked, only it wasn't Lily that you reached."

"What? I don't understand."

"You connected with Fern and her condition worsened." Aster's eyes glowed, reflecting the fire and the hatred I assumed she now felt for me.

"I'm so sorry," I whispered, then flung myself to the ground. I laid crying for a moment, letting the cold penetrate my bones as punishment, then pushed up off the floor.

There was nothing else I could say or do, so I crawled into bed and prayed to the Goddess to deliver us from the mess I created. And more pointedly, to deliver me from the darkness waiting just beyond my lies.

Twenty-Six

Alder

General Niasin led my Guard for a reason—he was great at his job.

Despite Lily disappearing under his watch, he'd already arranged two patrols who had scoured the woods by the time I arrived, and he'd tracked the trail from which Lily disappeared.

Giant footprints led higher into the mountains. Under the General's instruction, the rest of our troops were mounted and ready to continue up the main path that led to Glenmiere.

"With it being our original destination, it seems like the best play. Most of us will arrive and pretend we're unaware of the Queen's disappearance, while a small group of warriors will sneak in and begin their search." The General held my stare, confident in his plan, but I saw a wariness in his eyes.

I laid a hand on his shoulder and offered my reassurance. "I agree with your plan. And I do not blame you for what happened here."

He visibly relaxed and bowed his head.

"Let's mount up!" I called out to the men, but paused when I caught Aster's gaze from across the camp.

Standing outside the royal tent with a fur blanket draped over her shoulders, she looked like an avenging angel with her corn silk hair flying loose in the wind and her arms crossed over her chest.

"We're getting ready to leave and will hopefully return with Lily by nightfall." I nervously adjusted the sword hanging at my side as I closed the distance between us and waited for the argument I assumed was on the way.

"Good luck. I'll pray to the Goddess for your success." Her words were sharp and measured.

"You don't want to accompany us?" I asked, surprised.

"No. There are things with Daisy I need to attend to here."

I couldn't imagine what those things may be, but I wasn't going to look a gift horse in the mouth. "I see. Then good luck to you, too." With a dip of my chin, I returned to my horse, vaulted onto Samson's back, and quickly joined my men. "Lead on!" I called out to the General, then tucked into the ranks a few rows back.

Glenmiere was still a day's ride away. I just hoped we weren't too late.

Aster

The frigid morning air nipped at my nose as I stood outside the royal tent and watched the Guard take to the trail. Of course I wanted to go with them to search for Lily, but something in my gut held me here. Since arriving last night, I found Daisy to be *off*. She wasn't acting like her usual self, and I needed to find out why.

The smell of coffee wafting from the cooks' tent had me stalking across the camp.

"Morning, ma'am. Help yourself." A kind-eyed soldier nodded toward a selection of cups set out on a table, making it clear that Alder had left a significant group of guards behind.

I raised my chin in appreciation and took one of the cups, sipping it slowly as it warmed my hands.

"Morning," Daisy's tentative voice floated over my shoulder.

"Morning. Did you sleep well?" I turned and looked at my sister, noting the bags under her eyes.

"Not particularly. You?"

I shrugged. "Well enough."

We drank our coffee in pained silence, then returned to the tent once the cook informed us he'd bring our breakfast over in a bit. I reclaimed my seat in front of the fire, recognizing the luxury of having one inside the tent and the effort it took for the men to dig out the in-ground chimney.

Daisy flitted around behind me, straightening the fur blankets on her bed and then occupying herself with any fake task she could think of. She wiped off the desk with the sleeve of her dress, then picked up debris from the floor that our shoes had dragged in… anything and everything that kept her busy and not talking to me. Our breakfast arrived shortly thereafter, and we spent the next few minutes eating in silence.

"This is better than I imagined, given our location." I smiled between bites.

Daisy mumbled her agreement through a closed-mouth grin.

"All right, out with it!" I couldn't stand it anymore. "There's something going on with you, and I want to know exactly *what!*" I tossed my fork onto the plate, cringing at the sharp sound.

Daisy stared at me with wide eyes before gently placing her fork on the table. "Fine. I'll tell you, but you have to promise not to be mad."

I hitched a brow and tilted my head, trying my best not to react before hearing what she had to say. "Has that sentence ever worked with me, Daisy?"

She took a deep breath and folded her hands in her lap. "I think Lily wants to move back into the Dark castle."

I frowned. "That's it? *That's* what's wrong?"

Her head bobbed in response. "Ever since we returned to Dartmoor, there's been something off about her. She keeps talking about freedom and told me she doesn't want to marry Alder yet. I think she wishes she wasn't even Queen."

I sat back in my chair and studied my little sister from across the table. Maybe she was telling the truth—that she and Lily had shared a concerning heart-to-heart—but when she shifted nervously in her chair and glanced at something near her bed, I knew there was more to it than that. Growing up, Daisy was the worst of us at keeping secrets, especially near Yule when Mama hid our gifts in the same spot every year. Daisy was always the first to peek *and* the first to tell.

I made an exaggerated gesture of following her attention and asked point blank, "What are you hiding, Daisy? And don't tell me this is about Lily wanting to move."

She straightened in the chair, her head shaking infinitesimally. "I…" she stumbled for words. "I don't know what you mean."

I stood up and crossed the room, coming to a stop at the end of her bed. "I know you, Daisy. And I know you're not telling me the truth. So whether you're hiding something here, or simply know more than you're letting on, let's just get on with it." I crossed my arms over my chest. "I don't have time for these games, and neither does Lily."

Daisy

"I don't have time for these games, and neither does Lily."

Sometimes I hated how perceptive my big sister was, and now was one of those times. Hovering near my bed, she stood with her arms crossed and looked down on me like she always had. I knew I should tell her everything, but whenever I thought about Bennett's pleading eyes, I knew it wasn't my secret to tell... so I opted for another.

"Fine. I told a little lie to the General."

I hoped revealing my shortcomings would satisfy her enough to leave the rest alone.

"And what lie was that?" she pressed.

"I told him Lily was here when I went to bed, and that she took her walk in the morning. But in reality, she went to check on Luna the night before, and I fell asleep before she returned." I sank into the canvas chair, ready and waiting for Aster's inevitable disappointment.

"What?!" Aster stomped to the front of the tent but stopped at the opening. She looked back at me with a snarl of disgust etched across her face. "I can't believe you'd do something like this. Lily loves you, and your *little lie* might have just cost her life."

I gasped in shock. My sister had never spoken to me like that before.

Tears flooded my eyes. I could only pray Bennett had already saved Lily, and Aster, for once, would wind up being wrong.

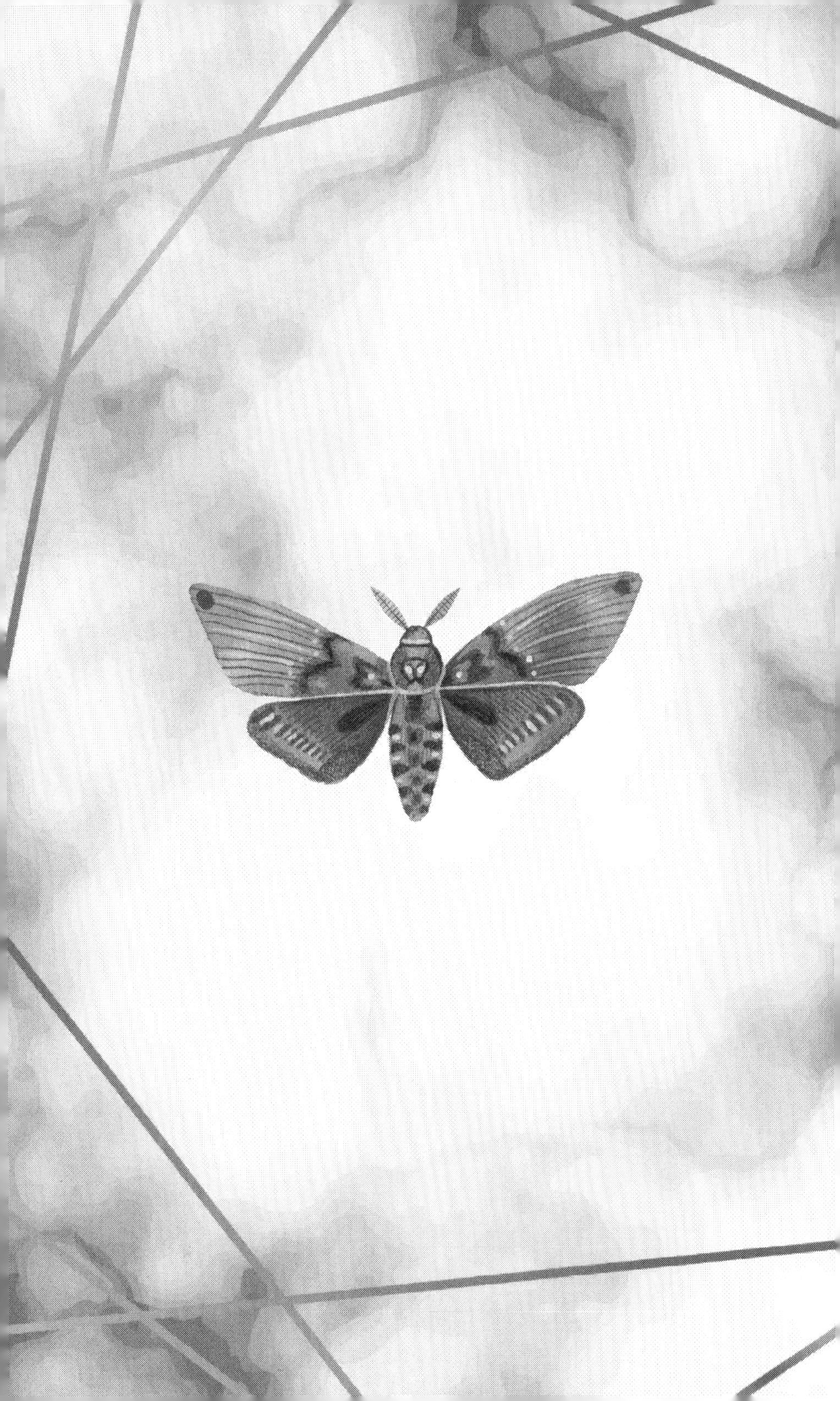

Twenty-Seven

Bennett

There was no way to tell what time it was this deep inside the mountain, but going by my internal clock, we'd made it to another day.

Lily was still asleep on the stone slab across the cell, shifting gently as I groaned and pushed my way up and away from the wall. Once on my feet, I crept to the barred door and looked past its metal grate, hoping to find anything useful within reach. There was nothing but more carved cells as far as I could see.

"Morning." Lily's voice was groggy; it reminded me of our night together at the Sessile Oak Inn. A memory forever burned into my heart and mind.

"Morning," I replied before moving back to my post against the wall. "I'd ask if you slept well, but…" I pointed to the stone slab and shrugged.

"Yeah, not the most comfortable bed I've ever had." She stood and stretched her arms above her head, revealing a slice of skin below the bottom of her cream-colored sweater.

I quickly looked away.

"Any more visits from our burly friend?" She continued to bend and twist, stretching out her muscles while I contemplated the best way to share what was in my heart.

"Nope. But I assume they'll have to feed us pretty soon." *Goddess, I'm such a coward.*

I'd gone over this conversation in my head multiple times, but now, standing in front of her with nowhere to escape, the words stalled on my tongue.

"Can I tell you something?" I blurted out, still wishing I had access to my magic to show her the truth behind my words.

"Sure." She sat back down on the stone slab and gave me her full attention.

I started to pace our cell, walking a few steps in each direction before turning around like a pinball bouncing off the walls. "I… I have a secret I need to tell you, and you're not going to like it." There, at least I'd started the conversation.

"And what secret would that be?" She leaned back against the stone wall and casually crossed her arms.

"This is so hard to explain without my magic," I whispered under my breath.

"Sorry, I didn't catch that."

I shook my head. "I just said this is a hard thing to discuss without the aid of my magic."

"Why would you need magic to tell the truth?" Her question was simple, innocent even, but the answer felt like a hundred boulders weighing down my soul.

"Because without it, I don't think you're going to believe me." I stopped pacing and leaned back against the wall.

She straightened. "I don't know you, but I'll be able to tell if you're lying. Magic or not."

I shook my head and a light huff of laughter escaped my breath. Like this was some kind of easy banter between friends, not the end of my fucking world. "That's just it, Lily. You *do* know me... very well."

Lily

"No. NO!" I shook my head, pulling my knees tight against my chest and wishing I could disappear.

The man before me did not look like the Bennett I knew, but the stories he told and the words that were shared only between us made it an undeniable fact—one with which my head and heart struggled to come to terms.

"I'm so sorry, Lily, but everything I'm telling you is the truth. This is my true form—minus the uniform—but I swear to you that everything I did was to save my mother's life." He dropped to his knees in front of me. "I promise you; Daisy has the crone's book back at camp right now. I've been trying to reach you to return it for months." He hung his head and begged, "Please, can you ever forgive me?"

Forgive him? I didn't know if I could. But right now, in the predicament we were in, what choice did I have? He was my only hope of getting out of here, and despite his betrayal, knowing his true identity was almost a small comfort, instead of being locked up with a stranger whose intentions were unclear.

I wiped my wet cheeks, sniffling and shaking like a leaf. My mind understood what he claimed, but my body was still in shock. Once my head started to clear, one remaining question bubbled to the forefront. "What did our captor mean when he said you have Dark Elf blood in your veins?"

Settled fully on the floor, he scooted back against the wall and shrugged, the movement miserable and deflated. "I have no idea, I swear."

We stared at each other in silence, probably afraid of what the other would say next. With measured breaths, I looked deep into his eyes and finally saw *my* Bennett there. Beneath the fear and sorrow, his stormy gaze held the truth of who he really was. "While I may not forgive you just yet, I do believe you."

He dropped his head and exhaled a relieved breath. "Thank you, and I understand. But Lily, know this…" He looked up again, his gaze serious and intense. "I'll never stop trying to prove myself to you. I know you're with Alder and being the Queen comes with certain responsibilities, but if you'll have me, I would like to remain with you as a real Light guard, in service to you both."

"Well, well, well. Isn't this a real heart-to-heart?" The gravelly voice of our captor interrupted at the worst possible moment. If he'd been listening for any time at all, he knew I was the Queen.

Bennett scrambled to his feet, then blocked me from the brute's view with his wide shoulders. "Tell us why you've brought her here," he demanded.

"Because..." the Dark Elf sneered, "there's someone here I think she'd like to meet."

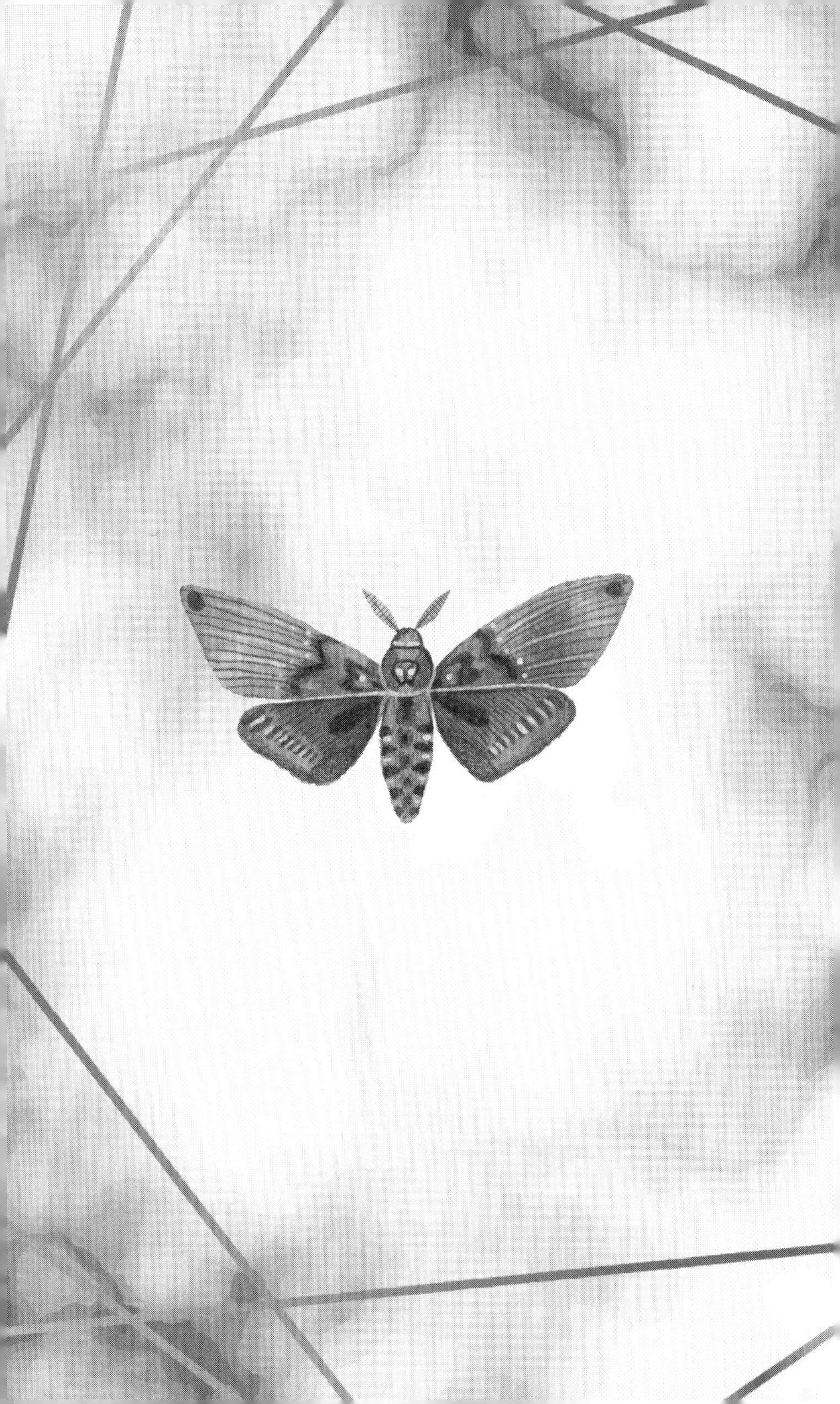

Twenty-Eight

Alder

The trudge up the mountain path to Glenmiere was longer than I remembered. Only once as a boy had I been this close to the Dark Elves' stronghold. And while our horses were battle-ready, the incline of the trail was beginning to take a toll.

"Hold here!" General Niasin called out, then flagged for our men to dismount and take a break.

The mid-day sun was high in the sky and finally visible from beyond the treetops. I stared at it, forcing myself to endure the blaze, and thought of Lily trapped somewhere in the cold, miserable dark.

"We'll be back on the road in a half-hour, Sire." With a firm nod, the General turned and left me alone.

I understood the men needed to eat and drink, but all I wanted to do was push Samson faster and harder up the hill, and the General knew it. In fact, if I possessed another portal ball, I would have already used it to arrive with my sword in hand on the Dark Elves' front steps. But I didn't. So, like the rest of the men, I dismounted and took a swig of water, stretched my back, and rummaged through my pack for something to eat.

I spotted Dylan, the young guard I'd sparred with a few days ago, standing among the other soldiers at the edge of the road and waved him over. "How did you end up here? I thought you stayed behind at the castle," I asked.

"I rode in with the other men the General requested to follow the messengers back."

"Ah."

"I'm sorry about what's happened to the Queen." He looked around nervously, like he didn't want anyone to hear him expressing concern, then quickly took a bite of his sandwich.

"Thank you. I appreciate that." I looked out over the men now gathered before me and waved the General over to address a concern of my own.

"Yes, Sire?" General Niasin asked as he approached.

"Have you decided which soldiers you'll be sending in to conduct our search for the Queen, and which ones will stay behind as the emissary crowd?"

The General offered a clipped nod. "Yes. I've selected fifteen soldiers who will sneak in and infiltrate the core of the stronghold and search for the Queen, while the rest of us stay above ground to address the leader as you instructed."

I glanced at the gathered men and the cacophony of sounds coming from the group. "I'll be altering your plans, General. I hope you don't take offense."

General Niasin bowed. "Never, my King. We are *your* Guard. Do with us as you please."

"Please let the rest of the men know they will be staying topside with you, while Dylan and I sneak into the mountain."

The General's mouth hung agape.

"We need quiet. Stealth. And fifteen stomping, chattering men won't do the trick," I explained.

"Sire, respectfully, these men are trained for missions such as this. They can become as quiet as the shadows if need be."

"That may be, General, and I do not doubt the abilities of your men. But we have no idea how the mountain stronghold is laid out, and it will be far easier for their guards to spot a group of fifteen, versus two. Don't you agree?"

General Niasin rubbed his chin, then nodded his head in reluctant agreement.

"Great. It's settled then." I looked down at the young guard, who straightened. "Dylan, give me a moment with the General alone. Then, you're coming with me."

Lily

"Damn that guy! Why did he have to say something like that? '...there's someone here I think she'd like to meet,'" I mocked.

"Because he knew it would get a rise out of you," Bennett quipped in return.

I huffed, my nostrils flaring. "Well, it definitely worked." I paced to our cage's door, wrapped my hands around the metal, and rattled it as hard as I could. "Let us out of here!"

A low chuckle sounded in the distance. If I had my magic, he wouldn't be laughing much longer. I let the thought trail off and focused again on why I did not. I could move and talk since the Dark Elf lifted his spell, but I still couldn't access my magic.

"You said your magic isn't working in here either, right?" I turned back to Bennett, who continued to shift away from me after sharing the secret of who he truly was. His way of giving me space, I guessed.

"Yeah, that's right. Ever since the elf poked me in the chest with his staff."

I climbed back atop the stone slab and stuffed the last bite of our breakfast into my mouth. The brute had arrived hours ago with a heavy wooden platter piled with fresh meat that smelled like boar, warm flat bread with steam still rising from the loaf, and a heap of oddly-shaped purple vegetables, none of which I recognized. Regardless, that didn't stop me from digging in. But only after Bennett insisted on tasting everything to check if it had been poisoned first. Apparently, his need to protect me had already kicked in again.

"What if it has something to do with this place?" I ran my hand up the white-flecked stone pressed firmly at my back.

Bennett's eyes narrowed as he followed my train of thought. "You think the stone of the mountain blocks fae magic?"

I leaned back against our immovable problem. "Yes, and there's no way we're getting out of here without it."

The emotion on Bennett's face told me everything I needed to know. We were stuck here, without magic, and with no means of escape.

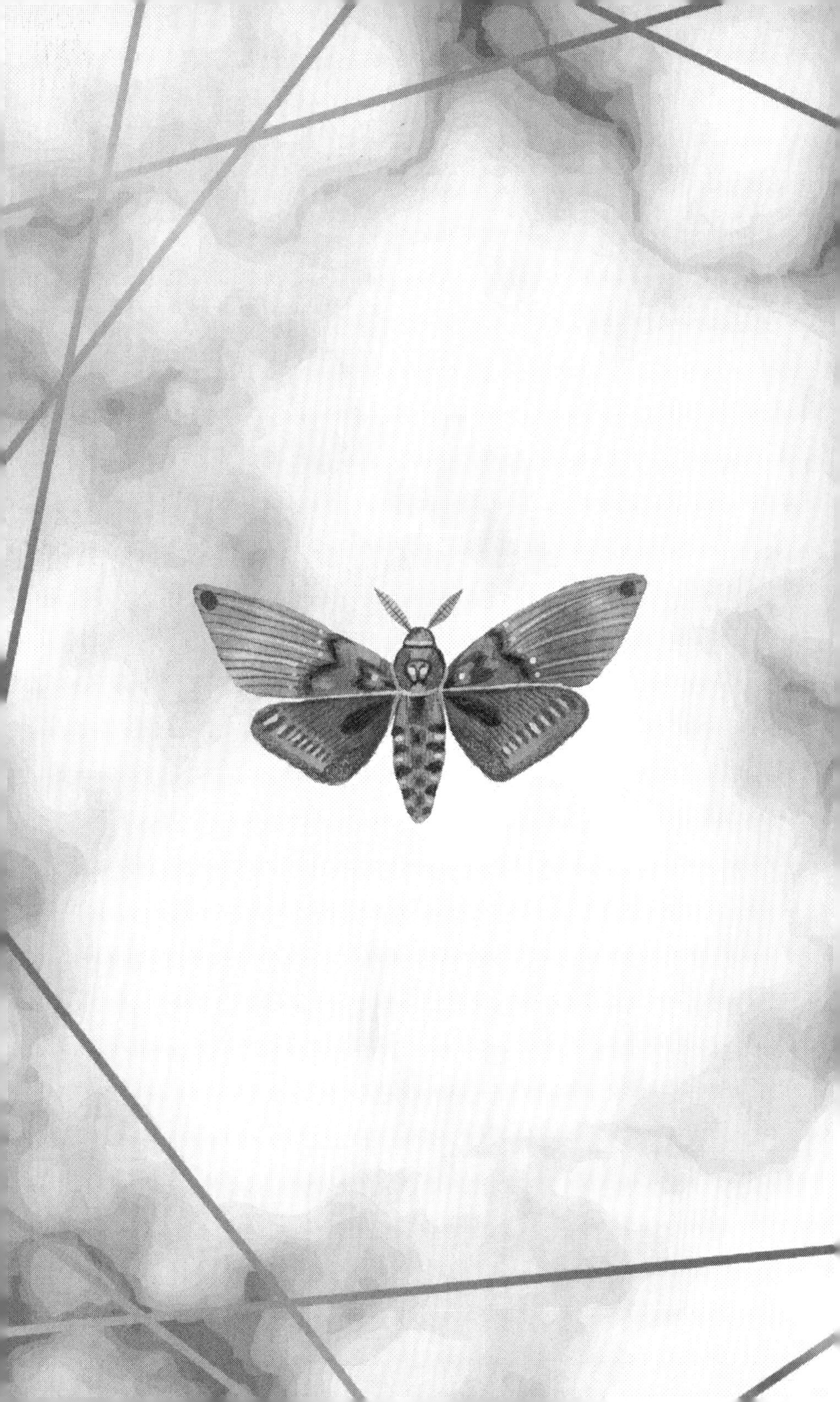

Twenty-Nine

Alder

Back on the road by mid-morning, Dylan and I followed General Niasin and the rest of the troops at a steady pace for the rest of the day. With dusk now upon us, Glenmiere's stronghold could finally be seen in the distance. Like a beacon, it stretched toward the sky, rising out of the forest with its white rockface glittering in the moonlight. The road we traveled on led to the main entrance carved into the side of the mountain, but Dylan and I would be veering off to a different path.

Leading Samson from the road and into the trees, Dylan and I wove our way down the hidden trail my father showed me when he brought me here as a kid. Moonlight flickered, and the soft rays of night switched to day as my mind drifted to thoughts of Gideon. A memory of my mother running through the trees in her deer form invaded my mind. Laughing, Gideon hoisted me onto his shoulders and gave chase through the woods. I remembered feeling like I was flying.

Snapping out of it, I smiled. It was one of the few good memories I had of us together as a family before everything changed.

Now, with Lily's life at stake, I stood at the precipice of losing another piece of my family, which I utterly refused to do.

Nearing the base of the mountain keep, I dismounted Samson and tied his reins to a tree before motioning for Dylan to do the same. "We'll need to go by foot from here. Follow me and stay quiet." I crept forward, pressing my sword close to my body to hold it still.

The frigid temperatures had hardened the snow, making it easier to walk on. But there was no hiding the footsteps we'd leave. It was a risk, but from what I remembered, the elves didn't patrol outside their keep. Why would they? The mountain was impenetrable... to most.

Being a half-shifter had its advantages. All shifter magic came from the Dark Elves, and while I couldn't fully transform like my mother, it lay dormant in my veins and would give me access to their world. It was another reason my father brought us here when I was young... to broker peace between the Dark Elves and the Dark Fae, with me as the pivot point. It worked, for a while. But when Gideon disappeared from the realm, the elves refused to acknowledge the Fae Kingdoms as long as Thadius was in control. After he had my mother killed, our realm was left with neither a Light or Dark Queen, and the elves retreated into their mountain once more. Now, for the first time in centuries, we had both in Lily again. A united kingdom and one Queen to rule it all.

The leader of the Dark Elves was a burly man named Craven, but despite the ominous sound of him, he was actually a good man.

I'd told General Niasin all this and instructed him to parlay for a peaceful meeting at the main gate, while Dylan and I snuck in and retrieved Lily before he knew she was gone.

I had no idea why Craven took my queen, but I was eager to find out.

"Just up ahead," I whispered, easing my footsteps as we inched closer.

Along the mountain's base sat a small crack, unnoticeable to the naked eye unless you knew where to look. Sliding my fingers inside the crevice of stone, I felt the rock react to my shifter magic and grinned when the secret door opened beneath my hands. It was a rare thing for a fae to possess, and I sent a mental thank-you to my mother, for it was her magic that aided me here.

I held a finger to my lips and gestured for Dylan to follow me inside.

The hidden entrance opened onto a precarious set of stairs that ran in both directions along the inside of the mountain wall. The space was cavernous, hollowed out on both sides with a honeycomb of large holes carved into the stone. I held my position as my eyes adjusted in the low light. Belatedly, and with a mounting sense of dread, I realized they were prison cells, complete with metal bars on their doors.

The urge to call out Lily's name nearly drowned me. I wanted run head-long up and down the stairs, rattling every cage, but I refrained. I wouldn't risk her's or Dylan's lives by exposing myself in a fit of desperation. Instead, we silently crept down the stairs, dropping further and further into the dark.

The blackness became suffocating and phantom noises echoed off the stone the deeper we descended. Soon, I wouldn't be able to discern anything, let alone see who resided within the cells.

Nearing what felt like the bottom, I spotted a tiny fairy light flickering up ahead. Gripping my sword, I padded forward, unsure who or what I'd find.

With Dylan watching my back, I approached the cell and squinted to see inside. Forcing back the gasp clawing from my throat, I stared at a woman crouched in the dark. Thin and disheveled, she barely noticed I was there.

"Hello? Ma'am, are you okay?" I whispered.

Through long, scraggly black hair, a pair of blue eyes turned and met mine. "Alder?" The sound of my name scratched past the woman's lips.

Holy shit and heaven above... How is this possible? I pleaded to the gods as I stared into the eyes of Lily's sister, Fern.

Iris

Lifting the cool rag from Fern's fevered skin, I was thankful her muttering had at least stopped. Picking off the plate of fresh fruit, I finished my lunch with a sip of the wine Gretta had brought in earlier, then continued sending prayers to the Goddess.

Mighty Goddess of love and light, reveal to me my sister's plight. Release her now from the spell within, bring her back to us again.

When Fern thrashed on the bed, I hoped my spells were working. With no way to communicate with Aster or Daisy, all I could do was sit here, tend to my twin sister, and hope they'd all return soon.

Once we had the vilenflu flower, Fern would be able to break free of whatever dark spell had a hold on her mind. Then we could finally start to concentrate on finding Bennett and the crone's book again. It was the whole damn reason we'd come to Ferindale in the first place, but now, it seemed so trivial.

Seeing my twin in this distraught state, I honestly could not care less where Bennett had disappeared to or what his clan planned to do with that stupid book. All I wanted was for my sisters to be returned and for all of us to go home. As selfish as my thoughts were, I didn't care. Living in the fairy realm was definitely not for me.

I missed our magical shop and our customers. I missed the cobblestone streets of the familiar town we grew up in. And most of all… I missed our mom.

If she was here, she would know what to do.

Fern convulsed again, and I swore I saw her lips peel back to reveal her teeth.

Good. She must be fighting whatever has a hold on her.

Thirty

Bennett

Lying on the floor with Lily only a few feet away was even more excruciating now that she knew who I was. It had taken hours for her to believe me, and even now, she maintained a cold demeanor for which I couldn't blame her. After we'd pieced together that the stone of the mountain must be suppressing our fae magic, she fell silent and forced herself back to sleep atop the stone slab bed.

I'd already failed her again.

The entire situation proved more frustrating than I expected, and I realized now how ridiculous my plan was. As if I'd simply be able to use my glamor to stroll into a mountain dungeon and rescue the damsel in distress. *Stupid!* Why I thought it would ever work was beyond me. The one thing nagging at my brain, though, was the Dark Elf's tantalizing words... *"Where do you think your shadow magic comes from? You've got Dark Elf blood running through your veins, boy."*

I still didn't understand how it could be possible. My mother never would have turned her love away from my dad, but without knowing the truth, the only thing I could do was test the elf's theory and see if it could aid me in any way. Closing my eyes, I reached for my usual magic, but again, felt it blocked, like a piece of the stone mountain resided inside me, trapping my magic behind its impenetrable wall.

I thought about how easily I'd gained access to the stronghold and chalked it up to being glamored as a Dark Elf at the time. But if what the brute said was true, maybe it was because their magic *did* reside in my veins. If so, I needed to figure out how to access it, and fast. Maybe then, I'd be able to prove myself useful to Lily again.

Shifting to get more comfortable, I readjusted Lily's pack beneath my head. A sharp edge poked me in the back of the neck and I sat up and checked to see if she was awake. I didn't feel right rifling through her things, but she hadn't mentioned the pack yet or demanded that I hand it over since we'd been shackled here together. Then again, the bag looked the same as every other soldier's in the Guard, so she probably thought it was mine. I had practically forgotten about it too, seeing as I had other, far more important things weighing on my mind. But as I ran my hands over the outside of the pack, curiosity got the best of me.

From what I could tell by feel, I couldn't distinguish anything besides a square block with sharp edges. Perhaps, whatever it was could be used as a weapon the next time the brute brought us food. Easing the pack open, I reached inside and pulled free what turned out to be nothing more than an old leather book. Rough creases marred the entire cover, and from what I could see in the dim light of our cell, there were no words to provide a title for the tome.

"It was supposed to help release my sister from the state she's in." Lily's soft voice drifted to the floor.

I looked up and met her gaze as she peered over the edge of the slab. "I'm sorry, I didn't mean to go through your things without asking; I just didn't want to wake you while you slept."

"It's okay. Honestly, I forgot all about it." She rolled further onto her side with a cringe as her bones cracked against the unforgiving stone. "Have you opened it yet?"

"No."

"Do it and tell me what you see."

Squinting, I lowered my eyes and did as she asked. The cover creaked open, and I swear I heard the book exhale. As I flipped through the first few pages, I sat there confused when they had nothing to reveal. "There's nothing here."

"Okay, good. I thought maybe it was just me." Lily sat up, still struggling to get comfortable on the hard stone bed. "Let me see." She held out her hands and I placed it in her grasp. Flipping back to the front of the book, she ran her finger down a particular page. "Do you know who Gwenlyth Trelayne is?" She twisted the book so I could see the name scribbled in black ink in the bottom corner.

"Holy shit! *Yes...* that was Gideon's grandmother. The last true Dark Fae Queen to rule the entire realm."

Scrambling off the slab, she dropped to her knees in front of me. "You're kidding! Tell me everything you know about her, Bennett!"

I opened my mouth to relay the history we'd all been taught as kids, but stopped short when an ominous shadow of sharp horns appeared on the wall outside our cell.

"Yes, *Bennett*... tell us all about my great-grandmother and how she was betrayed by the witch clans to give up her throne." Alder's cold voice sliced through the stone as he approached our cell, emerging from the darkness like a great beast of the forest.

Lily flew from the floor and raced to the door, wrapping her hands around the metal bars. "Alder, you came for me! Thank the Goddess you're here! I..." Words stalled on her tongue when she noticed the young woman lying motionless in her lover's arms.

Lily

The woman in Alder's arms looked emaciated and weak, but I couldn't stop staring at his beautiful face long enough to pay her any attention. "I'm so glad you're here." A tear ran down my cheek as he stared silently into the cell.

"Is that really Bennett?" he whispered so only I could hear.

"Yes, but there's so much to explain."

"Correct, wee one... there *is* so much to explain," the brute's scratchy voice sounded from behind Alder's back.

"Run, my love!" The words stung my tongue, like a combination of fire and ice.

"There's no need to run, my dear." Alder turned to face the brute. "Hello, old friend. It has been a very long time."

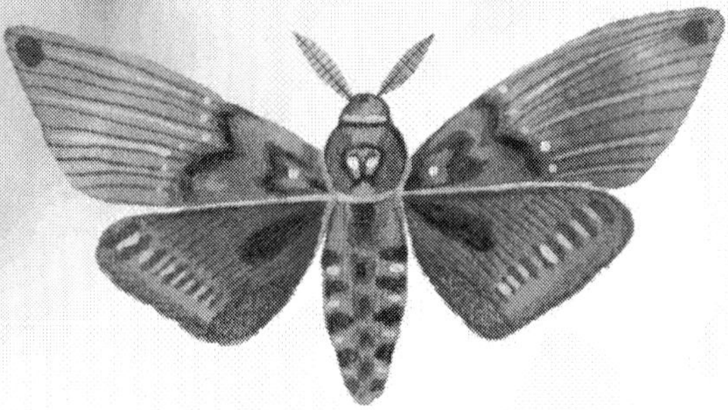

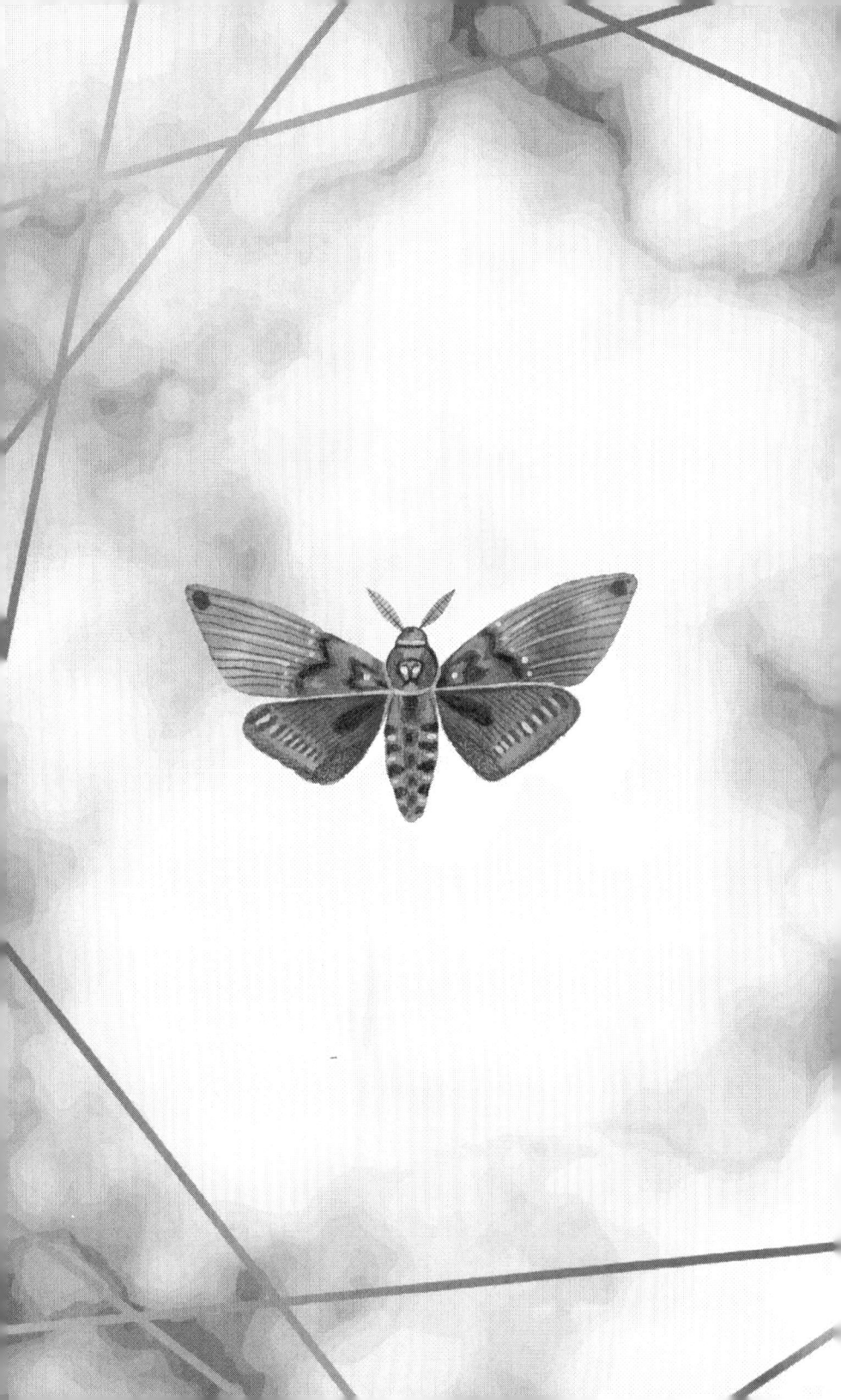

Thirty-One

Alder

I turned my back to Lily and faced Craven. "Hello, old friend. It has been a very long time."

"Indeed it has, my boy. It's good to see you. I just wish it was under better circumstances." He gestured to the woman in my arms, then touched the tip of his staff to the cell door. Metal clanged against stone, ringing throughout the mountain as Lily and Bennett were immediately released. "Follow me, and I'll explain."

I was waiting for the outburst, but surprisingly, Lily remained quiet as she tiptoed behind me with her body pressed against mine. I nodded at Dylan to follow Bennett when he emerged from the cell, looking very different from the man I knew. Thankfully, he, too, must have thought it best to keep his thoughts to himself.

Craven led us out of the prison cavern and into the main hall. I heard Lily gasp as she took in the massive pillars and sparkling floor of the Dark Elves' stronghold. The same light that reflected off the mountain outside shimmered here, blanketing the space with a softer, sparkling edge, while intricate etched carvings of animals and trees cut deep into the stone of the ceilings and walls.

"Here." Craven marched into a large meeting room off to the side and pointed to a deep chocolate cot set against the far wall. "Lay the woman down there."

Lily remained silent, but I knew as soon as she recognized Fern, all of that would change. *"Prepare yourself. This is going to be a shock,"* I sent through our bond, grateful it was working again.

Lily gasped at my unannounced intrusion into her mind.

"Everything will be all right. Trust me."

She squeezed my side, then I heard, *"It's not you I don't trust."*

"Just stay calm. Please. I have to know the reason he took you, and how..." I paused, dreading revealing Fern's identity, *"your sister ended up in the darkest part of his prison while she also remains unconscious in our bed."* I laid Fern down and smoothed back her dark hair to reveal her face.

"Fern! Oh my Goddess!" Lily collapsed to her knees, stroking her sister's hair as tears began to fall in earnest down both cheeks. "What the hell is going on here?"

"I'd be careful, lass. We're not sure if that's your sister or the crone herself," Craven warned.

Lily gasped and jumped back, grabbing me by the arm.

"Please take a seat, and I'll tell you what we know." Craven motioned to the large stone table in the center of the room, his gravelly voice at odds with his kind demeanor.

Collecting herself with great effort, Lily marched over and pulled out the thick wood chair right next to Craven, then dropped into it and folded her hands in a very Queen-like manner. "Tell me what happened to my sister, and how she came into your possession... Please." She looked over her shoulder and waited for the rest of us to join them, but all I could do was gawk at her beauty and strength. I could sense she was on the edge of losing it, but no one would know it except for me.

I slid into the seat beside her and noticed Bennett and Dylan both taking positions on the opposite side of the table. Taking a deep breath, I stared at the man who betrayed my wife and somehow managed to be back in her good graces, or so it seemed.

"I'll remind you of the same thing, darling. Just stay calm. Please. There is much to explain." Lily sent the words into my mind when she sensed my rising anger.

"I apologize for the circumstances in which we took your Queen. But after finding this one..." Craven gestured to Fern, "alone and left for dead in the woods a few months ago, we didn't know who we could trust." He rolled his shoulders and stretched his thick neck from side to side. "Or to be more precise, who amongst you were impostors after what happened to both your Kings." Lifting his chin, he pinned Bennett with a knowing stare. "We discovered this one as he attempted to free your Queen. His shadow magic was strong, but as you know, no magic besides our own is allowed within these walls."

I felt Lily tense and reach for magic, and sensed her annoyance when she couldn't access it still.

"I remember," I stated, hoping to get us back on point and moving this conversation along. "Until now, I was unaware Bennett possessed shadow magic, but I swear on the life of my father, no one else here has been compromised. We are our true selves."

Bennett stared at me from across the table, probably itching to speak for himself, but thankfully he recognized now was not the time. Our conversation would come to a head soon enough.

Craven nodded to show he accepted me at my word. "After rescuing the girl, we nursed her back to health the best we could, but she quickly became inflicted by some kind of dark spell. We had no choice but to keep her imprisoned, especially once she began to call out to Macha. It was then we assumed she had a connection to the crone or perhaps was the crone herself."

"Wait," Lily spoke up. "I don't understand. Who is Macha?"

I opened my mouth to explain, but Craven beat me to it. "Macha is the Fae goddess of death. A dark witch, and the one upon whom the crone calls."

"She's also the one your *sister* is muttering about back at our castle," I added, squeezing Lily's hand beneath the table. "We must find out if this is really Fern or not, because if it isn't… I fear our entire realm will soon fall to the mercy of the crone again."

Lily

This could not be happening! First, Bennett wasn't who he seemed, and now, Fern may have fallen victim to one of the crone's own changeling spells. *"My heart can't take much more of this,"* I privately admitted to Alder.

"I know, my love. We'll get to the bottom of everything soon. But first, I need to know how you came into possession of my great-grandmother's book of shadows?"

"So, it's true? Gwenlyth Trelayne was Gideon's grandmother?"

"Yes. What Bennett told you is true, though there's so much more to it. But we can't get into that now. When Gwenlyth ruled the entire Fae realm, the book was regarded as her fairy handbook to spells and salvation, and it may be exactly what we need to save Fern now."

My head snapped to Alder, and with his acknowledgment, I turned back to Craven and asked for the one thing we came here for in the first place. "Is there any chance you have a crop of vilenflu flower growing somewhere in Glenmiere?"

A smile pulled at the brute's thick lips. "As a matter of fact, we do."

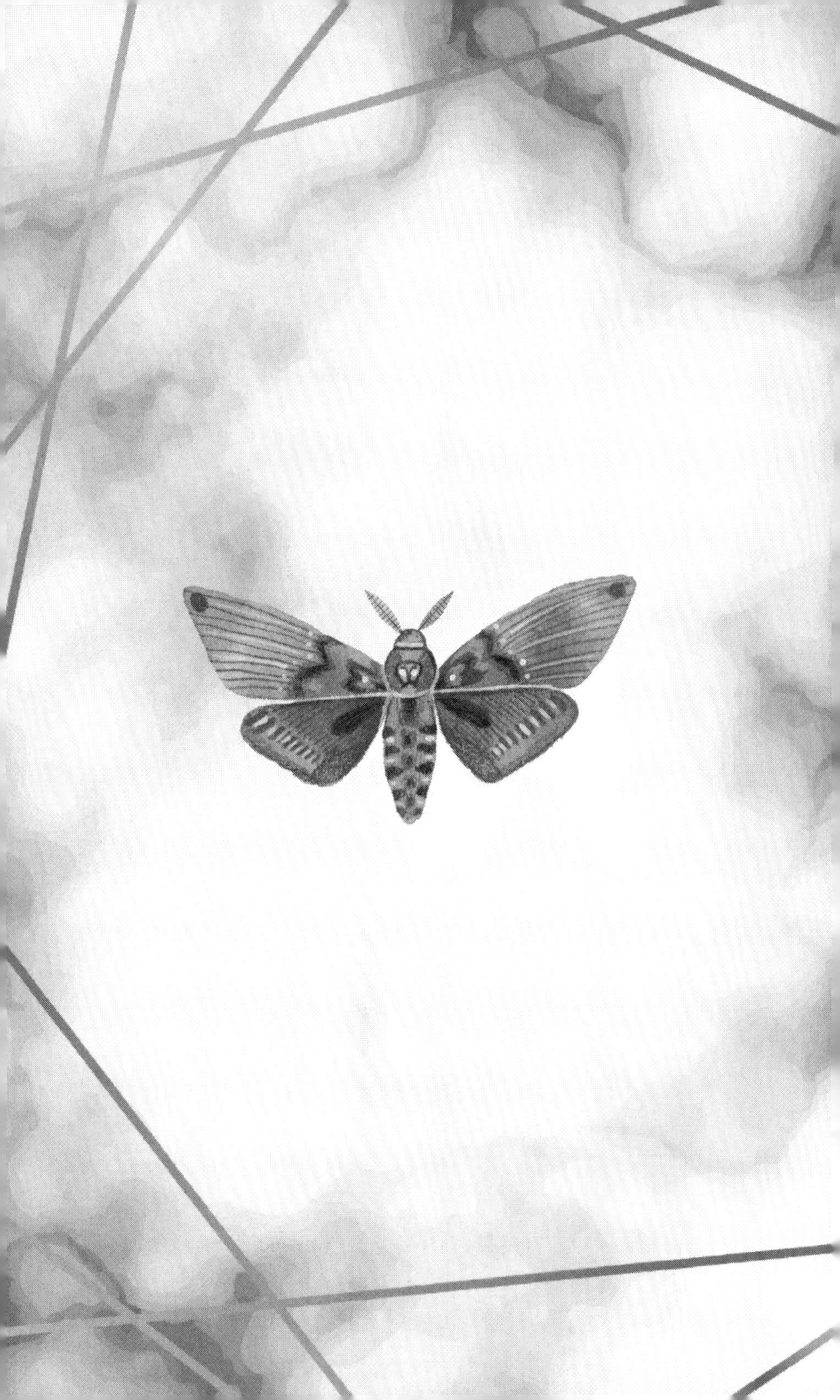

Thirty-Two

Lily

Shivering beneath a fur cloak, I stood in a field of red, sharp-petaled flowers hidden behind the Dark Elves' home. "My goodness, this is beautiful. How do they grow this well in the cold?" Spread out between a small grove of pine trees, the vilenflu flowers pushed their vibrant blooms up through the snow, blanketing the hidden grove and even climbing up the rock face to take root between the cracks and crevices of the mountain itself.

"When the Light King started burning our crops, our healers absconded with a sample of every variety they were able to save. They brought them inside and nursed them back to their original stock, the transplanted them again as soon as it was safe." Craven crossed his arms over his barrel chest. "It took years to hone the space for them here, but it was worth it to regain something so special and solely our own."

I gawked at the secret oasis, mesmerized by the play of colors between the black barked trees, the white snow, and the crimson flowers existing together in a perfect balance. "It's truly stunning." I faced the leader of the Dark Elves. "All I can do is apologize for my birth father's horrific behavior, but please know, nothing beyond his blood flows through my veins. You will never have anything to fear from our kingdom again."

"*Our* kingdom?" Craven questioned.

I looked to Alder, who simply smiled, allowing me to share the good news.

"Yes. It was Gideon's final wish that we unite the kingdoms and make them one. No more Light or Dark, only a single Fae realm governed under our banner of peace."

I lifted my chin, proud for the first time that I was Queen. The Elves may have magic all their own, but they were still Fae, and an integral part of a world I was now excited to learn everything about.

"If you would allow me to harvest some of your vilenflu crop, I can find out which version of my sister is truly her, and which, in fact, is the crone." I paused. "But it will require access to my magic, which I'm not sure is possible here." I looked up at the mountain face and turned back to the stronghold.

Craven chuckled. "Yes, the stone here is what blocks your magic, not me. But I give you my blessing to take as many vilenflu flowers as you need, and will happily accompany you back to Dartmoor to keep the woman subdued." He lifted his staff topped with a large chunk of stone in the air. "Once there, you can perform your spell."

I looked at Bennett who stood quietly against the large wood door that would lead us back inside. Smiling, I raised my eyebrows in a 'told you so' gesture. I was right about the stone. "That would be wonderful, if my King agrees." I turned to Alder and he bowed his head, giving the plan his blessing.

"Fantastic!" Craven boomed. "We'll leave in the morning. For tonight, let us return inside and feast as friends."

Bennett

Watching Lily and Alder together was painful, but I meant what I said about serving them both. I wouldn't go back on my word again.

Craven and Alder showed us to our new quarters for the night and then went to address General Niasin and his troops. After sharing his intentions, Alder ordered the troops back to the camp and was now seated across the dining table from Lily and me. I leaned down and whispered in her ear. "Perhaps I should eat in my room."

She snapped her head to the side, her green eyes piercing me as she shook her head. "What? No. Stay and eat with us."

I cringed when all eyes turned toward me.

"Yes, *Bennett*. Stay and eat, and perhaps share the tale of how you managed to earn the Queen's trust again." Alder's eyes flared in challenge.

While I would always respect the King of our realm, I wanted to smack that pompous smirk right off his face. "If you insist." I met his gaze across the table and scooted closer to Lily as I adjusted my chair. I'd hoped this was a conversation she would have with him in private, relaying my situation and how things had changed. But seeing as it was my story to tell, I lifted my chin and shared my truth.

"I was born into the witch clan of Támar. And like I told Lily, I grew up a witch and warrior, but with a special kind of magic not often seen in our clan."

"Shadow magic," Craven interjected.

"Correct. It's why I was tasked with obtaining the crone's book in exchange for my mother's life."

Alder straightened in his chair and rolled his shoulders. I hoped he felt the sincerity in my words, because I seriously doubted I could best him in battle.

"I never meant to hurt anyone. I only did what I had to do to save my mother. Turns out, the crone's blessing was no longer needed by the time I returned, so I stole the book back and gave it to Daisy when I learned Lily was missing from your camp. I shifted into a Light Guard and set out to rescue her, but when Craven caught me, I ended up a prisoner as well."

Craven tapped the head of his staff on the table. "Your shadow magic is strong, but inside these walls, no magic trumps our own."

I looked at the Dark Elf and grinned. "Any chance you could explain how I have access to your shadow magic at all, since both my mother and father were witches?"

"All shifter magic comes from the Dark Elves, and your shadow magic is a form of that." He stabbed a piece of elk meat with his fork and slid it between his teeth with great relish. "Could be one of your parents had a shifter in their lineage, and you just so happened to inherit that gene."

I took a deep breath, grateful it wasn't because of some sordid affair. "Thank you for explaining." I nodded respectfully.

Alder lifted his glass in the air. "Thank *you* for explaining, Bennett. While I have many more questions that we can address later, I'm glad to have learned the truth."

The truth?

The truth was that I'd always care for Lily, but somehow, after sharing the burden I'd carried with me for so long, I could feel my destiny shifting. Now, it felt as if fate had something else for me in mind.

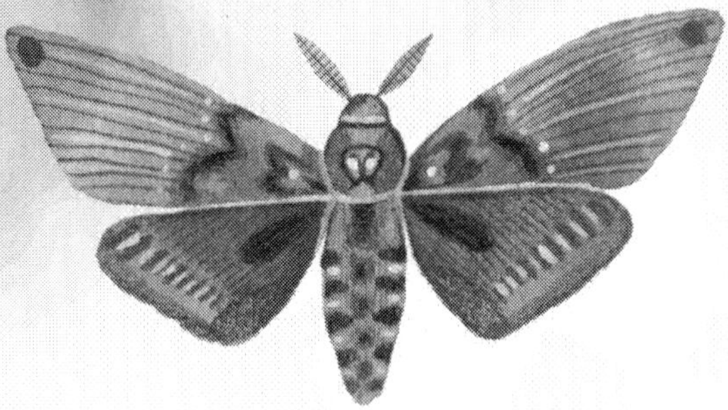

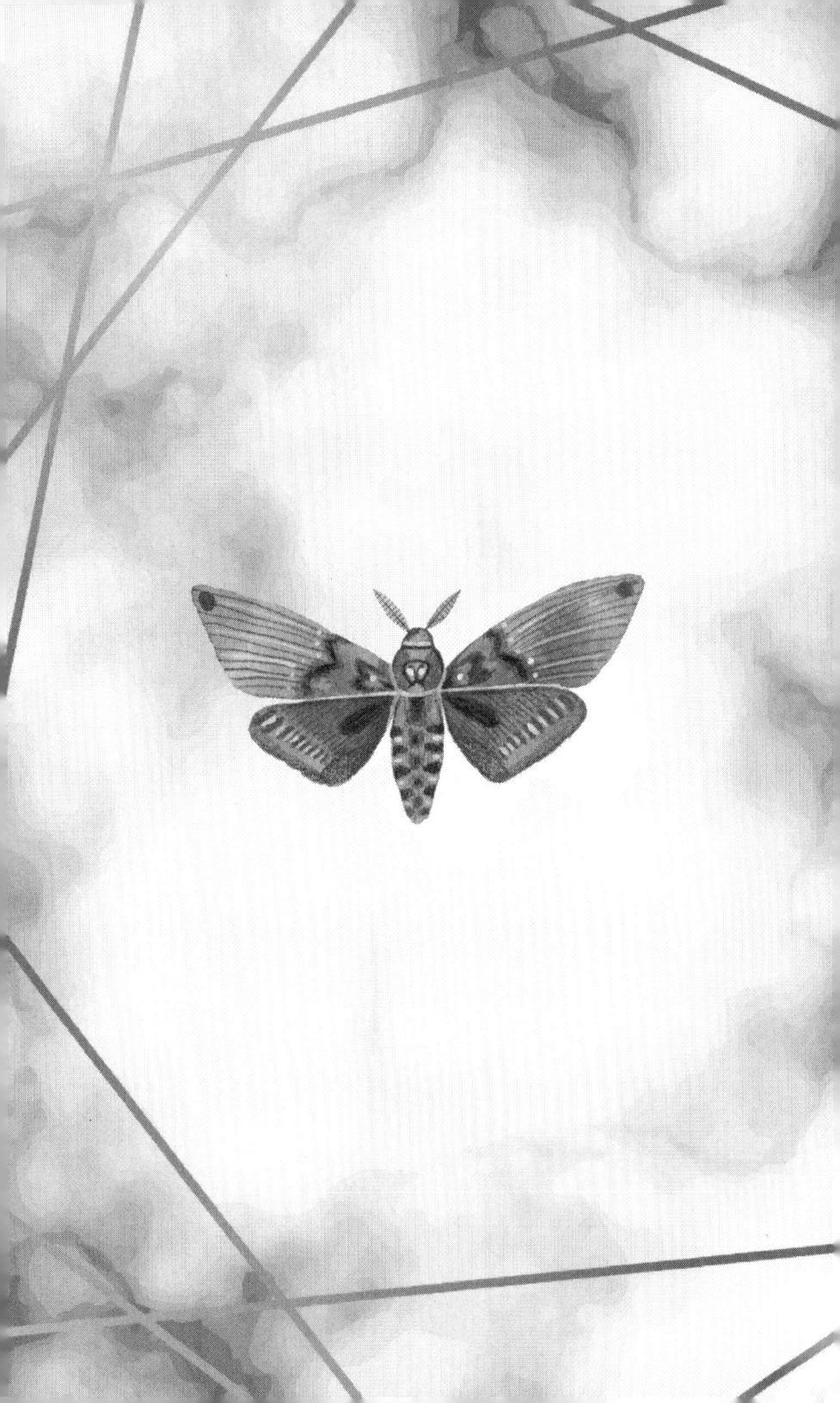

Thirty-Three

Lily

The room Alder and I were given inside the mountain was surprisingly warm. With a fireplace dug into one wall, the amber glow cast over the space reminded me of autumn back home. The yellow and orange trees were always my favorite sight to see.

"I'm sorry for the mess I caused." I lifted the sweater over my head, climbed into the large, fur-layered bed, and snuggled up next to Alder. With the stone of the mountain still suppressing my magic, I'd have to rely on his body heat instead of our shared elemental warmth.

"It's okay, my love. I'm just glad it all worked out in the end," Alder sent into my mind.

Rising onto my elbow, I asked, "How is it that our bond still works within this mountain, but our magic does not?"

"As I've told you before, as long as we're *together* the bond creates a connection between the blood of royals that nothing can break."

I lowered my head and rested it atop his broad chest. "That makes me feel even worse. I never should have taken off without you."

Reaching around me, he cradled me in his arms and pulled me closer. "Lily, you should know how hard this has been on me. It took everything in me to let you go without me in the first place, but I would never want you to feel trapped here. I vow to always grant you the space you need."

My eyes stung at the emotion I felt in his words. "Thank you. That's exactly what I needed to hear." I stared at the flickering flames across the room, losing myself to the sounds and rhythms of their sensual dance.

Despite my need for independence, Alder would always be there for me. Protecting me, loving me, and doing whatever was necessary to protect our realm.

"Are you really ready to forgive Bennett?" I asked after a moment's pause.

Alder took a deep breath, his chest rising and falling beneath me in measured waves. "Yes, I think so… Are you?"

I'd thought about all Bennett had shared—the special magic he possessed, the mission given to him by his clan, and of course, the reason behind it. "Yes. If faced with betrayal or my mother's death, I would have done the same thing."

Alder tensed. "If I'd been given the chance, I would have, too."

I snuggled closer into his side and thought about all the horrible things my father had done—Fawn's death being the worst among them. It was still hard to fathom how twisted my father had become. How he robbed Alder of his mother's love and the chance to grow up in his own kingdom. How he forced him into servitude in the Light Guard instead.

I shuttered and sent my next thought to Alder in a rush. *"I think I want to move into the Dark castle."*

"Hmm... Interesting." His hand caressed my bare back. *"I always did prefer you in the dark."*

A moan slipped past my lips as I sent an image of me naked, cloaked only in a sheer black robe while standing in the Dark realm garden under the moonlight.

I stifled a laugh when Alder pulled me on top of him. His tanned skin and gleaming antlers made for a stunning visage. With our bodies ready for each other, I realized I couldn't wait to be his wife.

"I love you," he said out loud, at the same time I sent the words into his mind.

"I love you."

Lily

Morning came too soon, but with so much at stake, Alder and I rose from the bed, shared a lingering kiss, then dressed for the day before heading back downstairs to the main hall.

Fern had been placed in the care of the healers for the night—her magic still subdued. Despite the shrunken state she was in, Craven assured me she'd been fed daily while in the dungeon. I wasn't so sure. Lifting her like she weighed no more than a feather, he cautiously positioned her in front of him on his horse. He was convinced this was the crone and not my sister, but unfortunately, we had a day's ride ahead of us before we would learn the truth.

"Do you have everything you need?" Alder asked privately.

"Yes." My jaw flexed as I gathered a fur lined coat around my shoulders. *"Let's get out of here."* I was sick of being stuck without my magic.

Mounted and leading the way, Craven motioned for us to follow as he started down the winding road that would carry us out of Glenmiere and back to Dartmoor.

With Luna still at the camp, I rode atop Samson with Alder's reassuring presence at my back. "Do you think after all this is over, we'll still be able to enjoy the Ball?" I asked over my shoulder.

His answering whisper tickled my ear. "I don't see why not. Especially if Craven accompanies us all the way back to Ferindale."

"Why would he do that?"

"Because I asked him to. Until we know which of these women is the crone, we'll need the suppressing magic from the stone in his staff to keep them both subdued."

I flinched.

"Do you not agree?" Alder gently asked through our bond.

"It's not that I don't agree, but after what I just experienced, it's hard to fathom anyone's magic being intentionally suppressed, especially one of my sisters."

Alder took a deep breath. "I understand how you feel, but it won't be for long. Besides, once this mess is over, Craven asked if he could stay for the Samhain Ball as well. He likes the idea of us uniting the Kingdoms and thinks it might be time for the Dark Elves to rejoin our realm."

"That's fantastic news!" I shifted excitedly in the saddle.

Adjusting himself behind me, Alder laughed. *"If I knew you'd react like that, I would have told you sooner."*

I shifted my hips backwards and arched my back. *"And what if I told you I wanted to marry you at the Samhain Ball?"*

Alder's gasp and his thrusting reaction told me everything I needed to know.

"Hiya!" he called out to Samson, picking up our pace and taking the lead as we raced toward Dartmoor—our soon-to-be home.

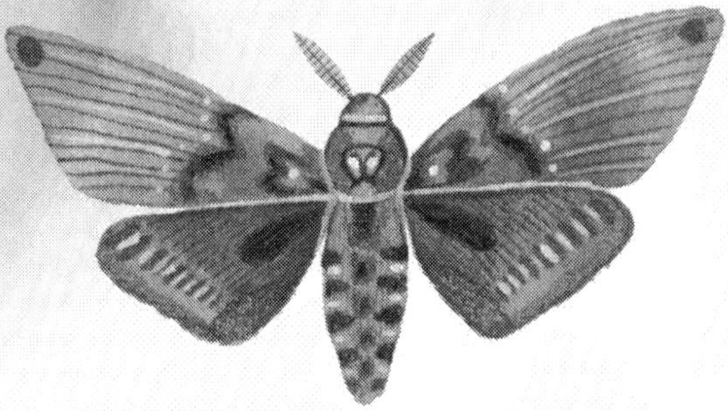

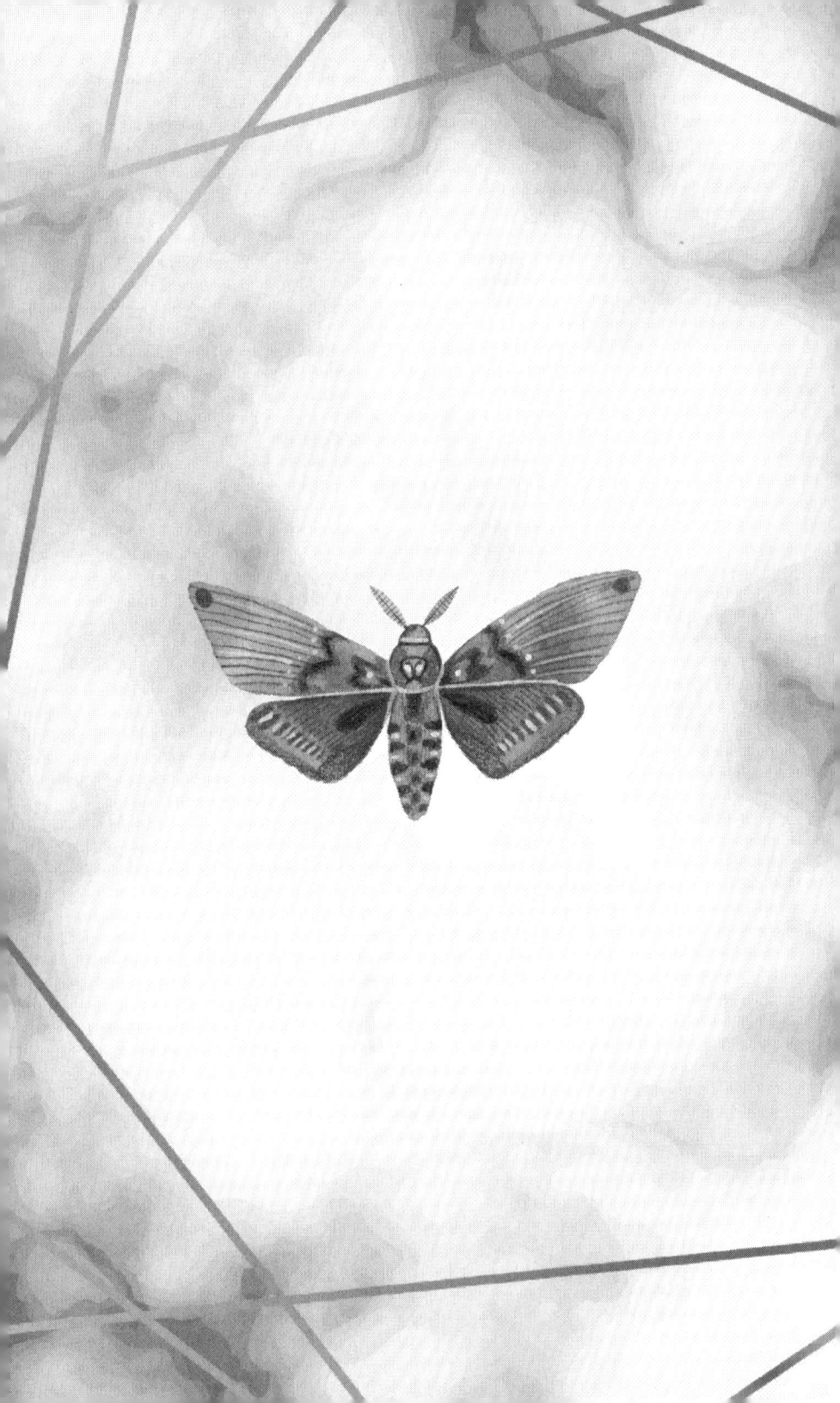

Thirty-Four

Daisy

The soft light of dusk blanketed the forest as the sound of hooves grew louder in the woods. Aster rushed to join me outside the royal tent, and we watched together as General Niasin and his troops rode back into camp.

"Lily and Alder aren't among them," Aster stated flatly.

Neither is Bennett, I thought to myself.

I still hadn't told Aster of his presence here or how he returned the crone's book after confessing who he truly was. Looking up at my big sister with her arms crossed over her chest, my heart sank. I knew it would be yet another reason why she'd never forgive me.

"Let's go talk to the General." Aster started forward but before she could take two steps, the General held up his hand to indicate that she should wait. Stalled like she'd been slapped, she returned to our tent with an angry scowl on her face.

Following her back inside, I stayed quiet and took a seat in front of the fire while she frantically started to pace. Moments later, General Niasin entered the tent and Aster froze, lifting her chin like she was expecting bad news.

The General raised both hands in surrender, palms out. "You can relax. All is well."

Aster visibly softened but remained standing, while *I* collapsed into tears. "Thank the Goddess!" I whispered.

General Niasin motioned for Aster to take a seat in the other chair at the desk. "Your sister is safe and has been reunited with Alder. They will arrive in Dartmoor tomorrow night with a small party of others to explain. We are to leave camp first thing in the morning and wait for them there, as instructed by the King."

Aster lifted her chin, then offered him a quick nod, her eyes as hard as steel. "We'll be packed and ready to go before breakfast. Thank you for letting us know, General."

As soon as he left, Aster placed both hands on the table, lowered her head to the wood, and whispered her thanks to the Goddess. It was the first real emotional display I'd seen since her last reprimand of me.

I sniffled. "I'm so happy Lily's okay."

Aster lifted her head only far enough to meet my gaze. "Yes, so am I." Her tone was as cold and sharp as the wind outside. I knew nothing would ever be the same between us again.

Crawling into bed, I closed my eyes and imagined Lily, Alder, and Bennett sleeping somewhere in the dark, wishing more than anything I could be with them instead.

Bennett

Staying in the Elves' stronghold over night, sleep came to me in restless waves. But once I sat atop Soven in the crisp morning air, I was filled with energy and a renewed sense of purpose.

Alder and Lily had both accepted my apology and agreed to keep me on as part of their Guard. It was everything I'd hoped for when I left my village behind. They also assured me my mother and the rest of our clan would be invited to the Samhain Ball where they would be welcomed into the kingdom again. I didn't know if the Elders would appreciate it, but I knew my mother would be proud of the peace I'd won for us all, book or no book.

As we rode behind the King and Queen, Dylan and I became fast friends on the trek back to Dartmoor. For the first time in my life, I felt that I may have something to look forward to besides being a spy for my clan.

I would always have feelings for Lily and think fondly of the time we spent together, but after seeing her and Alder together, and witnessing the respect they garnered as King and Queen, I no longer felt jealous or longed to keep them apart. In reality, Lily was never my lover, but had always been more of a best friend. The realization settled happily in my heart.

I gasped, startling Soven, when Daisy's sweet face popped into my head. Like a spell being woven, her kindness and understanding had formed an impression on me—one I was only now starting to see. Catching her eye in the hallway back at the castle and remembering the way she smiled at me while riding up the trail... I had noticed and appreciated her interest, of course, but I never expected to feel like this. My heart raced when I thought about how she so willing kept my secret after I revealed the truth to her in that tent. How selfless she was in our plan to get Lily back. She had no reason to trust me then, but she did.

Overwhelmed with emotion, I looked ahead to where Lily and Alder rode together and wondered if the Queen had developed yet another new power—that of a matchmaker. Or maybe this was the work of the Goddess, who had something else in mind for me and was now guiding my path. Picturing Daisy's chestnut hair and sparkling brown eyes again, I would never pressure her or expect anything back in return, but as the thought of a life together bloomed in my heart and mind, I couldn't deny I hoped she might feel the same.

Shaking off the vision and refocusing again, I knew we needed to confirm which version of her sister Fern was which before anything of the sort could be explored. But with a smile on my face, I welcomed the task and would use my magic to protect them all.

"Halt!" Alder called out, then motioned for us to gather our horses at the edge of the road.

Riding up next to us, Lily smiled at me, brightening an already good day.

"We can reach Dartmoor by tonight, but it will be a hard press from here. Water your horses and grab something to eat. We move out in ten," the King instructed.

Dylan and I entered the clearing first and confirmed it was safe for the Queen and King. Dismounting, we secured our horses and then stood watch as Lily passed out a handful of berries and nuts she'd gathered before leaving Glenmiere—with Craven's permission, of course.

I smiled as she placed the snack in my hand. "Thank you."

"You're welcome."

"Can I ask you something?"

"You just did," she teased.

Cocking a brow, I enjoyed the playful energy between us again. It felt real. Normal. And helped give me the confidence to follow this new path. "Did I see you and Daisy talking about me on the ride up?" I dropped my head, still embarrassed for asking.

Lily laughed. "Oh my goddess, yes! She's slightly obsessed with you. Well... *this* version of you."

I looked up, my eyes going wide. "Really?"

"*Really*." Lily placed a hand on my shoulder and leaned toward me, bringing us almost nose-to-nose. "I will always care for you, Bennett, but you deserve to find a love of your own. And if Daisy is it, I wholeheartedly give you my blessing. She's funny, loving, kind, and one of the smartest witches among us."

I reached up and laid my hand on top of hers. "Thank you. I can't tell you what that means to me."

"What's going on here?" Alder approached with a smile on his face.

"Oh, just some light matchmaking." Lily laughed and glided into his embrace. "Daisy has a thing for Bennett, and let's just say… there might be something there."

Alder took Lily in his arms with a lighthearted smile tinged by surprise. "All right! Then let's wrap this up and get back on the road. You know what they say… Love waits for no one!"

I should have been mortified discussing my love life with the King and Queen—my rival and my previous crush—but hearing Alder's declaration and seeing the look on Lily's face only solidified the life I wanted for myself.

With a genuine smile, I replied, "No, I suppose it doesn't."

Thirty-Five

Lily

Riding into Dartmoor felt like coming home. After feeling the rush of my magic flow back into my veins the further we traveled from Glenmiere, I shrugged out of my fur coat and rode comfortably in front of Alder the rest of the way, feeling free and powerful again. After dropping the horses off at the stables, our small group made our way inside the Dark castle, unannounced. Alder didn't want to alert the town or the staff to our presence until we'd figured out what was going on with Fern. He directed Craven to stay with whichever version of her he was carrying in a room off the main hall, giving me a chance to meet with Daisy and Aster first.

Crying and pleading for my forgiveness, Daisy raced across the dining room and fell into my open arms.

"There's nothing to forgive, sister. You did nothing wrong."

Her shaking hands held mine as she lifted them to her lips, whispering, "Aster doesn't feel the same."

I looked across the dining hall and found our other sister seated on the black onyx steps. Holding my gaze, she rose and strode across the space with a firm set to her spine. "I'm glad you're all right." Her words were clipped. "But I cannot believe the risk you took by wandering off alone."

There it was… a typical Aster reprimand. With a softer heart and wiser mind, I threw my arms around her. "I appreciate the concern, but you don't have to worry about me anymore."

When I pulled back, I saw a shine of tears in her eyes and understood. She loved us *so* much; it was the basis of all her fears. "You need to forgive Daisy. None of this was her fault."

Aster turned and searched for my sister, who was happily conversing with a certain blond-haired guard across the room. "Who is that?" Aster asked.

I took a deep breath, not ready to open that can of worms just yet. "Someone important who helped us more than you know." I glanced back at Daisy and Bennett and noticed each still wore heavy packs on their backs.

"Can you two bring those packs up to me?" I called out, then walked up the stairs to stand at the altar atop the dais at the front of the room. Gliding my hands across the carvings I knew Alder had created, I pulled the books from each pack, placed them atop the altar side-by-side, and took a deep breath.

"There is so much we need to discuss and explain, but first, I want to release *all* of our magic so we can be prepared." I met Aster's impertinent stare. She was going to freak out when she recognized the crone's book or saw Fern in the state she was in.

While I had no idea if the knowledge coming to me was from Gwenlyth's book of shadows or from the Goddess herself, I knew without a doubt, I needed to do this first. "Alder, will you please join me?"

Daisy, Bennett, and Aster stood at the bottom of the stairs, while Alder climbed up them to stand by my side. "You said this book was your great-grandmother's book of shadows—otherwise known as the fairy handbook to spells and salvation?"

"Correct."

"I believe it might just be our salvation, too." Guided by a wisdom far more ancient than my own, I opened the book to reveal the page with Gwenlyth's signature at the bottom. "Please place your hand on the page." Alder did as I asked and gasped when words started to bleed across the parchment. Flipping through the book, I smiled as the rest of the pages filled in. "It required someone in her direct bloodline to reveal the book."

"Brilliant!" He kissed the top of my head and moved away to join the others.

Letting the full power of my fae magic flow through me, I felt our royal bond strengthen as I concentrated on the book. The history of Gwenlyth's reign flooded my mind, showing me her downfall and what Alder meant about the witch clans betraying her.

What he didn't see, however, was that their uprising was orchestrated by the same crone we faced now. Younger but just as power hungry, she knew if the clans banded together and convinced the Queen to split the realm in two, she could manipulate her way to the crown by aligning herself with one of them. Light or Dark, she would pit them against each other in a secret plan of her own.

Gwenlyth agreed because she felt she was honoring the will of her people, but doing so came at a terrible cost. Relinquishing her reign of the entire realm diminished her powers. Soon after that, war ensued and there was nothing she could do to stop it.

I shared all this with Alder through our bond and meet his gaze as tears welled in his eyes.

"This ends now!" he snapped as he whirled around and marched to the door to retrieve Craven and Fern.

I looked to my sisters. "Daisy and Aster, please prepare yourselves. What you're about to see has to do with the crone. It will be a shock, but you must trust me." I barely got the words out before Alder led Craven and Fern into the room.

Cradled in the Dark Elf's arms, my sister's fragile form laid limply against his massive chest. I pulled the vilenflu flower from my pouch and ground the petals into dust before calling the rest of the ingredients to me from the stockpile in Daisy's pack.

"Lay her on the steps," I instructed Craven.

Aster moved aside, but as soon as Fern was revealed, she rushed forward. "What the hell is this? Lily, tell me what's going on this instant!"

"Easy, ma'am. While the woman before you may look like your sister, she may very well be the crone herself," Craven kindly instructed.

Aster jumped back, her eyes going wide as she fought to maintain control.

"Aster, meet Craven. He is the leader of the Dark Elves, and the man who found this woman who had been left for dead in the woods after you all were cast back home," I rushed to explain.

"I... I don't understand," Aster stammered, her eyes flickering back and forth between Fern and me.

"Remember what Mom told you? That there was something off with Fern ever since she returned home?"

Aster's head bobbed infinitesimally.

"I think that's because she never returned at all." I finished grinding the ingredients in the mortar and carried them down the steps. Sprinkling the fae potion over Fern, I asked Craven to remove his spell. "Do it." Somehow, I knew this was really her.

With the tip of his staff he released Fern's magic, and I called out the ancient spell whispered to me through the book. *"Vilenflu reveal thy twine, remove the shadows from all who are mine. Release their fae magic from within, igniting our true power again."* Fern's body thrashed against the onyx steps, and I dropped to my knees. "Fern, it's okay. Just hold on."

Gwenlyth's spell, combined with the vilenflu powder's healing traits, meant not only would Fern's mind be released, but it would also free her half-fae side. I sprinkled some over Daisy, hoping to do the same. Fern sputtered and coughed as she came to, and I could instantly see an improvement in the color of her skin. "Sister, is that you?" I asked.

Pushing her long dark hair away from her face, she forced out the words, "Yes, it's me." She looked down at her arms, turning them over in the light. "I can feel Gideon's powers flowing through my veins." Struggling to sit up, she reached for Daisy's hand.

The instant their fingers touched, Daisy's head whipped back and she let out a blood-curdling scream.

"My God, what's wrong with her?" Bennett rushed forward and cradled Daisy in his lap.

Black smoke rose from Daisy's mouth, and we all gasped as Craven raced forward with his staff in hand. "This one has been touched by Macha. Beware, as she still may be connected to the crone."

Thirty-Six

Lily

With all of us standing over them both, Daisy and Fern had nowhere to go. We watched in silence as Macha's influence left Daisy in a violent exodus, only relaxing once she and Fern were magically returned to full health.

Throwing their arms around me, they both cried their thanks into my ear. "Thank you for releasing me! I never thought I would see any of you again," Fern said.

"Lily, yes, thank you! I'm so sorry I used a spell from that book to try and reach out to you when you were gone," Daisy confessed.

"What book?" Aster snapped.

I held my sisters tight and met Bennett's gaze from across the room.

The three of us stood still as he marched up the steps and retrieved the crone's book from atop the altar. "This one." He handed it to Aster, who gasped in confusion. Using his shadow magic again, he shifted into the version of Bennett she would recognize and held his chin high. "I've told my story a lot over these past few days, but what you need to know is I've never regretted anything more than betraying Lily. I did it only because I had no other choice." Bennett walked over to Alder, where he shifted back to his warrior self and shook the King's hand. "Alder and Lily both understand and have agreed to keep me on as a member of their Guard. And as a gesture of my sincerest regret, I've returned the witch's handbook to magic and mayhem to them. I hope you, too, can begin to forgive me."

Daisy squeezed my arm, making it obvious she certainly had.

Aster stared down at the book, then looked up to meet my eyes. "And you believe this story he's told you?"

I smiled sadly, knowing whatever I said wouldn't matter. I could see it in her eyes—she felt betrayed by us all. "I do." I walked to my sister and took the crone's book from her hands.

Climbing the stairs again, I laid it back beside Gwenlyth's and pulled on the power of the one true Fae Queen. Letting my blood bond rise, it acknowledged that the same power now flowed through me. Combining the realms meant I was Queen of all, just like she had been.

Pushing a surge of elemental energy through my right hand, I allowed the flames to combine with the royal magic in my blood and smiled when the crone's book of shadows burst into flames.

Blue fire licked the edges of the dark tome, eating all the way to the spine until there was nothing left. With a cleansing breath, I blew the ash from the wood and opened the fairy handbook to spells and salvation, centering it on the altar alone.

I met Alder's proud but concerned gaze from across the room as he addressed our small crowd. "Thanks to the power of my great-grandmother, Lily's spell has revealed this version of Fern to be the true one. Which means... the crone is lying back in the Ferindale castle, fighting to maintain her guise."

"Iris!" Fern gasped, her twin's name falling in a whisper from her lips.

"Gretta is with her, and General Niasin and the rest of our troops are already headed back there now. She'll be safe until we arrive. But once the crone is exposed, we need to be ready." Alder turned his focus to Craven. "Do you still agree to accompany us to the Samhain Ball?"

The Dark Elf nodded, and I immediately knew what Alder had in mind.

"You're going to use the Ball to draw her out?" I sent through our bond.

"Exactly."

"Then how about we take a short cut back to the castle?" I lifted a brow, then gathered everyone to me at the top of the stairs to explain Alder's plan.

"If we keep Fern hidden and continue as planned, we can use the vilenflu powder to remove whatever spell the crone is using to stay masked. I believe she put herself into that coma because we were getting too close. Our spells were having an effect on her, and while she played her part well, she couldn't combat our combined magic once you all arrived in Ferindale to help."

Aster hovered at the edge of our small group, but she was listening intently to every word I said.

"Aster, you are the one who discovered the vilenflu spell. It only makes sense that you be the one to reveal the crone." I smiled and continued when I caught the look of pride in her eyes. "As soon as we're back, Alder and I will announce our wedding, which will take place at the Samhain Ball. The crone bided her time in the real world, but she came back with an evil purpose. I think it's high time we put a stop to her treachery once and for all."

Cheers of agreement erupted around the room, and Alder came to stand behind me at the altar, in front of the book. "So, what's this short cut you mentioned?" he asked.

I pointed to the open pages and laughed when he gasped.

The drawing of a silver metal ball and a hovering portal were scrawled across the page with notes of the spell and the materials needed to make more. "Have I told you how amazing you are?" he whispered into my ear.

"You can show me later, after we're husband and wife."

"That's a deal, my Queen. One I will hold you to."

I looked out at my family and friends and knew I was exactly where I was supposed to be. "Let's finish this!"

Thirty-Seven

Lily

With a new stock of portal balls in each of our bags, we bid goodbye to the horses and the stable master of Dartmoor and ventured slightly into the woods on foot.

"All you need to do is imagine where you want to go, and the portal ball will take you straight there." Alder gave us the instructions, then tossed a ball onto the ground, creating the only portal we'd need.

Filing through with Dylan and Bennett in the lead, we emerged back in the training facility where Alder rushed to inform General Niasin of our plan.

Craven and Fern were whisked away and placed in the home of one of the soldiers until they were needed.

With the use of Gwenlyth's book, we'd discovered many long-forgotten spells—one of which would allow me to communicate with the other side of my family through a bond of our own. With only a whisper into her mind, Fern would know when it was time to join us at the Ball.

Alder rejoined the group and asked, "Is everyone ready?"

We each nodded in return.

"Good luck," Daisy whispered.

"You too." I smiled at my baby sister, grateful for all we'd gone through. Having Fern back was a miracle, but getting to know the lengths to which any of my sisters would go for each other truly warmed my heart. Even Aster, who walked ahead of us as we entered the Light castle, fierce and protective as always.

The halls were lined with silver streamers and ornate decorations in preparation for the Ball. The palace glittered with a brightness that almost outshone Daisy's smile. *Almost.* The look on my sister's face as she stared at Bennett's back made it obvious there was something developing between them.

"I'm happy for you, ya know," I sent into Daisy's mind through our newly woven bond.

She gasped and returned the thought, *"I'm really happy, too. So much so, that I don't think I'm ready to go home, even after we get rid of the crone."*

"So don't! Stay here with Alder and me."

As Daisy's eyes scanned the hall and its overwhelming opulence and autumn decor, her smile widened by the second. "Oh, Lil. I think I would like that very much."

A thought dawned on me, and I sent the next thought into Alder's mind. *"If we're moving back to the Dark castle, how would you feel about giving this one to my family?"*

"My darling, as soon as this mess with the crone is over, I'll do anything you like."

"Hmm... I'll remind you of that later," I teased.

"See you at the altar, wife." Alder leaned down and kissed my hand, then we broke apart as planned.

Bennett and Dylan accompanied Aster, Daisy, and me back to my room, with Craven's staff hidden within Bennett's shadows. With Dark Elf magic flowing in his veins, he'd be able to wield the stone to suppress the crone's powers, if need be, but I hoped it wouldn't come to that.

I opened the bedroom door and rushed inside, where I hurried to the table against the far wall. "We got it! We got the vilenflu flower."

"I'm so glad you're okay," Iris muttered softly, not sounding like herself at all.

I turned around and stifled a gasp with my hand. Sitting in the chair beside the bed, Iris looked just as emaciated as the real Fern had been back in Glenmiere. Her cropped black hair was plastered to her face and neck, and it looked as though she'd lost twenty pounds.

"She's been withering away to skin and bones ever since Aster left to come find you." Gretta's words floated to my ear as she replaced the bowl of water on the side table next to Iris.

"Why didn't you notify us?" I snapped.

"How, my lady? None of you were at Dartmoor, and even if I could get word to the camp, you were no longer there."

The guilt of my rash decisions struck my chest like an arrow shot through my heart. "I'm so sorry," I apologized to Gretta. To Iris, and Aster... To *everyone*. "I never meant to put any of you at risk."

Aster walked across the room and pulled me into a hug. "Don't apologize," she said out loud, then whispered, "The crone is draining Iris's life force in an effort to stay alive. Remember, the real Fern is safe with Craven. Trapping herself in this coma was a bad idea, and the stupid witch knows it."

I pulled back and realized she was right. The crone made a panicked decision when she feared being discovered, and now, that decision could cost another of sisters' lives.

"We cannot wait!" I sent the frenzied thought to Alder. *"The crone is draining Iris's life as we speak. We must expose her now!"*

"No, my dear. Stick to the plan. It will only work if the crone feels comfortable enough to reveal herself. If what you say is true and you threaten her now, she could kill Iris before she wakes."

Dammit! He was right.

"Okay, then here goes nothing," I sent back, then quickly gathered myself again. "Daisy, combine the rest of the ingredients with the vilenflu powder so we can lift the magic of whatever's been keeping Fern's mind locked away. Maybe then, Iris will start to feel better too, since they share a twin bond." I voiced my fake idea into the room, hoping the crone would take my words and try to use them to her advantage.

Daisy handed me the mortar and pestle with the vilenflu powder inside, but like we'd discussed, I handed it off to Aster instead. "Here. You do it, Aster. You're the one who discovered the potion in the first place."

Aster approached the bedside and took the wooden vessel from my hand. Sprinkling the powder over the faux Fern's body, we made a show of holding hands and closing our eyes like Aster had suggested.

"Please work," Daisy pleaded, adding an element of sincerity to our act.

A moment passed, then *Fern* miraculously started to wake. "What... what happened?" she muttered.

We rushed to her side, fussing over her and Iris like the concerned sisters we were supposed to be.

"Oh, thank the Goddess!" Daisy cried, earning her a raised brow from Aster and me.

"How do you feel?" Aster asked, far more reserved.

"I think I'm okay." The crone scooted up in the bed until her back rested against the wall. Looking at Iris's depleted form sitting next to her in the chair, she faked a gasp. "Oh no! What's wrong with Iris?"

My fingernails bit into my palms as I squeezed both fists at my sides. Thinking about her working with my wretched father and all the damage they'd inflicted on my family and the realm as a whole, it took everything in me not to rip out her throat right then. Her ruse had been exposed, but we still had to maintain our act for Iris's benefit. "We're not sure," I replied. "Gretta said she started wasting away while tending to you."

The crone shifted to the edge of the bed, still playing the role of a concerned sister. Grabbing Iris's hand, she closed her eyes and made an elaborate show of praying to the Goddess to heal her twin. We all stood frozen, ready to jump into action, when suddenly Iris perked up and her eyes started to clear.

"Iris!" Daisy leapt forward and snatched our sister's hand out of the crone's grasp. "Oh, thank goodness. We were all so worried about you."

Iris spotted Fern on the bed and smiled up at her twin, still the only one of us painfully unaware of the truth. I debated sprinkling her with the vilenflu powder to release her fae side and create our new family bond to bring her up to speed, but from the look of her, she'd need to rest before learning the truth. "Now that we're all together again, I have an announcement to make," I started, opting for good news instead.

All eyes turned to me.

"I'm getting married tonight at the Samhain Ball, and I'm so grateful you're all here!"

Everyone's face lit up, but especially the crone's. This was the break she'd been waiting for. Little did she know, she was walking straight into our trap.

Thirty-Eight

Lily

I stared into the bathroom mirror and almost didn't not recognize myself. My skin and eyes glowed with the full power of the Fae.

I had absorbed all of Gwenlyth's knowledge and power, and as I looked down at my wedding dress and ring, I couldn't be more elated. Once we united the kingdoms as one, I would be the Queen of the entire realm. The magic running through my veins burned like a beacon from inside my soul.

Wanting to acknowledge our move to Gideon's castle and welcoming back the Dark Fae into our world, I opted for the dark green, almost black dress that hung in my closet, thanks to Gretta. It hugged my curves with a sheer beaded layer stitched over the top that fell to the floor in gently shimmering waves. I felt like a star floating through the forest under the night sky with every step I took.

My ring was a gift from Alder *and* Craven, and was one I'd cherish forever. Honed into the largest diamond I'd ever seen, the leader of the Dark Fae had honored me with his skill and presented me with a piece of his mountain and its magic-subduing properties in the most delicate form imaginable. Alder said he wanted me to be the most powerful ruler in the history of the realm, and with this gift and him by my side, I actually believed I would be.

"It's time," Aster's softened voice drifted to me from inside the bedroom.

I emerged to see a look of awe on her face and held up a hand as tears began to pool in her eyes. "Please don't. If I start crying now, I won't be able to stop," I joked.

She shook her head and quickly gathered herself, then led me out of the bedroom and down the halls that would bring me to the beautifully carved doors my soon-to-be husband had created and was now waiting beyond.

Pulling both handles, Aster opened the double doors.

Alder's caramel eyes were pinned to mine the moment I stepped into the room. Standing at the front of the Light castle ballroom in his dress leathers, he took my breath away. He was the most gorgeous man I'd ever seen, and in a few moments, he'd be all mine.

"I've been yours since the day we met." He smiled proudly as I glided to meet him in front of our gathered family and friends.

I winked. *"I didn't realize I thought that out loud."*

"Don't beat yourself up, princess. You're still getting used to the bond, but I wouldn't have it any other way. You're a loud thinker, and a lot of your more colorful thoughts tend to drift through." He shifted on his feet, clasping his hands in front of him.

"What?" I was mortified. *"My goodness. I'm so sorry."*

He sent a memory of us naked in bed, and the illicit images that were running through my mind at the time. I almost stumbled to the floor. *"Like I said… I wouldn't have it any other way."*

I laughed out loud, and the entire crowd stared at me like I was crazy. Maybe I was. I never dreamed of getting married, but here I was, Queen of the united Fae realm, in love with the sexiest shifter-King alive, and we were using our wedding as part of an elaborate scheme. *Crazy!*

"Scheme or not… this is the happiest day of my life. You look beautiful, bride." Alder sent an image into my mind and showed me the room from his point of view.

I spotted my sisters and the crone right away. *"Is everyone ready?"* I sent to each member of my family except Iris. As soon as the crone revealed herself, she would catch up soon enough.

"Yes," Aster sent back tightly, concern emanating through the bond.

"Yes, sister," Daisy replied sweetly but with a strength that was awe inspiring.

"Yes. Just call when you need us to appear," Fern confirmed from the hidden place where she and Craven waited.

Continuing down the aisle, I straightened my back. This truly was the most important day of my life.

The ballroom looked nothing like it had when Thadius hosted me here. Today, it was warm and vibrant with white, silver, and gold mixed throughout the warm autumnal tones of Samhain. It was beautiful and reminded me why I loved being a witch.

Suddenly, tears flooded my eyes. I realized even though this was a ruse to draw out the crone, my wedding day shouldn't be happening without my mom.

"*What's wrong?*" Alder sent, sensing my distress.

"*I wish my mom was here,*" I admitted honestly.

He lifted his chin with a glowing smile on his face. "*I was hoping to keep it a surprise, but your mother is here, my love. Aster demanded she be present and retrieved her earlier today. She's hiding with Fern until we call them to join us. She's going to be our ace in the hole.*"

Tears flowed in earnest down my cheeks, and I didn't even care who noticed. Aster knew I'd want Mom here, and she was the one to make it happen. "*Thank you,*" I sent, directing my gratitude straight to her.

"*You're welcome. Now focus. The crone is starting to get fidgety.*"

I continued forward and forced my eyes to remain on Alder's. We joined hands and waited for the priestess to begin, or for the crone to make her move.

We didn't have to wait long.

As soon as the ceremony started, *Fern* rose from her seat and stood defiantly in the center of the aisle. "The new King and Queen, ready to join their lives and unite our kingdoms as one... How romantic." *Fern's* smooth voice quickly faded to the scratchy rasp of the crone's as her disguise melted away.

With a startled gasp, Iris covered her mouth and almost fainted in her seat. Thanks to the pouch of vilenflu power I had Daisy sprinkle in her pocket, I was quickly able to put her mind at ease.

"Iris, don't worry, sister. We knew who she was all along. The real Fern is safe. Stay close to Aster, and this will all be over soon." I held Iris's gaze as she took in the scene and immediately moved to stand behind Aster and Daisy, who were already in position behind the crone.

Bennett stood to Daisy's left and revealed Craven's staff in his hands, while I sent a message to the real Fern. *"Now!"*

In a blinding flash of silver light, our true sister emerged with our mother by her side and Craven at her back. Bennett tossed the Dark Elf his staff as we all tightened our circle around the crone.

She looked surprised for a moment before she cracked her neck and stared me down with a snarl marring her face. "You think you've beaten me, child? Discovered my deception and gathered your friends to put an end to my meddling once and for all?"

"Damn right." I tossed my bouquet of lavender and white roses to the side, confident I'd be picking them up again soon. With my family here, plus Craven and Bennett offering their aid, I knew we wouldn't fail.

As we closed in on the crone, I saw her sly mind spinning, desperately searching for an escape.

"It's over. There's nowhere to go." My mom stepped forward and approached the crone as Craven pointed his staff at the hag's chest.

"Mom, wait!" I was grateful to see her, but concerned for her safety as the crone slithered in her direction.

Just then, the crone lunged forward and gripped my mom's arm in her gnarly hands. Pulling a knife from within the folds of her cloak, she held it against Mom's neck. "Back up, or she dies!" she screamed, spittle flying from her wretched mouth.

We all froze, stunned by the basicness of the move. We'd expected the crone to fight with magic, which Craven had already subdued. But as a witch from the old ways, I should have known she'd prefer more violent means.

Mom met my terrified gaze with her usual calming presence. "It's okay, Lil. I'll be fine. Just let us leave."

Alder stiffened beside me, sharing my gut reaction of *No fucking way*.

"Lily," Aster's steady voice resonated in my mind. *"Trust Mom, and let them go."*

I shook my head, unable to stop my rising fear.

The crone snarled, "Do it girl, or I'll bleed her right here!"

I watched helplessly as the malicious witch edged them toward the exit. Alder lifted his hand and signaled for the guards to let them pass.

Cackling as she pulled Mom toward the door, the crone pressed the knife deeper against her skin, drawing blood before disappearing from the ballroom.

"NO!" I roared as I lifted the hem of my beautiful wedding dress and raced into the hall.

The crone stood at the other end, ready to disappear into the portal through which Mom, Fern, and Craven had arrived. The memory of our last encounter here flooded my mind, and miraculously, just like before, Sybil stepped out of the portal and into the hall.

My mind spun and my heart raced with wicked glee as the leader of the Acrucian Coven plunged a silver blade straight through the witch's back.

Mom fell away and we all rushed to her side.

"Sybil, oh my Goddess, am I glad to see you!" I threw my arms around her neck while my sisters helped our mother to her feet.

"Oh, my babies." Mom pulled us into a group hug, only releasing her loving grip when Alder cleared his throat.

"You did it. With the crone's book of shadows destroyed and her magic subdued, you were finally able to kill the witch who betrayed my great-grandmother and who has plagued these lands for centuries." Alder stalked forward, grimacing down at the shriveled body of the crone as she started to decay right before our eyes.

Like the falseness of her dark magic, the shell of her vile being crumbled into dust, leaving nothing behind but a heap of blackened soot on the sparkling marble floor.

Daisy emerged from the group and twisted her hand in the air. I gasped as a blast of wind blew down the hall and scattered the crone's remains until nothing was left. Daisy grinned. "It seems when you unlocked our fae magic, I received an elemental power."

Fern stepped forward. "Me too." Cupping her hand in front of her, a small pool of water gathered out of thin air.

Iris joined us and snapped her fingers, creating a crystal in the center of her palm. "Looks like I did, too."

"Earth, air, fire, and water. Gideon's prophecy has finally come true!" Mom laughed, and we turned to see her and Aster beaming with pride.

"Prophecy?" I questioned.

"Yes. That the magical span of your births would unlock the elemental powers of your fae ancestors, once you realized your true potential. Or in this case, when Lily unlocked the magic of your fae side." She approached the four of us and gently touched each of our cheeks. "You still have so much to learn and can only do that here."

I looked at my family and felt the connection of our bond deep within my bones. "I was going to wait until after the wedding, but I'd rather tell you now. Alder and I are moving back to the Dark castle, and we want to leave this one to all of you."

Daisy giggled and smiled at Bennett from across the hall. Fern and Iris embraced each other, while Aster reached for my hand. "Let's get you two married for real."

Alder

Shifting our family and friends to the back garden, I stood under the delicate pink blooms of white-barked trees and exchanged vows with my beautiful bride. Bells rang out across the land as we sealed our love with a kiss. We walked back inside, hand-in-hand, and gathered everyone on the balcony of the Light castle one more time.

Waving to the crowd below, our union was celebrated with the boisterous cheers of fairies far and wide. I introduced my half-fae sisters and announced our plan to move to the Dark castle—or as it would now be known, the *Dartmoor* castle. There was no more Light and Dark; only one Fae realm as Gideon dreamed.

A knot formed in my throat. *"We did it, Dad."* I sent my thought to the heavens, finally proud to take my place as King.

"Let's go, my love," Lily whispered before guiding me back into the stateroom and picking up a metal ball from the small table sitting next to the white leather couch. Turning to her family, she hugged each of them in turn, then confirmed that her mom, Sybil, and Aster would stay a little longer to help the girls get settled in. Tasking Bennett and Craven to watch over them all, Lily walked back to my side and tossed the portal ball to the floor. A dazzling blast of silver light burst open in the center of the room, and my stunning bride took me by the hand.

"Let's go, my King… It's time we find our way in the dark."

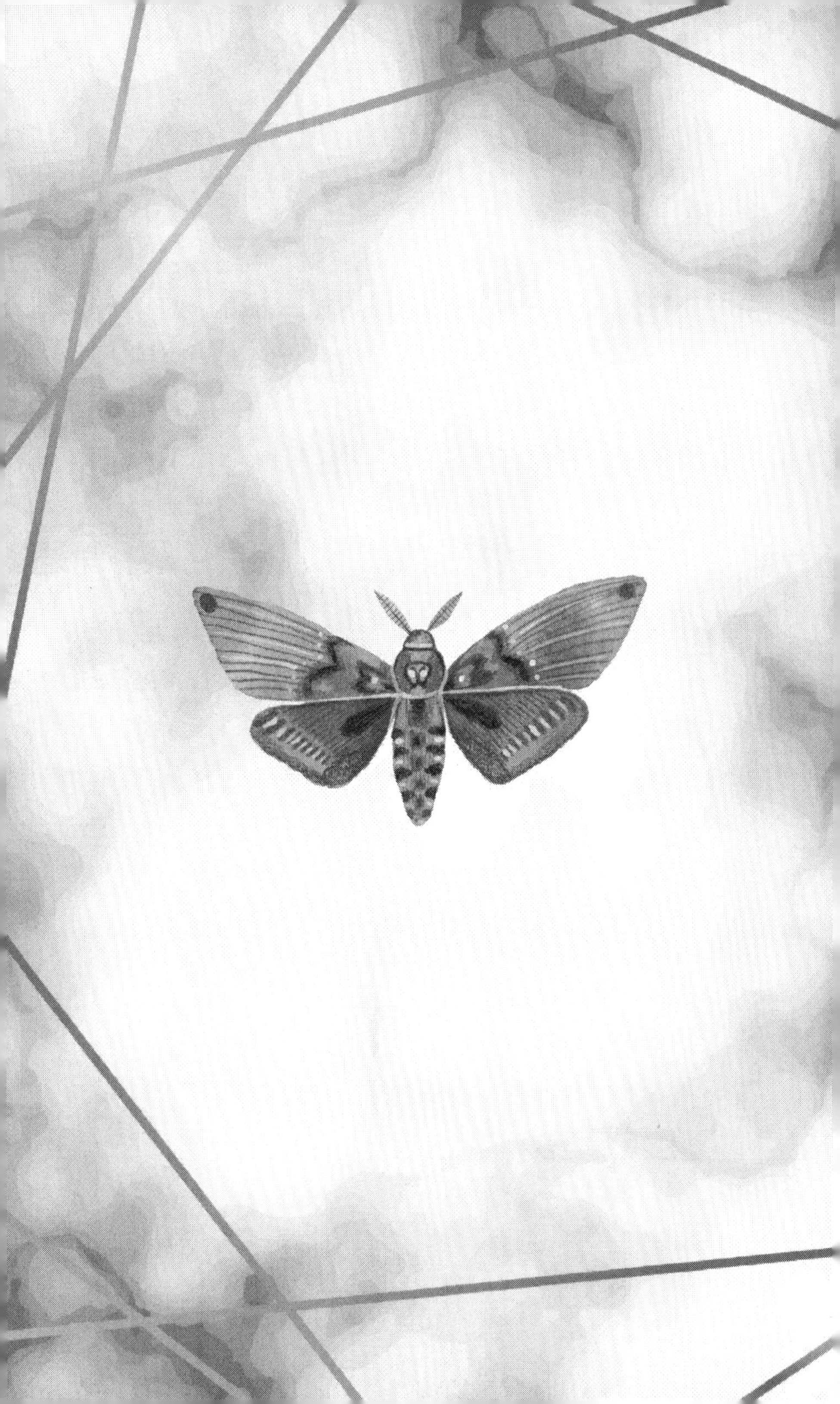

Keep reading to continue the adventure with Lily and Alder in the next novel of the Stolen Spells series.

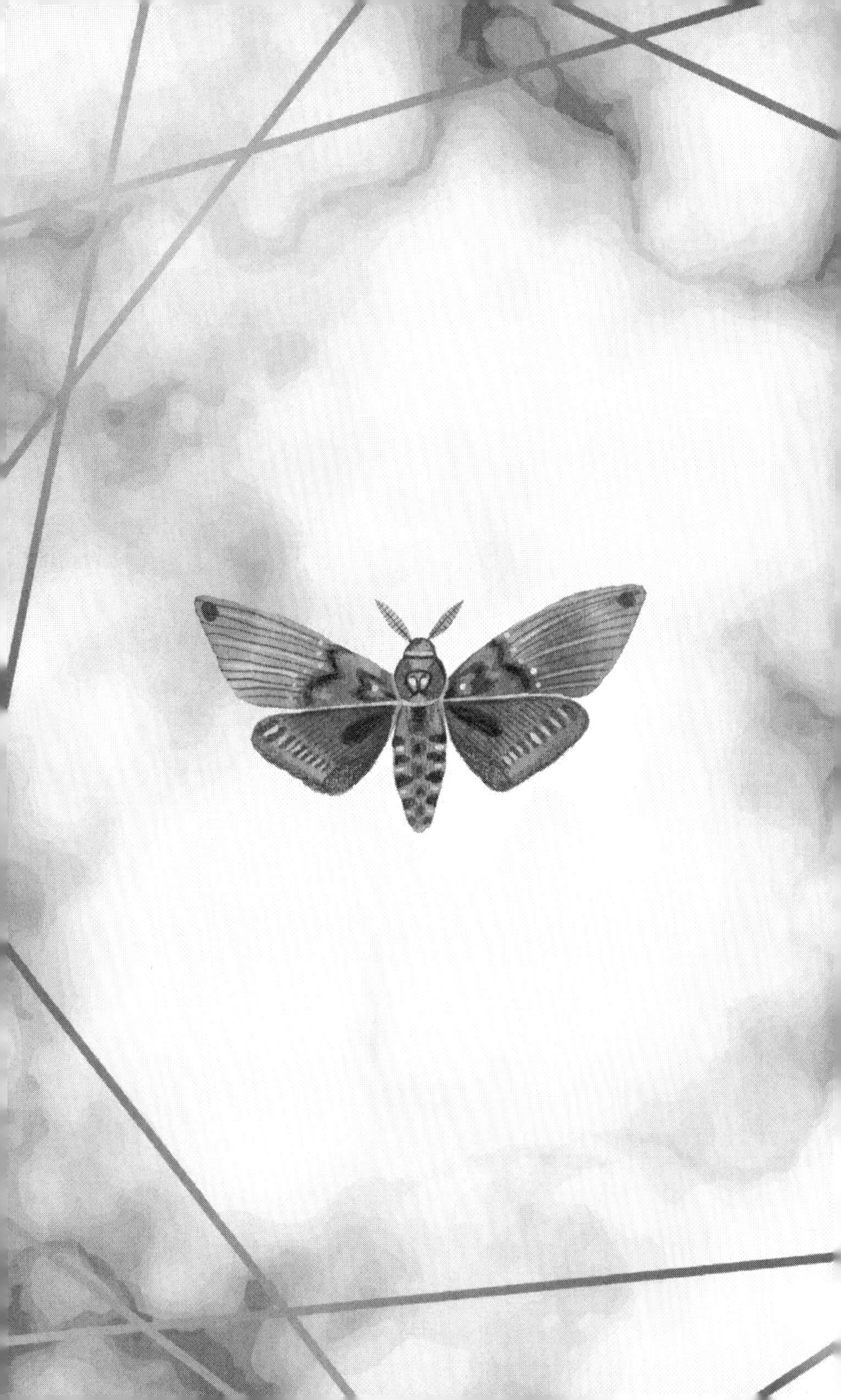

THE QUEEN'S HANDBOOK TO ESSENSE AND EMBERS

(Book 3 in the Stolen Spells series)

by

Tish Thawer

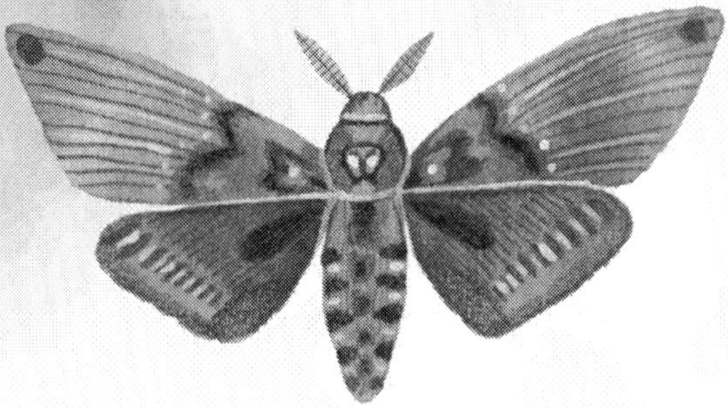

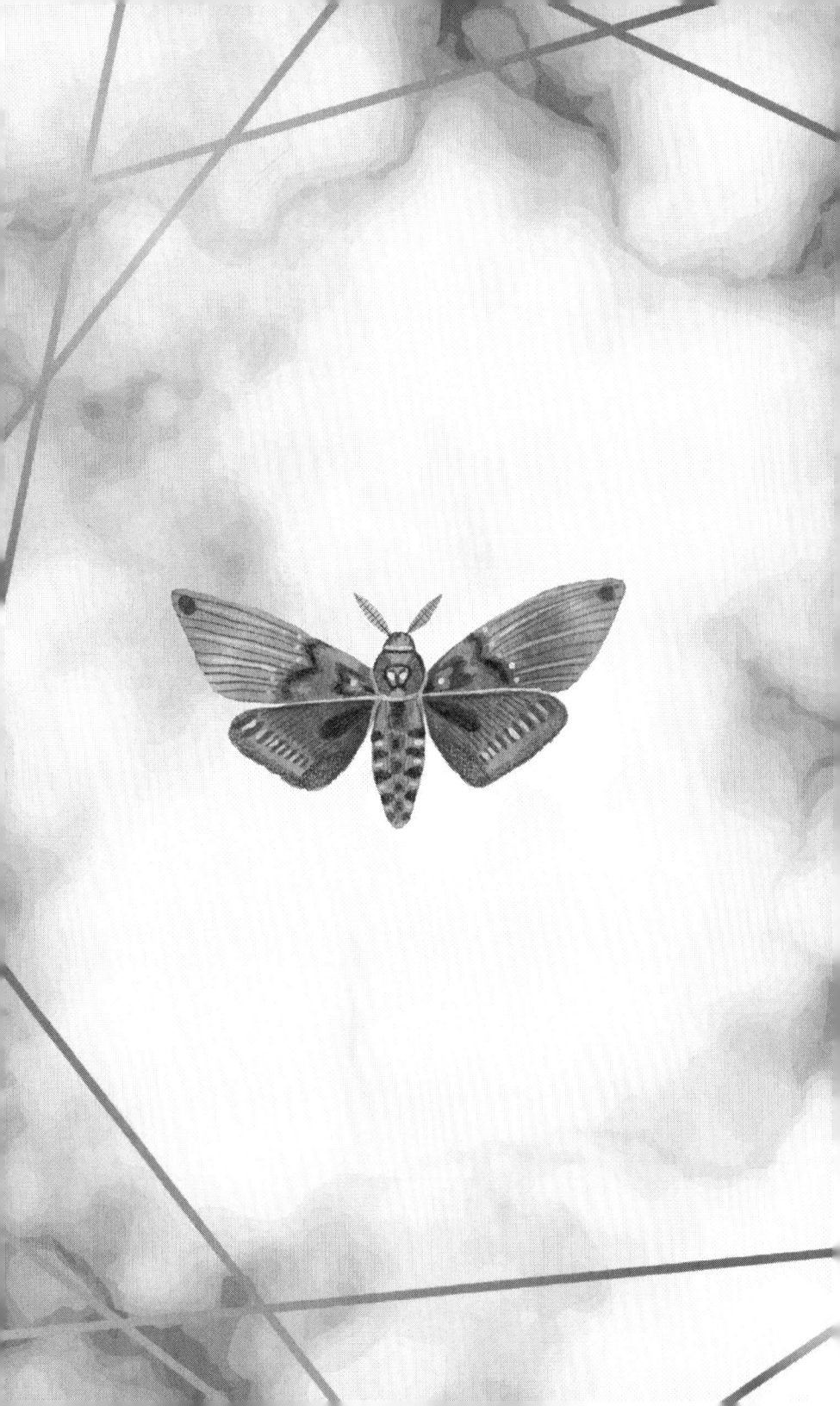

One

Ferindale - Present day

Lily

Flames licked the tops of the trees, singing their pink petals black as I tried again to control my element.

"Goodness gracious, Lily! You're going to burn down the whole damn castle!" Aster's panicked response was one of many I'd heard over the last hour and a half.

"I'm sorry. I really am trying my best." Gaining control over the elemental power I shared with Alder was paramount, but despite my efforts, I continued to struggle, and it seemed Daisy was, too.

Whipping the flames into a frenzy, Daisy's wind blew uncontrolled through the trees, snapping branches and sending charred limbs down upon our heads.

"Look out!" she screamed.

Thankfully, Fern and Iris were there.

With a twist of their wrists, the twins worked in unison to douse the flames and spare us from the burning foliage thanks to Fern's water and Iris's earth affinity.

"Wow. You two are getting good," I beamed.

Fully recovered after the crone was destroyed, Iris and Fern's twin bond had returned, and with their fae powers released, they both seemed to be thriving here.

My heart thumped in my chest.

Having my family with me in our united realm was a dream come true, one I never thought possible. After moving back to Dartmoor with Alder, we relinquished this castle to my sisters who stayed in Ferindale and made it their home.

Mom, Sybil, and Aster had stayed through the winter, helping them to settle in, but when spring broke, our mother and the leader of the Acrucian Coven returned to our original world to attend to their duties there.

We all missed Mom every day, but with the portal in our old basement now secure, she could return anytime she wanted, but her visits had been happening less and less. I think she still struggled to be here with Gideon gone, but it was a subject we hadn't talked about yet.

The years the Dark King spend in our world, and the bargain he made to keep me safe, hinged on his and my mother's relationship, but I knew there was more to it than that.

I think she truly loved Gideon, and with time, I hoped her heart would heal.

Acknowledgments

To my husband: For all the sacrifices you make… thank you never feels like enough. I love you!

To my children: Even as adults, you remain the light of my life. I love you with all my heart!

To Molly Phipps: Your inspired work helped bring this series to life. Thank you for always being there, and for being amazing!

To my editor, Stacy Sanford: Thank you for putting up with me. LOL. Your professionalism and dedication always shine through.

To Cortney and Sharon: Thank you for reading *TFHSS* before publication and providing your feedback and editorial reviews. I'm so grateful to have such amazing friends in this industry. You are all the best!

And finally, to my readers: I hope you find this expanded world one you never want to leave! As always, thank you for your support and your willingness to take a chance on me! I get to do what I do because of you.

About the Author

#1 Bestseller in Historical Fiction
Top 100 Bestselling in Paid Kindle Store
Best Cover Award Winner
Readers' Choice Award Winner
Best Sci-fi Fantasy Novel Winner (x2)

Author Tish Thawer writes young adult fantasy and paranormal fiction for all ages. From her first paranormal cartoon, *Isis*, to the *Twilight* phenomenon, myth, magic, and superpowers have always held a special place in her heart. Best known for her *Witches of BlackBrook* series, Tish's detailed world-building and magic-laced stories have been compared to Nora Roberts, Sam Cheever, and Charlaine Harris. Tish's books have been featured in *British Glamour* and *Elle* magazines. She has worked as a computer consultant, photographer, and graphic designer and has bylines as a columnist for Gliterary Girl media, *RT* magazine, and *Literary Lunes* magazine. Tish currently resides in Missouri with her husband and two of her three wonderful children, and operates Amber Leaf Designs, an online custom retail store, and Amber Leaf Farms, a lavender and flower farm they opened in 2022.

You can find out more about Tish and all her titles by visiting: www.tishthawer.com

Connect with Tish Thawer Online:
Instagram: @tishthawer
Facebook: www.facebook.com/AuthorTishThawer
Twitter: @tishthawer
Pinterest: www.pinterest.com/tishthawer/

If you'd like an email when each new book releases, please sign up for my mailing list. Emails only go out about once per month and your information is closely guarded.
http://www.tishthawer.com/subscribe.html

Also, to get an email for new releases, book updates, and special sales, follow me on BookBub and Goodreads at the links below:
www.bookbub.com/authors/tish-thawer
https://www.goodreads.com/tishthawer

Again, thank you for reading. If you'd like to stay connected and hang out for more magical adventures, you can join my private reader group here:
https://www.facebook.com/groups/TishThawersBookCoven

Blessed be,
~ Tish

Also by Tish Thawer

Stolen Spells
The Witch Handbook to Magic and Mayhem – Book 1
The Fairy Handbook to Spells and Salvation – Book 2

The Witches of BlackBrook
The Witches of BlackBrook - Book 1
The Daughters of Maine - Book 2
Lost in Time – (A Legends of Havenwood Falls novella, and a Witches of BlackBrook side-story – Book 2.5)
The Sisters of Salem – Book 3

The Women of Purgatory
Raven's Breath - Book 1
Dark Abigail - Book 2
Holli's Hellfire – Book 3
The Women of Purgatory: The Complete Series bundle

The TS901 Chronicles
TS901: Anomaly – Book 1
TS901: Dominion – Book 2
TS901: Evolution – Book 3
The TS901 Chronicles – Complete Set

Havenwood Falls Shared World
Lost in Time – (A Legends of Havenwood Falls novella, and a Witches of BlackBrook side-story)
Sun & Moon Academy – Book 1: Fall Semester
Sun & Moon Academy – Book 2: Spring Semester
Havenwood Falls Sunset Anthology

The Rose Trilogy
Scent of a White Rose - Book 1
Roses & Thorns - Book 1.5
Blood of a Red Rose - Book 2
Death of a Black Rose - Book 3
The Rose Trilogy – 10th Anniversary Edition

Also by Tish Thawer Cont'd

The Ovialell Series
Aradia Awakens - Book 1
Dark Seeds - Novella (Book 1.5)
Prophecy's Child - Companion
The Rise of Rae - Companion
Shay and the Box of Nye - Companion
Behind the Veil - Omnibus

Stand-Alones
Weaver
Guiding Gaia
Handler
Moon Kissed
Dance With Me
Magical Journal & Planner (non-fiction)
Found & Foraged (non-fiction)

Anthologies
The Monster Ball: Year 3
Fairy Tale Confessions
Losing It: A Collection of V-Cards
Christmas Lites II

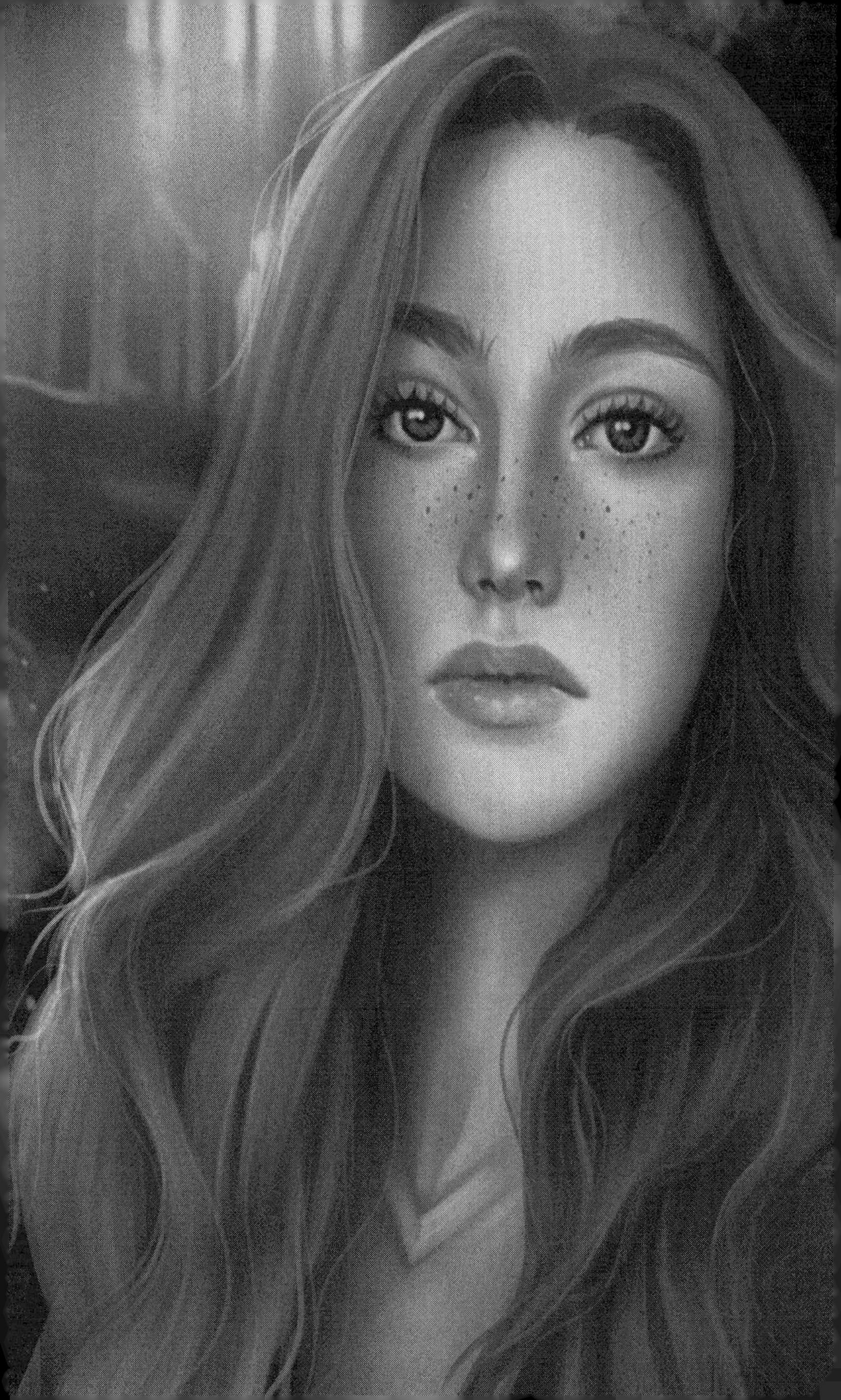

For another adventure

please enjoy this excerpt from *Guiding Gaia*

She awoke to save us, but it may already be too late.

The world is in chaos.
Stars are falling from the sky. Floods, hurricanes, and fires rage across the land. And the only being strong enough to stop it is stuck in teenage form ... again.

***

Reborn, Gaia has come to Earth to battle through the strife and discover if the world is worth saving.

***

Tasked with guiding her, it falls to me to help her weather the storms, and hopefully, find a place where she can be at peace. But time is running out, and her patience is waning. Now, I fear if the human race doesn't destroy the world ... she will.

The sky is her love, the trees pulse with her blood.

The air is her breath, and the sea her tears.

Only through Gaia's treasures can we be saved.

~Tish Thawer

Prologue

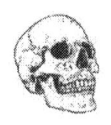

*S*creams pierced the air, but I kept swinging my sword. Souls of the damned swarmed the field, released from their fiery home in an attempt to keep me from achieving my goal. But after years of training, I was ready. Dropping to the ground, I spun in a circle with a wide sweep of my weapon, slicing through five at a time. Scorched earth crackled beneath my feet, dry and brittle as I slayed the next one.

"No matter how strong you become, you will not succeed," a deep voice reverberated from behind me, clearing the field with his godly presence alone.

"Are you here to stop me?" My long, dark hair blew across my face, hopefully hiding the fear elicited by his words.

"No. But I am here to punish you." Lightning coursed between his fingers.

"Punish me?" I stood with my sword propped against the curve of my hip, its hilt heavy in my hand as the tip sank deeper into the ground.

"Look around, my darling. In your desperate attempt to save your daughter, you've neglected your duties, and the world has fallen into chaos because of you."

Taken aback, I raised my eyes to the horizon. Fires raged in the distance, their sparking fingers reaching into the churning sky. Violent clouds rolled, filled with lightning and ill intent. It was as if the sky and the earth were reaching for *one another, determined to explode together, destroying everything in one final embrace.*

"It will be up to you to guide the only one who can fix this. For that is your punishment, and the only way to secure a deal to save the one you love."

Chapter One

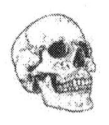

~ *Varanasi, India* ~

Rain pounded against the hotel windows, jolting me from the nightmare of my reoccurring memory, the force almost cracking the stained-glass as another monsoon raged outside. "Gaia, please. You need to calm down," I pleaded with the young goddess now under my care.

"I know, but it hurts."

"What hurts, honey?" I ran a hand down her auburn hair, offering comfort as if she was my own daughter—a habit we'd slid into over these last four months since our return to Earth.

"My blood. It feels like it's flowing the wrong way in my veins. It pushes and pulls." Gaia sank onto the gold duvet of the four-poster bed, dragging the heel of her hand back and forth along her forearm. "I need to get out of here." Her eyes snapped to mine as another wave of the unnatural storm thundered against the windows, their arches highlighted in sharp contrast by a kaleidoscope of colors reflected against the wall.

I didn't question her request. If Gaia needed to go, we'd go. Unfortunately, until we reached our destination here, we couldn't leave this portion of the world just yet. "I'll arrange transport to the final town on the map, but it is the middle of the night, so I'm not sure how easy that will be. It's unlikely the concierge will drive us himself." I set our bags near the door, then pulled my long, dark hair into a ponytail at the nape of my neck, knowing the storm wouldn't be the only thing I'd have to face outside.

"Fine. I don't care, just get me out of here, Demi."

The thin glass of the window shattered as the storm reached its peak, soaking the cream, patterned carpet and the antique wood furniture filling the room. Three hanging, multicolored lanterns crashed to the floor, extinguishing the candles the moment they fell. At this point, I couldn't tell if Gaia was upset because of the storm or if the storm was upset because of her.

Desperate to fulfill the oath of protecting my charge, I raced into the hall, the heels of my boots digging into the carpet as I dodged silver trays of discarded dishes lining the floor. Sharp scents of curry and chai permeated the air as I pushed into the stairwell and jumped over the edge. I dropped three floors in a single leap, straightening just in time to see a group of men heading straight for me.

The Crags were here.

Two months after Gaia's rebirth and our return to Earth, they cornered me in the dark alley between the hotel and the restaurant Gaia had started to favor. Pizzeria Vaatika Café sat minutes from the Ganges, but was now underwater, as the river had flooded and overflowed its banks just three days ago. They offered some of the best pizza and banana honey pancakes I'd ever tasted, but on the night of the attack, our takeout ended up on the ground while I battled the *men* sent to stop us. Seven continents, seven treasures of Gaia, all placed in sacred spots around the world at the time of creation—it was our mission to retrieve them, and the only way to save Earth from destruction ... or from Gaia herself.

Smashing through the hotel side-door, three Crags rushed inside. While they resembled human men in their current form, their lumbering movements and lanky limbs told another story. I reached into the folds of my black leather trench coat and unsheathed my sword from its magically hidden pocket. Metal clanged while they tried to best me, my muscles tensing as two more poured through the battered opening—all determined to reach the goddess three stories above our heads.

"Not gonna happen, boys." I rushed forward into the onslaught, matching their strikes, blow for blow. Blood rained down, coating the white tile floor in the darkened stairwell as the Crags scrambled to escape my wrath. After slicing through the stomach of the nearest man, I turned to see the final one slip past me, his red eyes glowing in triumph as he raced up the stairs.

"She's mine now, bitch," he snarled.

I crouched down, pushed off the ground, and flew into the air, snagging the handrail above me. Before he could reach the second floor, I flipped into his path. One swipe through his neck, and Gaia was safe again ... for now.

The wind howled through the broken glass below, reminding me of the task at hand—transportation out of here. I dropped back to the main level, my boots hitting the floor with a thud. Stepping over what remained of the Crags, I was happy to see their bodies disintegrated already. Minding the protruding glass of the shattered door, I crept out into the storm and smiled. The bad guys drove a nice car.

Rushing back inside, I toed through the Crags' remains until I found a set of keys lying in the dust. *Score*. With all the elements of our escape in place, I raced back upstairs, concealing my sword again before reentering the room.

"Let's go," I shouted, grabbing our bags from the floor.

Gaia looked up, her green eyes pinched in pain. "What happened? What took you so long?"

"Nothing happened. It just took a minute to arrange our rental." I looked to the floor, drawing attention to the drips of water falling from my drenched hair. "And as you may have noticed, it's a little wet outside," I teased—my usual attempt to hide anything was wrong.

"I'm aware." Lightning streaked across the sky, backlighting the eighteen-year-old goddess as she stood silhouetted against the maelstrom outside. Her auburn hair was wind-whipped and plastered to her neck and face, and though newly reborn, her divinity was something she could never hide ... at least not from me.

"How far is it to the temple?" she asked.

"Five hours, but hopefully, you can get some sleep along the way. You'll need your energy for when we arrive."

Gaia pulled her jean jacket over her soaked cotton tee and followed me from the room. She was oblivious of the Crags and their intent to kill her, and it was my job—and part of my punishment—to keep it that way. To protect her from everything ... even knowing they exist.

After losing my own daughter, and the training I forced myself through to try to get her back, this was a task I would not fail again.

Chapter Two

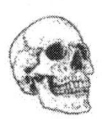

Hues of pink and orange sliced across the horizon, the colors bleeding into the early morning sky. We would reach the Mahabodhi Temple in just over an hour. Located in the Bodh Gaya area of Bihar, India, it was a mecca for tourists, welcoming visitors from all over the world for well over two-thousand years. However, for our purpose, we'd be forced to sneak in before anyone here had a chance to wake.

"Hey, where are we?" Gaia looked out the passenger side window of the Crags' black Jaguar, her voice groggy with sleep but much more even than it had been during the storm.

"Just outside of Gaya City. We're almost there. Are you ready?"

"Yes, I think so. I feel much better. Thank you for getting me out of there, D."

"Of course. It's my honor and duty."

"Come on, Demi. Stop with that shit already. I get that you were sent here with me—bound to protect me or whatever—but we're more than that, right? I wouldn't want to be on this quest with anyone else." The young goddess grinned, a sweet smile lighting up her face.

"Yes, Gaia, we're more than that." My heart clenched in my chest.

Our initial four months were hard. The dynamics of bringing back a goddess beyond her own will required a certain amount of *cosmic* interference—hence her being reborn a teenager instead of simply awakened as the true goddess she was. With myself an eternal thirty-five, I'd been able to witness the world throughout the centuries. However, the moment she awoke, we were deposited on Earth together, and found Gaia's powers and memories to be limited, forcing her to learn all she could about the modern world and its customs today. Luckily, money wasn't an issue, as I'd been divinely gifted a limitless amount in the form of a little, black charge card I'd been putting to good use. But no amount of computers, books, or even the iPod I bought her could negate the frustration of being cooped up in a hotel for four months while learning to ease her way back into a world she, herself, had created. Hence the random storms due to her emotional outbursts.

How could the gods put something like this on a teenager? I rubbed a hand over my face. "Honey, I know things haven't been easy, but I'm truly honored to serve as your guardian, and it's not something I take lightly."

"Ugh ... you're always so uptight." Laughing, she turned back to the dark-tinted window, her red hair shining in the soft morning light. "It's so beautiful here."

I took a quiet breath, swallowing my sigh. Watching her process this world anew was often a heart-breaking task. She was the ancestral mother of all life, consort to Uranus—the creator of the heavens and the sky, and mother to the Titans themselves. She created all we see and know, and was now tasked to evaluate the chaos that enveloped that same world, deciding if it was worth saving or not. So far, I couldn't tell which way she was leaning. It would take us completing our mission before she regained her full powers and all of her original memories—both of which she'd need to make her final decision. So, in times like these, when she still noticed the beauty around her ... I took note.

"With this being our first stop, why don't you tell me all you've learned about the temple," I prompted. The world had changed so much since Gaia buried her treasures; recon and research had become a significant part of our mission.

"The temple itself is a straight-sided pyramid with a round stupa on top." Gaia broke into her Wikipedia, internet voice. "The main shikhara tower is over one hundred and eighty feet high, with smaller ones surrounding its base. The construction is typical Hindu architecture, originally made from bricks covered in stucco. The towers rise into the sky like mountain peaks, which is the literal translation of the Sanskrit word shikhara, that's used to describe the style."

I laughed. "Good. Now tell me about the interior and the history of the site."

"Siddhartha Gautama was a philosopher, medicant, meditator, a spiritual and religious leader in the 5th to 4th century BCE, and is revered as the founder of the world religion of Buddhism. As a young prince, he saw the world's suffering and wanted to end it, and found himself wandering the forested banks of the Phalgu River. That's where he sat in meditation under the Bodhi tree for three days and three nights, and achieved enlightenment and the title of the Buddha after finding the answers he was searching for. After his awakening, he spent seven weeks at different spots in the vicinity, which are now all marked in specific ways." Gaia paused for a moment, counting on her fingers.

"The spot where he achieved enlightenment and spent the first week under the Bodhi tree is where the temple was built, with the sacred tree still inside." She cast an ornery look in my direction. "And we both know why he was drawn to that spot, right?" She lifted her hands and pointed both thumbs at her chest.

"Yes, Gaia, I'm fully aware your treasures are what made all of these sites special to begin with." I chuckled. "Now please, continue," I urged her on.

"Fine." She faked a huff and turned back to the window. "During the second week, it's told that the Buddha remained standing, uninterrupted and unblinking, staring at the Bodhi tree from a spot on a hill to the northeast. That spot is now marked by the Animesholcha stupa—the 'unblinking Buddha shrine'." She looked over her shoulder at me. "My favorite thing is how lotus flowers sprung up along the path he walked between the two locations. It's now called Ratnachakrama, or the jewel walk."

I glanced over, noticing a spark in her eyes.

"I hope we get to see that part." She turned back to the window, the longing on her face reflected in the glass.

"Me too. It does sound lovely."

"During the third week, though, things got hinky."

"How so?"

"The Buddha saw through his third eye that the devas in heaven weren't sure if he'd attained enlightenment or not. So, to prove himself, he created a golden bridge in the air and walked up and down it for the rest of the week."

I burst out laughing. "Wow, I guess that showed them."

"Absolutely. He then spent the fourth week near Ratnagar Chitya to the northeast, sitting inside of a beautiful, jeweled chamber he created, where he meditated on what came to be known as his 'Detailed Teachings'. It's said his mind and body were so purified that six rays of light burst from within him. Yellow for holiness, white for purity, blue for confidence, red for wisdom, and orange for desirelessness, with the combination of them representing the sixth and the whole of his noble qualities."

"That's incredible."

"I know, right? This has been one of my favorite sites to research," she continued. "On the fifth week, he answered questions of the Brahmins under the Ajapala Nigodh tree. That's the spot where the Buddha stated that people were not born as Brahmins, but their work defines them as one. There's a pillar there which marks the spot where he sat. During the sixth week, Buddha meditated by the lotus pond, then rested under the Rajyatna tree for the seventh, which is outside and behind the temple. Some say it's even more beautiful than the Bodhi tree itself."

Gaia fell quiet as we entered the complex, her focus solely on the massive temple looming straight ahead. Its imposing figure dwarfed any description ever written. Even pictures couldn't do it justice. There was no way to adequately describe its beauty or notate the spiritual energy radiating from its sheer presence without standing in front of it yourself.

I pulled the car to a stop in the deep shadow of a giant banyan tree, cut the engine, and slid out of the seat. With my senses on high alert, I did a quick sweep to make sure we were alone, then rapped on the window for Gaia to exit the vehicle.

"Do you know what to do?"

"I think so. I can feel it ... here." She placed her hand over her heart and shuffled toward the entrance as if being pulled inside by an invisible cord.

I followed closely behind, scanning our surroundings with every step. Other small structures, beautiful in their own right, lined the main thoroughfare. Detailed carvings slinked up and around the curved pillars and square columns like snakes carrying secret messages to the gods upon their etched backs.

Nearing the main temple's large door, Gaia stopped and looked up, taking in its full expanse. The carved wooden entrance was over ten feet tall and held caricatures and symbols—none of which I could decipher, but Gaia could.

"The world has changed so much," she whispered, turning back to me with tears in her eyes.

"It has, but isn't that why we're here?" I gave her an encouraging nod, then turned around and prepared myself to guard the temple while she ventured inside. I had no doubt more Crags were bound to rear their ugly heads. "I'll be here, making sure you remain alone, but if you need me, simply call out."

Gaia took a deep breath, then opened the door and disappeared inside. I caught a glimpse of the large Golden Buddha at the front of the sacred space right before the door clicked shut between us.

The sound of bells rang out in the distance, and I looked over the wall to the nearest hill sloping away from the complex. A group of monks in orange robes all knelt upon individual prayer rugs, their vibrant colors lighting up against the green grass under the early morning sun. I felt my body relax as their monotone chants reached my ears. Closing my eyes, I let their ritual wash over me, stunned into a reverent state as I thought about where I was.

Assigned to protect the goddess here on Earth, I still couldn't believe I was actually here … a witness to it all. The scent of fragrant blooms of jasmine and parijat reached my nose, once again awaking in me a deep-seated guilt. However, as their chants died away, a thick silence descended, heavy and unnatural.

The Crags had arrived.

Pulling my focus back to the complex, I knew they couldn't enter the sacred space. Protected by her treasures, the sanctuaries were impenetrable to the Crags. Yet, as soon as she stepped outside, they'd seek to claim her prize and wouldn't hesitate to destroy her in the process.

Sliding my sword from its hiding place, I crouched low and prepared for their attack, but nothing happened. Darkness wavered in the shadows of the trees, yet no one made a move. Then again, it wasn't me they were after.

Easing behind the nearest column, I squinted to locate the heart of the threat and spotted them in the trees. Six Crags hovered above our car—perched in the branches like jaguars themselves.

After re-sheathing my sword, I unhooked the custom bow from my back and aimed triple arrows in their direction instead. Singing through the air, my arrows hit their targets—disintegrating the first three Crags into dust. The other three dropped from the tree in a panic and began their retreat, only making it a few steps before another volley pierced each of their hearts.

Scanning the area again, I found no further threats and quickly stowed my bow. I moved back into position to await Gaia's return, and moments later, the heavy door creaked open, revealing the goddess with a burlap bag grasped tightly in her hand.

"Any problems?"

"No. Its energy was clear and pulled me to the exact spot where I left it. Granted, I had to destroy a few tiles and a section of the base surrounding the tree, but once inside, it was smooth sailing." Smiling, she lifted the bag. "And don't worry, I repaired all the damage. The sacred site remains exactly as it was."

"Good. Now let's get out of here before anyone shows up."

"The monks live outside of the main walls, and the complex is currently closed to tourists, so we should be fine," Gaia reassured me, pulling more information from her online studies.

"Still, we have a long drive ahead of us, and you need your rest." Swallowing my anxiety, I shot her a quick smile, then led her back to the car.

"Eww, what's all this dust from?" She lifted her hand from the door handle and blew it clean.

"Hmm, maybe another monsoon blowing in?" I slid into the driver's seat, avoiding her eyes and hiding the truth.

Gaia let it drop as I pulled back onto the main road, her attention focused on the bag resting in her lap. She pulled back its edges, reached in, and lifted out her treasure. "It's been so long," she murmured.

Glancing to the side, I watched in awe as the goddess ran her hand over the smooth skull resting in her palm. For the most part, it looked human and perfectly preserved, except for the crystalline veins embedded into its side, which were pulsing vibrant blue. "One down, six more to go." She winked. "Next stop ... Australia."

Printed in Great Britain
by Amazon